Time Is A Gentleman

Time Is A Gentleman

Ellen Anderson

The Pentland Press Limited
Edinburgh • Cambridge • Durham

© Ellen Anderson 1994

First published in 1994 by
The Pentland Press Ltd.
1 Hutton Close
South Church
Bishop Auckland
Durham

British Library Cataloguing in Publication Data.
A catalogue record for this book is available
from the British Library.

ISBN 1 85821 255 3

Typeset by CBS, Felixstowe, Suffolk
Printed and bound by Antony Rowe Ltd., Chippenham

CHAPTER 1

'Pass the gulley,' Edie said and Roberto nipped his knees to repress the shiver of anticipation surging through his body. The knife glinting in the afternoon sun had the same curvature as the scullery window sill where it had been worn down by Danny Marr's daily sharpening. Edie always sat alongside the large square kitchen table, opposite the window where she could monitor the up and down traffic in the back lane. The dusty lace curtain was dragged to one side so that no one passed unobserved. Roberto thought of the next door curtains, whitened by starch and dolly blue and stiffly folded, to back-stare any curious neighbour. Olive would disapprove and her mouth would give its thin-lipped down turn if she knew he was spending Sunday afternoon with Edie. From her carbolicked floors to white-washed ceilings, her house could not have been more hygienically distanced, instead of being next door in the same street; of course, Olive always had the edge as hers was the end house. There was no criticism today as Roberto knew she spent every Sunday afternoon in solitude in the front room.

He moved the pint pot aside, half full of peat brown tea, to reach the knife.

Inside the pot the dentures stirred uneasily and the upper half barely surfaced with a grin before settling down among the tea leaves. Danny Marr firmly believed that the daily tannin bath stained his teeth to make them look more natural. After his pint of tea he would dislodge his dentures into the pot and empty the tea pot over them. By then the tea was always stewed near black and anything lighter he contemptuously dismissed as 'maiden's water'.

Roberto held his breath as Edie seized the knife with her right hand and settled the large home-baked loaf between her breasts, deeply clefted by her cross-over pinafore. Holding his breath he watched the swift right-left movements and the smart one hundred per cent turn of

1

the loaf when exactly halfway through. The repeat performance saw each slice neatly tipped on to the table with the precision of a factory machine. There was nothing stable holding the loaf for Edie was a big woman and the undulating movements of her capacious breasts made the exact timing a skill known only to herself. If the knife should slip there would be two red-lipped gaping mouths. Roberto dragged himself away from these gut-clenching thoughts to listen to Edie's monologue. It was her family, apart from the back street traffic, it was always her family. There was Jonty, the darling of her heart and womb, always laughing, always dodging out of trouble and women's beds, fooling his way around people and life, so that very often the duped person would reluctantly agree that he was 'a card'. And Michael – Edie showing her nervous pride in her second son, talked of his strange political opinions, 'he had a bust of some foreigner called Lenny on his bedroom mantleshelf'. Michael restrained and silent spending his spare time reading in the Mechanics Institute and going to Worker's Educational classes; even the priest had reluctantly, but with secret curiosity, abandoned this strange man so dedicated to his Union's principles and the only dark-haired one in the Marr brood of blonde to ginger tousled thatches. To his shipyard boss he was well understood – a menace.

Edie looked up to the window. 'There goes Vinegar Lill, she's a bit early to buy her two pennorth at the fish shop.' Her mother stopped her getting it at the corner shop; with his back against the wall he conjured up and then dismissed the tall, thin vinegar addict. The untidy kitchen was hot, for even on this summer's day a big colliery coal fire was halfway up the chimney back. Sunday afternoon was the only time in the week that such peace and quietness reigned in the Marr household, with the menfolk sleeping off the double effect of beer and the huge Sunday dinner, the twins out with the dogs and Maisie out fluttering her Sunday finery. The third living creature in the untidy kitchen was the cat. By leaping from the shabby couch back he could reach the top of the kitchen press where he had made a retreat in the folds of a moth-eaten fox fur, caved out of the litter of old boots, newspapers and old caps. To see his head alongside the fox mask gave the impression of circus freak, a two-headed animal, and as his tail undulated over the press top it gently animated the fox's brush. His yellow eyes gazed down upon the empty clippy mat as if wondering where were the two dogs that ousted him daily from the fire side. Safe from both the dogs and the tormenting twins he purred and kneaded the pelt, as long dead as its owner – Edie's mother.

Roberto loved it, for it was only in the Marr house that he felt comfortably warm for Olive's cold house was scarcely heated by the small grate fire fuelled by spare coal bought bucket by bucket, from the miner's free coal allocation. Usually they would leave, for free, small coal and dust for Olive to shovel up, knowing that she was widowed, had no man in the house but that foreign lodger; the collected coal dust was later dampened in a bucket, packed into used blue sugar bags and burnt as coal bricks.

'There's Bessie,' said Edie, 'she must have fallen wrong again – she's been to church every morning this week.' Some of the colloquial sayings had puzzled Roberto for a long time after he had arrived with his few dictionary-culled words of English. For a married woman to be with child and yet said to 'have fallen wrong' was surely a contradiction in terms. But it was not the child but the appearance of the child that caused Bessie to spend much of nine months on her knees. She had a large wine stain over the left half of her face, covered usually by a woollen scarf. The gratitude to her husband for marrying her, expressed itself in a cornucopia of children and for each she prayed that her shameful scar would not be inherited. And after six blush-free children she still worried and prayed.

With a jerk Roberto realized Edie had reached the twins. Had he missed Maisie? Strange that, because between Maisie and the twins there was a seven-year gap, filled by five little Marrs either born dead or early deceased, and Edie never failed to list these in chronological order, with medical details interspersed with sighs, religious crossings and exact catalogued references. He listened without interest to Edie's troubles about the twins. They were known in the street from wild to wicked, some adding, with hesitation, that one of them was weird. They had plagued him in his early days by following his ice cream barrow, the one chanting while the other mouthed the words:

> 'Hokey pokey a penny a lump
> The more you eat the more you pump'

and with a quick sleight of hand never hesitating to steal wafers and cornets while he was busy serving.

Edie was silent now, staring out of the window, dewed with heat and exertion. The huge plates of bread and tea cakes were all buttered beside the pot of jam and the cut fruit loaf. Easing herself in the chair she hitched the cracket from under the table and thankfully rested her feet. For such a big woman she had small, well-shaped hands and feet and a small round head covered with fading fair curls. Roberto thought she must have been beautiful when young with such a pale, fair skin and large hazel eyes.

Edie switched suddenly from her family troubles. 'I heared tell you'll to be married – is that a fact?' There was no use denying it for that old witch of the Priest's housekeeper must have been whispering in the aisles. 'Yes, Maria, a girl from my own village. Now I've got the shop it's time I had a family. When she gets here I'll be living at the shop while she stays at Olive's.'

'Well, I hope she will be comfortable,' she said sarcastically. 'By God, you've kept her behind the door, but I'll say this for you – you've done well for yourself.' She leaned forward and winked. 'I know two women who will miss you and one's next door.'

Roberto smiled and was saved from bait rising by the sounds of a bed creaking upstairs followed by a chamber pot being dragged from under, which brought him to his feet. Danny Marr was on his way downstairs and at this time of day was to be approached with caution, for his moods could swing from eroding familiarity on a descending scale to some, spiteful outbursts. He would have slept out his dinner time drinking and enjoyed his hour in bed with Edie.

Few women in Inkerman Street wore stays on a Sunday afternoon, which made Edie's bread slicing activity all the more fearfully fascinating. 'I'll be off now, Edie,' he said.

Roberto walked through the back kitchen past the set pot with a large, yellow bowl of left-over dinner vegetables in the corner, to be fried up for supper and served with cold meat. The set pot was empty because Monday was washing day. He negotiated a back yard cluttered with bicycles, frames and wheels all in various stages of assembly or disintegration, making closet and coal visits an obstacle course. The earth closet cornered by the coal house was self evident on this hot summer afternoon in spite of the daily layering of a bucketful of ashes. It never occurred to the Marr family to close the wooden shelf or outer

4

door when leaving – except for Michael, but he was different. Roberto skirted the bucket of night slops put down near the back gate and awaiting Jonty now sleeping in the back bedroom. He would after tea nourish the garden down on his allotment, for the weekend slops, he firmly believed, and had magnificent vegetables to prove it, were especially beneficial when the men in the house had been heavy on the beer.

Roberto walked past Olive's gate and wondered, not for the first time, why it was called No. 7 Inkerman. Where were the other six was a problem that had engendered much public house discussion from years back. A popular theory but never substantiated was that the previous six had tumbled over the cliff, past the fisherman's cottages and into the river Tyne. He lowered himself on to the cliff edge and looked down at the huddled cottages clinging to the bank side, right down to the fish quay. He pondered over the eleven years he had passed in this hard, rough-weather town. At seventeen years of age he had landed, a foreigner weighed down with a responsibility, into what had seemed, at that time, an alien world. He thought of those early years, of the hard, grinding, penny pinching years living with Olive at No. 7 and of Betsy down below in her tiny cottage. He smiled, 'Easy as two old shoes', as the local saying went, was Betsy.

Then, as the remembrance of that terrible, first dark winter's night closed in, he jumped up and turned smartly to walk away to the town centre. Roberto Denno was not the man to waste time on yesterday.

CHAPTER 2

T he winter of 1919 saw a weary town still crawling away from the misery of a Great War, a lethal influenza epidemic and now enduring a cold, raw winter. In the immigration room two men talked in undertones as they watched the young lad re-strapping a straw hamper. 'The poor bugger looks starved and come off that ship did he?'

'Aye, from Naples, his papers were all right but he canna speak but a word or two of English, he is seventeen.'

'What will we dae with him? I'm dying for me pint afore closing time.'

The two officers looked at the lad in the thin, blue blouse and shapeless trousers.

'What did he have in that bass bag?' indicating the straw hamper alongside the lad now huddled by the side of the fireplace.

'Nowt much, some bread and cheese off the ship, I think, and a few clean clothes.'

The other whistled softly. 'By God, coming to this climate he's swapped his fiddle for a gew-gaw.'

The younger officer stirred uneasily. 'It's a bloody awful night to turn him out.'

'Well, he canna stop here. Let's leave him at the Pollis Station.'

The lad who had been holding out his hands towards the fire, as if to clutch at its warmth, looked up as the officer fitted the half-domed fireguard in front of the open fire. The older man moved forward and said not unkindly, 'Howway, lad, on your feet, we're away now.' From the gesture the lad grasped the meaning of the words and silently picked up his straw valise.

The stout door of the customs house had muted the sound and velocity of the wind, although the squalls spat spitefully down the chimney on to the still glowing fire. As the men pulled on their thick, warm overcoats and wound rough dark mufflers around their necks, imperceptively bracing themselves against the wintry night, their eyes met and they turned to the stranger.

'He's nowt but a skelp of a lad and poorly clad at that,' there was a pitying note in his voice. 'Howway,' said the older man, 'I want my pint, we'll let the Bobbies see to him.'

The wet wind struck them with the viciousness of a snapped hawser, causing the lad to gasp as if in pain. Sheltering in the lee of the broad, short bodies of the customs men, the lad, numbed not only by the ferocious Northern gale that cut every breath as he toiled up the steep steps from the harbour into a maze of dark narrow streets, lit occasionally by flickering gas lamps, popping and gasping to stay alive in the storm, but by the one word he had recognized in the men's conversation 'pollis' – *polizia* – police station.

Inside the police station two constables were struggling to overpower a huge, drunken Swedish sailor, while the station sergeant, seemingly oblivious of the sweating, swearing commotion forcing the sailor down to the cells, looked up to the newcomers.

'Got an Eytie immigrant here, Bob, can you give him a bed for the neet?'

The sergeant, resentful of the custom man's over familiar approach, replied coldly, 'This is a Police Station, not an hotel,' and walked slowly from behind his desk to examine the shivering lad.

'Well, it makes a change from the bloody Irish,' and he nodded to the lad to a wooden form beside the wall.

'We're off now for our pint,' and the two customs men, glad to shelve the responsibility, turned quickly to the door.

While the sergeant eyed the lad, the background noise of the heaving guttural Swede, instead of receding into the distance, became a swelling roar and there were anxious cries of 'Serge' interspersed with thuds. The sergeant drew his stick and disappeared down the passage, whereupon the thuds multiplied until all that was heard was a drunken hiccoughing sound. Looking flushed the sergeant emerged to find the waiting room empty. The Italian had gone, leaving his straw bass bag behind the old wooden form.

Roberto Defino, panting and exhausted, slid down in the shelter of the wooden bollard. In a blind panic he had raced back to the docks and now he could see the ship that had brought him moving away out into the darkness of the River Tyne. Lights on the deck beckoned him back in vain and, as tears mingled with the squalling rain, he turned and looked about him. Wiping his eyes and peering up at what he thought was a bollard he now realized it was the statue of a woman with a long pack strapped to her back. The dockside was quiet except for the sound of singing from the public house in the corner. As the prospect of warmth and the longing for companionship washed over him, he wondered if he dared to enter. These people were his own kind – fisher folk, seamen, not like those terrifying men in uniform. He had fled from the police station leaving his few pitiful belongings, for fear of being searched made flight imperative. He fingered the lining of his waistcoat and was comforted by the weight of twenty golden sovereigns. An ache of loneliness swept over him as he remembered *La Mamma* carefully sewing each coin into small separate black bags and attaching them to the false lining of his waistcoat. His Father had sold *La Belle Virgine del Mare* to get him to England to carry out his orders and now there was only one boat left to fish for the whole family, and he knew, in anguish, that there was no going back until he had carried out his mission. He jumped in terror as two men approached. The tavern door had opened and in the seconds of light he saw two roughly garbed seamen; one carried a knife. He clutched the far side of the statue and instantly knew he would rather die than give up money that had cost so much family sacrifice.

'We'se that?' said one to the other as they gazed down at the crouching figure. 'Howway, Paddy, get your slivor and let's get on board.'

Incredulously he stared as the men turned the knife – not on him – but to cut a shaving off the wooden statue before setting off down the slipway. 'Pray they have a better journey than mine,' and he crossed himself as he remembered the awful voyage from Naples.

In the Cat and Bagpipes big Betsy Haddick was warm and flushed with drink and repartee. Even in this company of strong-boned fisherfolk she was exceptional. Her thick red hair piled carelessly on top of her head paled beside the fair skin now stained with heated blood. Her broad forearm rested on the round beer table to accommodate a knife-scarred hand, clutching a large glass of beer.

8

Betsy worked on the quayside and no-one could cleanse a fish as neatly or quicker – the mastering of a skill as the scars proclaimed. At the end of the week she was still able to hawk a full creel of cheap fish around the city of Castletown, ten miles away. Her broad, placid face contrasted strangely with the smoke-leathered complexion of her mother, whose hooked nose jutted out above a broken hafted clay pipe, seemingly impervious to the combustion process below. Rumour had it that Betsy was the product of a casual encounter with a Norwegian sailor who had generously pressed upon Sarah Haddick what she thought to be a five shilling piece, but later, under the lamplight, had turned out to be a Norwegian medal. More likely Betsy in a genealogical upsurge was the direct descendant of a red-headed border reiver for she certainly did not favour her mother or the dark man in the photograph on the mantleshelf, now long dead and dispassionately referred to as 'your Da'. In a society of strange, disturbing quayside characters Sarah Haddick was well known for she went to sea and served as a deck hand on the fishing boats. In summer as in winter, on land or at sea, she wore a long seal-skin coat with a keel man's hat. She puffed away at a short-stemmed pipe on a circular smoke cycle through the mouth and back down the nasal passage, thus gently igniting the tobacco for a re-run. She drank her quarter of rum from a stone bottle kept under the sink beside her wooden trestle bed. When ashore, in fine weather, she would stand at the cottage door with her pewter mug, removing the pipe only for fortifying gulps.

Betsy, the speculative issue, was known as an 'easy lass'. All of her friends would stoutly deny that she was a whore, just that she was easily led. She had an animal-like capacity for living life as it came and extracting as much physical enjoyment as possible on the way, whether it be food, drink or a sexual encounter. Sitting comfortably half drunk, her heavy legs encompassing the iron legs of the table, she enjoyed the fisherwoman's bawdy stories, while at the same time catching the ship talk of the old men in the corner: old men who had sailed in wooden ships and remembered when the Post Office would not entrust the mail to iron ships. They still argued that iron ships attracted weeds and barnacles more quickly and that iron upset the working of the compass by distracting the magnetised needle. 'Get out there,' said the young voices in opposition. 'They can carry twice as much in half the

9

time,' and so the old, oft-repeated arguments would go on – until the old men died and were no longer remembered. Betsy stood up, swaying slightly, crossed her shawl over her breasts and tied the ends in a knot in the middle of her back.

'Well, I'm away now for I've a creel of fish to hawk around Castletown the morrer.'

With that she jammed on the man's cap she habitually wore with the peak at the back and made her way to the door halting as the barman called, 'Want the old girl's rum then?'

'Naw, she's away with the fishing fleet and I've had my belly full.' She heaved open the heavy inn door and gasped as the wind made her stagger against the door posts. Head down she pushed her way across the square, only to halt at a sudden movement at the base of the wooden dolly. 'We'se that?' she called as she stooped down to peer at a terrified youth. 'For God's sake what are you deein there?'

Robert, wet, freezing with cold and agonizing over his last frightening encounter, looked up and saw in the light of the dim gaslight what looked like a wild creature; a broad red face with snake-like tossing strands of red hair loosened from under the cap by the wind. With tears streaming down his face he stood up and cried, *'Aiuto straniero.'* Betsy had never heard a word of Italian in her life, but the meaning was clear as the lad held out his hands clutched together as if in prayer. She had no fear of this stranger in the night for, as the lad stood up, he reached her only shoulder high and as thin as a lath; she could have felled him with one blow. 'God help us, it's nowt but a skelp of a bairn,' and pulling his arm she said, 'Howway, bonny lad, ah wouldn't leave a dog out on a night like this.' Leaving the square she led him down a maze of narrow streets and shoved open an unlocked door, for in that close fisherfolk community, locked doors were unheard of. Anyone doing so would have aroused the suspicion of – what have they got to hide?

Roberto was now weeping with relief as he met the warmth of the room. Such a small room with a sea-coal fire glowing in the grate, its occasional green-gold flame lighting up the room. There was a large cupboard, a small chest of drawers, two chairs with a curtained recess adjacent the large cupboard and, apart from a few mats on the floor, these completed the furnishings. Betsy lit a lamp on the chest of drawers, opened the large cupboard and tossing aside a tumbling of blankets pulled out a folding wooden frame and a feather bed. Sorting among the heap she handed him a blanket and jerking at his coat she yelled, 'Off, off,' and impatiently, as he hesitated, said, 'howway, you've nowt different.' Then she left him to reappear through the far door with a stone bottle. Into a mug from the mantleshelf she poured two large tablespoons of rum and topped it up with stewed tea from the tea pot on the hob. Roberto thought he had never tasted such a vile mixture but the warmth that spread through his body made him gulp it down gratefully. Betsy straightened the feather bed and threw a bolster and blankets over it. She turned and gathered up his wet clothes and hung them over a rope fastened above the mantlepiece. Roberto, covered by the blanket, was left naked underneath except for his knee-length, well-darned linen drawers, but under his arm he had securely folded his waistcoat. Poking her thick finger into his chest she demanded, 'Name – your name lad,' each word punctuated by a solid push. Looking up into the small, bright blue questioning eyes, the meaning was clear.

'Roberto.'

'Well, that's easy – it's Robert around these parts,' and jerking a thumb breast wise she returned, 'Betsy Haddick.' Crouched in the chair he watched with amazement as Betsy pulled both her thick guernsey and shift over her head with one quick movement and then waisted down skirt and drawers. In the firelight he watched open mouthed as, naked, she pulled off her woollen stockings. In a rosy dream, tinctured by rum, her broad back and heavy thighs lurched him back to the portraits of Titian-haired women he had lusted over in the picture galleries of Naples. Big, fine women with heavy breasts and strong, white limbs. The rum now seeping into his very pores caused a hazy lightness in his head and a heavy, urgent swelling between his legs. Betsy heaved herself into bed and patted the empty space beside her. Ashamed to expose his tumescence he edged towards the bed, the blanket covering his lower limbs. The warmth of her body drew him closer in the bed. The softness of the feather bed and the warm pillows of her body were irresistible. Hesitantly, he eased his hand into the warm cave between breasts and belly. Betsy pulled his body over, 'Howway then, you're not the first by a long chalk and, by God, I hope you won't be the last.'

In the early dawn hours Betsy cursed a full bladder and the beer that had caused it. With a hand reach she hooked the chamber pot from behind the curtained recess containing her meagre wardrobe and, turning up the kelly lamp, eased herself out of bed. As she relieved herself she noticed blearily a black note book had fallen from the bolster where Robert had placed his waistcoat. Betsy had had very little schooling; as she would have put it – 'didn't know B from a bull's foot' – and as the writing was in a foreign language her interest was desultory until she turned a page and saw a word instantly recognisable, the printed name of Fanshaw. That name she knew well because it was spread large over the biggest emporium in Castletown. Puzzled she looked from the sleeping lad to the name carefully spelled out before her and even in her half awake state she tried to tie up this homeless, newly arrived foreigner with the prestigious name of one of the most prosperous merchants in the area. Well, mysteries were made for clever folks; Betsy carefully replaced the pocket book and climbed thankfully into bed. As untroubled sleep came easily, her face on the bolster was peaceful enough and showed little evidence of her hard twenty-eight years of existence.

Except when lit by the oil lamp or a bank happed fire, the cottage always seemed to be in half light, mainly due to the small window scarcely raised above street-level, for in that narrow street no sun ever touched the front wall and only fleetingly warmed the back yard in late afternoon. Roberto, deep in the depths of a cloud soft feather bed, moved unwillingly from half dreams to a vaguely dreaded consciousness. Easing himself up he struggled to piece together the events of the past two days. Leaving the ship, the numbing cold and rain, the fear and loneliness touched his memory and catching his breath – the warmth and ecstasy of his first woman. Mildly he looked around the empty room and a strange name came to his lips – 'Betsee' – but there was no answer. He got up and dragged down his clothes from the line. Although the fire was out, the room was warm and as hunger clenched his stomach he warily opened the far door. Two shallow steps led down to an even smaller room where he faced a yellow stone sink with a board and mattress stretched underneath. A galvanised bucket stood under the sink tap containing a few gleaming herrings. Opening the cupboard on the opposite wall he found a loaf of bread, butter, cheese, a blue bag of sugar and a box smelling of the foul drink he had swallowed last night. As he drank water and ate the bread and cheese, the door opened and a man entered carrying a metal canister. With a brief 'How do,' he lifted the metal lid and ladled out a half pint of milk into a bowl waiting on the sink board and was immediately gone. Cautiously Roberto opened the back door to find in the tiny yard a heap of coal and wood covered by a piece of ship's old tarpaulin and on the wall a wooden safe fronted by an aluminium sieve door, but nowhere to relieve his urgent needs. The sound of chopping made him look over the low wall where a man, as the noise ceased, left his pile of sticks and crossing the dirt track between disappeared into a closet alongside a midden. Roberto waited in agony until the man emerged, passed him with a brief nod and, 'Now then,' and went about his business as Roberto thankfully went about his.

By the late afternoon Roberto had explored the cottage and waited uneasily yet with an assurance that Betsy would return. With the sound of the door sneck he turned to greet her with a welcoming smile but Betsy walked past him and dropped her creel in the yard. She came back saying, 'Well, not such a bad day but selling good fish to the miserable fancy folk in big houses was hard work for they would skin a louse.' Looking at the fire he had kindled she nodded with approval, 'Right, it's dinner time.' From a linen bag she laid on the table two thick slices of cod. Such lovely pieces of fish, glistening white, made Roberto's mouth water. Following her into the back kitchen he watched amazed as she took the bucket of herrings out to the midden and threw them on to the ashes, where it seemed from nowhere, an army of cats descended fighting and scratching among the ashes. Betsy placed peeled potatoes in a pan on the fire. Roberto watched with disapproval for the fish had not been boned nor skinned, a feeling that did not diminish as he sat down to white potatoes, soggy white fish in a thin milky juice with a dollop of butter atop the potatoes. Betsy enjoyed her meal liberally sprayed with salt, while giving him a non-stop revision of the day's activities, oblivious to the fact that Roberto had more understanding of her expressive gestures than her words.

No salad, no sauce and no herbs – just butter and salt – what a waste of that beautiful fish, thought Roberto.

He let the sounds flow over him as Betsy, still talking, lit the lamp, raked the fire to a brighter glow and sat down to ease her feet. He walked over to the chest of drawers and picked up a brush and comb,

13

together with some fine tortoise shell pins. Facing Betsy he placed a finger over her lips, effectively stopping her chatter in mid-flow. He took off the ugly man's cap and undid the carelessly tied plaits shoved up under it and began to brush the lustrous red gold hair that tumbled waist length down her back. Except in oil paintings at home he had never seen such beautiful hair and, as he slowly and gently drew the brush through, he marvelled how the firelight turned it to a burnished copper sheen. Betsy sat in silence, unable to understand the flow of mixed emotions engulfing her. A longing and a feeling of peaceful relaxation, together with a sweet gratitude, swept over her. Her experience of men had been limited to short, hard couplings and she had never before known such an aching tenderness. Roberto secured the glowing mass with pins and slowly undid the gathered shift, drawing it over her plump upper arms to rest just above her bosom. He went into the kitchen and lifted the small, looking glass from above the kitchen sink. Standing in front of her he raised the mirror and said, 'Betsee.' She shook her head slightly. 'It canna be me,' she said, for she saw a magnificent woman with round white shoulders, a crown of piled high beautiful hair. Placing the looking glass in her hand, he walked round and gently kissed the back of her neck.

CHAPTER 3

Quietly he moved the heavy weight of Betsy's arm from his chest, for sleep had long gone and had left a throat-sour feeling of guilt. He looked over at Betsy, her hair now tumbled over the bolster. What was he doing in this warm cocoon, he asked himself. His family would be incredulous that he lay with a foreign woman while they carried such a burden of shame. Confession, that was what he needed and quickly. To do penance to salve his conscience and to seek guidance from Mother Church. 'Tomorrow, no, it's today, I'll go and find a church.' And with that decision sleep came easily.

Betsy was already working on the quayside when Roberto awoke, and as he lay rehearsing his plans he became aware of a strange combination of a fish and tobacco smell. Dressing quickly he opened the back kitchen door and jumped back at a movement from under the sink. What looked like a long, brown sack turned a face towards him. Rolling from under with the ease of one long used to a ship's bunk, the tall figure straightened up. Ignoring him, the person, for at that stage the sex was still undetermined, walked through to the fire and raking aside the top coals placed three clay, short-stemmed pipes into the glowing centre. She, for it was Betsy's mother, poured tea into a mug, liberally laced it with condensed milk and sitting by the fire proceeded to light up yet another pipe taken from the mantleshelf. She seemed to be unconcerned and uncaring about the young man now staring at her wrinkled brown face with its enormous nose jutting out over the pipe. Boots projected from her long seal-skin coat, which stank of fish, and a strange hat covered her head. In the long silence that followed, broken only by the sounds of the pipes, now burnt clean of tar and gleaming white, being carefully removed by the small tongs and laid upon the hearth. Roberto decided first to ease his own problems and then to ask questions about this strange creature when Betsy returned later. It seemed to him that it was acceptable in Embleton for people other

15

than the family to walk in and out of the cottage.

He stepped out into the street, closing the door quickly behind him and noticed thankfully that, although it was cold, the wind and the rain had ceased. To keep warm he walked quickly away, aiming uphill towards the town centre. The old-fashioned shops he passed were filled with sea-going wares, chandlers, rope makers and provision merchants, but now he entered a more residential area. On the corner of a street he saw a large building with a blackboard notice on the side wall of the door, surmounted by a small gilt cross. The joy of finding a church was tempered with disappointment at the sight of such a plain, angular building. For a moment he thought of the beautiful cathedral in Naples, but the anxiety of his present position make him long for sanctuary, wherever it could be found.

Inside the Methodist Chapel the 'meeting women' had gathered as they did every Wednesday to what they called 'our Guild'. It consisted of long prayers, a cold appraisal of what everyone else had brought for the later tea, doleful hymns sang in untuneful voices and finally the shifting into cliques for the latest news and gossip, spread with pursed lips and passed on in undertones to wherever the two and threes were gathered together. During the closing hymn, when minds and palates were latched on to tea and cakes, there came the sound of the heavy door ring being turned and, as it clanged back to punctuate the closing phase of unmusical voices, all heads turned sharply, swivelling hard, black hats to stare at the young man standing in the aisle. Thin voices tailed away as the harmonium notes died with a groan. In shocked amazement they gazed as the young man fell to his knees and genuflected. He walked up to the communion rail accompanied, pew by varnished pew, by a hiss of horror. With his eyes fixed on the cross stitched to the purple velvet lectern cover, he fell to his knees and genuflected once more. The first woman in the front pew gathered the folds of her coat tightly around her and skirting the kneeling figure made for the vestry door. Outrage written on her face she beckoned to the Minister who had comfortably thought that his sole responsibility that afternoon would be to close the meeting. As he came through the door to a low babble of words – 'Popery', 'He crossed himself', 'Catholic' – assailed his astonished ears.

Roberto stood up and with outstretched hands called out *'Straniero,'* to the hostile faces in front of him. The call of 'stranger' may have touched the heart of Betsy Haddick but here in that icy atmosphere there was nothing but cold and fearful suspicion. Roberto appealed to the Minister: *'Non so che case fare.'*

At the sound of the foreign language a threatening murmur increased in volume and the Minister, seizing Roberto by the arm, hurried him through the gauntlet of disapproval. Outside he pointed down the road but the lad made no move to go and stood with his eyes mirrors of bewilderment and disappointment. James Brown, being a Man of God, could not turn away from that mute appeal. He walked quickly with Roberto anxious to be rid of this embarrassing situation. Well, the women would have a wonderful tale to tell and to think about before the next Guild meeting.

Even now, and he smiled at the thought, scrubbing brushes would be out to cleanse a suspicion of Papist contamination in his church. No doubt Adelaide Williams would with satisfaction take upon herself the honour of leading the congregation in closing prayers.

It was a short walk interspersed with right and left turnings. When on a cliff top, Roberto realized that previously he had put his foot into a wasp's nest, for here he realized was a Catholic church. They walked up the path to the manse door adjoining the church and James Brown rang the bell. It was answered by Agnes Cowen, the Priest's housekeeper. After his encounter with Sarah Haddick, Roberto thought that he could never meet a stranger looking woman – but he was wrong. The housekeeper believed dedication to the Priest, his home and his work had placed her in the nun category and she wore as near as was permitted a religious habit. This did not conceal a small, bitter face disfigured on the left side by a large mole sprouting a healthy grey-haired growth, rivalled only by one above her upper lip. Small, black eyes under thick, crescent-shaped eyebrows were equally disfigured by reddish inflamed eyelids.

'I wish to speak to the Priest,' said the Minister. Although he knew full well the name of the Priest, he could not bring himself to preface it with 'Father'. The grey mole moved downwards in shock and horror as she recognized the Protestant Minister and turning away she hastily crossed herself before moving rapidly down the passage. After a few moments Father Anthony Howard, with eyebrows raised, came to the doorway. They both knew each other very well by sight but religious practices had never allowed the other more than a nod in passing. The Minister on his walk had rehearsed what he should say and now, confronted with the Priest, he had nothing to say except, 'One of yours, I believe.' He beckoned the lad forward. The rising joy and relief Roberto felt at recognising his church and a religious mentor, burst forth and he fell to his knees crying, *'Mea culpa,* Father.' James Brown turned sharply and strode down the path, unwilling to witness more of this emotional scene. Father Anthony pulled the boy to his feet, equally embarrassed, and with a sharp, 'Get inside,' followed him in and shut the door.

CHAPTER 4

Father Anthony Howard's ancestral roots went as far back as the building of Rievaulx Abbey. His forebears had survived in spite of persecution and isolation over the centuries to make and lose fortunes while some ancestors had spent time in their lives living in priest holes. In spite of aspirations, he wondered sometimes at the years spent in this area of fishermen, colliers and ship builders and always with a 'forgive me' under his breath, he thought perhaps it was, unlike the Bishop, that his mother did not come from Ireland. At the end of his noviceship he had spent two years in Rome and had fallen in love with the eternal city, the people and the culture, so much so, that his evening solace was to delve into its history with a glass of whisky at his elbow. There was scarcely a church, and they were numerous, in that entrancing city whose history could not fill volumes and it was the life-long ambition, and Father Howard's silent pleasure, to trace them all. After the sins and sorrows poured daily into his ears and revolted by the sour, often beery confessional breaths, he would gladly hurry through his church, past the regulars such as Bessy Mayhew praying again for an unblemished child, to shut himself away after the evening meal in his study. He was now in his forties, a lonely man, although his daily needs were more than adequately looked after by Agnes Cowen, who cooked good food, well served, and who harassed the daily woman continually so that his house was kept scrupulously clean and polished. Perhaps it was just as well, for his Bishop, slender white fingers forming a steeple and looking through him into the far distance, had heavily advised the appointment of Agnes Cowen rather than Olive Harman. In his heart he knew he could neither flout the pointed advice nor follow the dangerous inclination of his heart by preferring the young widow's presence in the manse. In middle age, he appreciated the fierce protection of his privacy, although he knew Agnes Cowen had no respect for anyone's business but his own.

With the young stranger in front of him, he tried to commensurate his scholastic Italian with the thick Neapolitan dialect he was now hearing. He understood Roberto had come to England at the behest of his parents, but exactly why was difficult to understand as the lad gazed blankly when he pressed the matter and either did not or preferred not to understand. What Father Howard did understand, with increasing unease, was that the well-known quayside character Betsy Haddick had taken him home. In the close confines of the confessional box, he was not surprised at the carnal revelations, but was quietly amused at Roberto's incursion into the Methodist citadel. That must have put this pigeon among the sanctimonious cats. Later, as he watched the young man kneeling with his rosary, he decided that the immediate problem was to find a temporary lodging for Roberto while seeking advice from the Bishop.

Father Anthony did not often visit Inkerman Street, for he had long since decided that admonition was lost on the Marr household and, in the past, close contact with Olive Harman had disturbed his nights. The sporadic attendance of the Marrs at church was offset in some way by the frequent baptism and subsequent burials of infants. Edie Marr 'had turned' when she married Danny and now her religion was a mish-mash of converted Catholicism, superstition and the remnants of a Protestant upbringing.

Equally he did not house visit No. 7, knowing Olive's deep disappointment all those years ago, at losing the housekeeper post to Agnes Cowen. That the repulsive-looking Agnes had been preferred, it did not occur to her, in itself was an acknowledgement of her youth and beauty.

Today, seeking her help, the Priest turned into her back gate, giving in passing, a murmured blessing to the toddler twins sitting on the Marr doorstep. They were identical, except for the small yellow triangle in the grey lower right iris of the one and the lower left iris of the other. Looking at the twins, others might think crossed fingers more efficacious than a blessing.

The Priest knocked on the back door and walked through the scullery into the kitchen, knocking again on the inner door. Olive Harman sat by the table, carefully folding newspapers retrieved from the big house where she worked by washing clothes and scrubbing the front steps for two shillings and sixpence, for each of two mornings

20

per week. She was cutting a shell pattern that, when unfolded, would give a fancy edge to the pantry shelves. Beside her on the table was a neat pile cut into squares and ringed through the corner by a string and destined for the less decorative position of a nail in the earth closet. A bunch of rolled paper spillikins filled a brown jar to be used to light the gas from the fire flame, while tightly twisted circles necessary as firelighters half filled a box on the floor. Seeing the Priest she modestly pushed the squares under the shelf paper. After the surprise of seeing two visitors she motioned the Priest to sit in a wooden rocking chair against the wall. From thereon the lad felt he was living in a dream as the two held a long, incomprehensible conversation. As they talked, occasionally looking in his direction, he gazed around the room. Quite a big room, with a high ceiling, it was sparsely furnished with a large wooden table centred beneath a gas light with a circular patterned oilcloth stuck above it on the ceiling. In the recess beside a shining black-leaded stove a large, green-painted cupboard filled the space from floor to ceiling. A treadle sewing machine stood under the window and, apart from the chairs and table, the room seemed to hold more air than objects. A brass coal scuttle filled with blue paper bags stood alongside a burnished steel fender, doing its best to reflect some warmth from the small fire in the grate. The room was cold and Roberto shivered in his thin clothes. Suddenly he heard the name 'Betsy Haddick' and looked up guiltily to meet the disapproving stare of the woman in whose house he must now live. He blushed as deeply as his olive skin would allow and tried to remember all that the Priest had tried to explain to him. He was to stay temporarily in a good Catholic household and was never to approach Betsy Haddick again. To attend church regularly and to put behind him these unfortunate happenings since he'd arrived in the country.

'Yes,' the Priest told Olive, the young man, whose name was Roberto Delfino, had, he said, a little money, had agreed to pay ten shillings a week until he could find work.

'Then he'll be finding the same as many out there – there's not much work about,' said Olive.

The Priest agreed but added it was the best that could be done. The conversation passed now from Roberto's to Olive's problems and the Priest asked if she was still working for the Fanshaws. As he spoke the name Roberto started and shouted, *'Che cosa?'*

21

'Now what's wrong?' asked Olive but the boy had turned his head away and the Priest, ignoring the interruption, was more than anxious to end this troublesome business. Olive finally agreed to lodge Roberto but not, she pointed out firmly, in his present condition.

'Tell him he must wash himself down thoroughly before he gets into my bed.'

He smiled inwardly at the possessive not personal interpretation of 'my bed', and Olive left the room to return with a towel, a square of flannel and a piece of hard, blue mottled soap. The Priest led Roberto into the back kitchen, half filled the sink with water and handed him the washing articles, explaining meanwhile that to 'wash down' in Olive's vocabulary meant a complete and thorough cleansing of the body.

Olive said, 'His clothes will have to be washed – has he a change?' The Priest shook his head and explained that somehow he had lost his belongings since leaving the ship. Silently, Olive took a key from the drawer of the green-painted cupboard and left the room. He heard the sound of the front room door being unlocked and wondered why he had never been invited inside, most of his parishioners were more than keen to show off their parlour.

'Well, there's not much comfort here,' thought Father Anthony, 'but at least he will be well looked after and it might take Olive's mind off the irritating neighbours.' Tale after tale she had told him indignantly about the shortcomings, the rowing factions and the unhygienic habits of the Marr household but there was nothing he could do but listen. His reverie was interrupted by the sound of the front door being re-locked and Olive entered carrying a pile of clothes smelling strongly of moth balls. Without comment she laid them on the fender as if the feeble fire had heat to warm them. There was a pair of thick flannel linings and a vest. Over the back of a chair she placed rough sea-going trousers and a dark blue guernsey. She moved quickly away as the Priest put out a tentative hand as if to say thanks, for he knew these were from the sea-going trunks of her father or her husband, whose bones now laid somewhere at the bottom of the South China seas; both drowned in a coffin ship several years ago. He knew this gesture must have awakened painful memories but he also knew that she would not welcome any comment or thanks for the same.

In the icy scullery Roberto cried with both cold and misery as he washed in the cold water. Only the thought that he must obey the Priest prevented him from running away, as he had done in desperate fear from the Police Station. He stood silently waiting, draped in the small damp towel until the Priest opened the door and handed him the clothes. On a chair Olive had placed another pile of underclothes – 'to change next week,' she said. Roberto entered the room awkward in the unfamiliar garb and conscious that his returning body heat seemed to heighten the camphor smell. Olive handed him a pair of boots, thick sea-going wool stockings and he was glad of the latter as the boots were two sizes too big.

The Priest looked ruefully on, worried about the strange situation he was leaving behind, but after assuring Olive that he would return tomorrow, gave them a blessing and left the house. Olive motioned Roberto to a chair and silently they took stock of one another, one each side of the fireplace. Rising after a while, Olive took a note book and pencil from the table drawer and wrote down Number Seven, Inkerman Street, Embleton. With her arms she made an all embracing circle of the kitchen and she made him repeat the address several times. There would be no confusion over where he lived from now on. After a supper of bread, cheese and cocoa and in bed in his flannel underwear, Roberto still felt the all pervading cold of the bedroom and he longed for the warmth of Betsy Haddick's body and cottage. Drawing up his feet from the cold end of the bed he tried to concentrate on the Cross and the picture of Our Lady on the opposite wall, regularly illuminated by the flashing lighthouse beams, and wept because he received no comfort.

CHAPTER 5

Harriet Fanshaw permitted herself a thin smile of satisfaction as she smoothed from her trim waist the folds of her barathea skirt. As a young girl she had been forced to work as a cashier in what, to her distaste, her father called, 'the shop', while to Harriet it was the Emporium, and as descriptions go, hers was the more apt. Amos Fanshaw had, in his early days, been a packman selling miscellaneous goods around the moors and in the dales of Northumberland before setting up his first shop in Embleton. This first venture had been financed by the dowry brought to him by the girl he had deliberately impregnated in her father's barn, while supposedly selling her laces. Before marriage his wife had taught in the village school and as the only daughter among a brood of brothers she had been carefully parlour trained. The disgraced daughter was hastily married and brought her only child, Harriet, into the world. Now she was saddled with a man who had long since lost his rough attraction, who gobbled his food and disappeared every night to soften up, with free drinks, local councillors and dignitaries who, in turn, favoured him with inside knowledge of goods tenders. She dressed Harriet in finery as if playing with a doll, in the clothes she persisted in ordering from London shops. Amos Fanshaw stormed and shouted over the bills as he carefully extracted a trade discount.

And the best of the year's fashion was reserved for the May Day procession. For three years, Harriet, now sixteen and dressed in London fashions, had as May Queen led the May Day procession seated in a bower of flowers on a decorated cart. Even Amos played his part by more intrigues and deals to keep this coveted honour in the family. But after three successive crownings cautious councillors with their ears to the ground could not now ignore the muttered swell of complaints by the mothers, the same now transferred by the fathers to the field committee. Some members, as they shuffled their feet, shuffled

24

their allegiance from the powerful Amos Fanshaw, preferring to risk their store discounts to provoking more maternal wrath and their seats on the council.

In Embleton there was a cherished belief that the May Day celebrations always brought good weather and, although nine times out of ten they were proved wrong, nothing could dispel the optimistic myth. But this May morning certainly substantiated the wishful thinking for the warm morning promised a hot day. In the houses of the six finalists no royal Queen could have been less well attended as mothers, aunts, cousins and neighbours poured in by back and front doors to exclaim unanimously and with certainty, that here was this year's May Queen and the rest would be lucky as Maids of Honour.

In the square of beautiful Georgian houses situated well above the rest of the town lived many prosperous business men and rich retired ship owners, most of whom tried hard not to recall that the fortunes their forbears had made were founded in the slave trade. Had any of their work forces in the mines and the shipyards along the river been privy to the information, they would have insisted that times and conditions had not changed much. In the bedroom of one of the houses the two maids were unravelling Harriet Fanshaw from her rag hair curlers. Her mother laid the beautiful white silk dress edged with guipure lace and scalloped at neck and hem with tiny, pale rosebuds, on the bed. Harriet had condescended to allow the maids a preview, hastily warding off their workman hands as they made to finger the wondrous dress. Full of confidence she would have skipped in her white kid shoes had not decorum overcome her excitement as she remembered the elevated role she would be called upon to undertake. Spoilt by her mother, who fondly called her 'my English rose', and ignored by the father who resented the fact that his only child was a girl, Harriet did not deny her mother's cloying description, for with her fair hair, blue eyes and pink cheeks she had fulfilled a doll-child need for her doting mother.

In the field behind the Welfare Hall a canvas track led up to the dais to where six aspiring beauties were lined up. Alongside, a plodding horse was yoked up to the Co-operative cart decked out with an arch of flowers. Inside the bower, the royal throne consisted of a beer keg covered with a cloth and topped by a purple cushion, its gold tassels shining in the sun to complete the regal equipage. Five smaller seats

25

were arranged behind on the cart as a compensation to disappointed maidens. Each seat had its basket of paper flowers alongside to be thrown to well wishers and favourites lining the roadside into town. A group of committee men stood beside the dais trying earnestly to choose the girl least likely to cause offence. They had returned the strained smiles on the candidates' faces with, 'Never been such lovelies,' and 'a vintage year,' doled out to propitiate as they walked along the row. The last girl in the row was small and slim with brown hair casting a bronze glint in the sun. She was simply dressed and without ornament in a pale green silk shot through with a silver thread. Her dress had been made by her mother from a fine Indian sari brought back by her sea-going father. Its very simplicity contrasted with the ribbons, bows and bright colours of the other five competitors. After a huddled consultation the leader of the council squared his shoulders and, taking the wreath of roses held out to him, he declared the brown-haired girl to be Queen of the May. After all, there would be few complaints against a girl from Inkerman Street. With a scream of rage and disappointment, Harriet ran to her mother waiting under a parasol at the edge of the field and flung herself sobbing into her arms. They left the field, the one distraught and the other, while indignant, was also ashamed of her daughter's outburst in front of so many lower class people. Officials hastily got the procession underway and, as the newly crowned May Queen on her royal throne passed through the field gate, she was startled to see the bitter hate in the face of a girl being driven away in a car. As well she could not see that same girl in her bedroom slashing her splendid dress to pieces.

Harriet dated all her subsequent unhappiness from that fine May Day and channelled her hatred on the girl who had usurped her throne – a Catholic girl from Inkerman Street – for within six months her mother was dead from a heart attack. She mourned not so much for the loss of her mother as for the removal of a staunch ally, who gave in to her every whim and always overlooked her tantrums. Together with pursed lips or sly smiles they would sit in silent condemnation of her father's crude table manners and rough speech. One night after their evening meal Amos motioned her back to her chair as she rose to leave the room. Briefly, sucking at his moustache, he told her that from now on things would be different. He intended to sack those silly lasses his late wife had called servants and to install a housekeeper with only a daily help.

'As for you, young woman, you're now going on seventeen and it's time you earned your corn. Starting Monday you will work as a cashier in the shop with the same wages as the other shop women.' Almost retching with rage and fright Harriet screamed at him, 'You odious man – why ever did Mother marry such an oaf as you?'

'Well, she did and was glad of it,' he said coldly. 'If you won't work in the shop then it will save me paying a daily woman for you will do the scrubbing and washing.'

Looking into his black protuberant eyes Harriet realized there would be no appeal. 'You will have your wages, free board and lodgings, you have a wardrobe full of clothes and all you have to do for it will be to sit on your arse and collect my money.'

Shocked, Harriet rushed to her room and locked the door, determined to starve herself to death. As her father's daughter, two days lack of food and solitude brought a tougher Harriet to her senses. Sullenly, she accepted meals in the kitchen with the new housekeeper as drawing room and dining room were locked up and furniture shrouded in the spare bedrooms. Daily she sat on an elevated platform collecting wooden balls from an overhead runway, inserting the change and pulling a chain to send it on its way to the counter staff. Although she hated her work, she kept watch from her platform to ensure that no employee should arrive one minute late or leave, undetected, one minute early.

Miserable with longing for the pleasant, easy life she had held, she hated mixing with the shop assistants, especially sharing communal use of the bare toilet facilities. Any overtures of friendliness were met with a cold stare or a cutting remark. She felt she had forfeited not only her comfortable life but also the respect of the community since the day she lost her May Queen Crown.

CHAPTER 6

As Roberto stood outside his shop, the twins raced past on their ancient bicycles, handed down from the elder Marr brothers, waving as they went and with the two dogs trying to keep up to their speed. He knew they were going to keep watch for the pitch and toss men who would gather, illegally, in the late afternoon to play their games in the hollow on the other side of the Canny Hill bank. The boys free-wheeled down the hill out of town, thin legs outstretched from their knee-length trousers, to cross the road and see how far they could get up the Canny Hill without pedalling. Once on top they threw down their bikes and lay down beside the panting dogs. After watching the road behind them to ensure that no policemen were in sight, they looked over the other edge at the small groups of men converging into the hollow. Gathering together and sure that any approaching danger would send one of the twins hurtling down the bank side, they spread a blanket and began tossing pennies. On the ridge above the twins rolled occasionally from one view to the other. Identical, except for the small yellow triangle in the left eye of Jamie and the right eye of Joe, the lads lay in the sun knowing that the afternoon winners would drop them a few pennies on the way home. Jamie produced a half-eaten apple from his pocket and began to munch steadily.

'Save us the gowk,' said Joe for he was the one that could speak. Jamie handed over the skeleton of the core. Despite Jamie's lack of words there was a complete understanding between the two. They had instant rapport and communication with each other and, while Joe was both speaker and interpreter, no one could understand the complicated method of this bizarre vocabulary.

At the age of five Edie Marr had presented both boys at the Primary School where Mr Mitchell, the Head Master, a tall, thin man with a bobbing Adam's apple working continually above his celluloid collar, made his decision to take Joe but not Jamie.

'Why?' demanded Edie, ignoring the obvious.

'This is not the school for a child like him,' replied the august Mr Mitchell.

'You let her in every playtime,' and she pointed to a woman entering the school yard carrying a cracket, who, calling over her five-year-old son, began to breast feed. The spectacle of this woman's wide apart legs, as she suckled the child, had on week days occupied his morning break as he watched from behind a corner of the curtain. Alarmed when he realized that this had been noticed, he said sharply, 'That will be stopped,' and added harshly, 'take that one away – the other one can start school.' The twins glared at him and, realizing the inevitable separation, glanced at each other. Next morning Mr Mitchell found two windows in his heated greenhouse had been broken and his delicate and highly prized orchid collection was now black and dead from the cold of a late September night. Occasionally, education officials approached the Marr household concerning Jamie's future. Met with Edie's adamant, 'He's not going to the daft school in Castletown,' the hot, angry stare of Danny Marr and the menacing lowering of the *Sports Gazette* and *Evening News* by the elder Marr brothers, the file on Jamie was regularly postponed for further consideration. While Joe passed on to Jamie the benefit of his education through the channels known only to themselves, Jamie during school hours usually eluded the gate watchman and slipped into the shipyard. While a few warned of the work place dangers he was so quick, so agile and so useful in carrying bets to the bookie, Bacon Jack, that they were careful to motion him away when the bosses were about.

Roberto's return home coincided with the Marr twins homecoming. Racing ahead of him as they turned the far end of Inkerman Street, he heard a scream and a loud shrill outburst. Hurriedly turning the corner he saw the twins standing by their bikes as Hilda Mason, white with fury, gazed at her bespattered silk stockings. The lads had ridden through seepage from under the metal shutter of the earth closet and the mess was generously sprayed over her legs. The silk stockings were the gift of her lover, a baker with a shop and a nagging wife in the town. Returning from her tryst in the woods Hilda had literally had her path crossed by the Marr boys. Panting with rage she shouted, 'Stay at your own end of the street,' and spat out, 'Paddy's end.'

Turning to Joe while pointing at Jamie she said, 'Explain that to him – the dummy.' She walked away to her back gate and slammed it after her. The twins looked at each other and smiled, quickly they worked through a silent vocabulary in their thin-fingered language.

To calm her nerves Hilda put a teaspoonful of whisky in her tea and cooled her feet on the stone floor of the back kitchen. Smiling to herself she thought of the enjoyable love making in the wood and of the coming Wednesday when Alan James would call while on his bread and cakes round. Bare footed, she stepped out to make her late night call to the earth closet. In the yard, on the second step down her foot came heavily on to something furry and squashy. Her screams brought those lately abed to the windows and the back step dawdlers to their feet. Shouts and questions flew both ways up and down the street and faces appeared over adjoining walls. Voices exclaimed, 'What's happened?' 'It sounds like a murder,' and 'Who's screaming?' Neighbours rushed into Hilda's yard to calm her down and to answer the repeated questions with, 'It's only a rat.' Peace was gradually restored and many, disappointed that it was only a dead rat and not a wife getting the rounds of the kitchen, retired indoors.

Upstairs at No. 8 the twins, waiting by the upper window, hugged each other, one laughing quietly and the other mouthing laughter, both communicating quickly in their own finger language. Then peace and the warm night encompassed Inkerman Street.

CHAPTER 7

Herbert Platt changed his life style the day he decided to be measured for a new suit in the Gentlemen's Outfitters department of the Fanshaw Emporium. Until then, he had lived contentedly with his sister, a woman who knew well how to cook a plate or a pot pie rounded off with spotted dick or a bread and butter pudding. On that particular morning, as he passed on his way through the drapery to the Gentlemen's department, he looked up and saw what he thought to be an angelic vision in the shape of no other than Harriet Fanshaw. When she looked down and saw his fascinated gaze she turned coldly away with what Herbert interpreted as a very proper and lady-like response. There seemed to be an extra number of fittings for the suit and Herbert, each time, inched slowly past the cashier's desk. Piqued, but nonetheless curious, Harriet enquired his name from the oily floor walker, a man who was very careful to win the approval of the boss's daughter. Told that it was Mr Herbert Platt, the owner of Platts Brewery, at the next encounter Harriet favoured the stricken Herbert with a faint smile. Platts ale was well known in the North Country and enjoyed by farm workers to steel men; the latter, coming straight from the mills at dinner time with their heavy boots smoking, would down their pints already lined up on the bar counter from the moment the hooter went. More than a gallon or two had been carried mid-morning on to the furnace floor by bucket lads as water was forbidden as injurious to the sweating pores of hot-skinned men.

Herbert was a small, round, happy-natured man and a good advertisement for his strong ale and comfortable in possessing a solid bank balance. The latter information Harriet acquired by a cautious questioning of her father. When in due course a note arrived on her desk, inviting her to a Saturday tea at the Royal Hotel, she sent back a demure acceptance. From then on, it was a staid and steady courtship until the day Herbert asked Amos Fanshaw for his daughter's hand in marriage. Despite her sweet reluctance in courtship, Harriet had decided from first learning his name that Herbert Platt, the well-to-do brewery owner, provided the means of escape from her hated job as a cashier and from her loathsome father to the comfortable and easy life she had lost since her mother's death. Smiling tolerantly she listened to his long explanations of beer brewing, giving more attention to the profits than to the product. Somehow, she told herself, she would bear with the smell of beer for the sweeter smell of the money it earned. Amos was secretly glad to be rid of Harriet, both as a daughter and as a cashier. She warred continuously with each housekeeper, causing him frequent adjustments to indifferently cooked meals and household arrangements; in the shop her supercilious manner rubbed his assistants up the wrong way, except for Joshua Milburn, the obsequious counterhand, newly turned shopwalker. To Herbert, Amos showed a hypocritical reluctance at the prospect of losing a daughter and agreed to the marriage on one condition – that Herbert must change his name to Fanshaw. He had been blessed, he said with a twitch of his lips, with only one daughter and desired to ensure that the name of Fanshaw would be carried on. In his besotted state Herbert was prepared to agree to anything and willingly underwent the formalities of change from Platt to Fanshaw, thus creating for himself an identity problem both at work and at home. At thirty years of age he left the tidy little home, comfortably kept by his amiable sister, for the grander up-bank home Harriet had insisted he bought. By tantrum or by wheedling Harriet assumed command and Herbert found himself unable to drink his own beer in his own home and having to visit a public house and to pay for it, since Harriet forbade such a common drink in the house. He was happy when his son Reginald was born and, although Harriet's demands for money became more insistent, he sought to believe in his naive fashion that this then was married life.

Harriet Fanshaw smoothed down the folds of her grey barathea skirt and turned up the gold watch pinned to her chest. Ten minutes before her special pleasure, she noted. Rare were her smiles but today the thin lips were slightly upturned with inner satisfaction for she felt that at last life had given her well-earned rewards. Dear Reginald had married so well, the only daughter of Sir Nathaniel Dobson, the well-known Tyneside ship builder, and even now a child was on the way. Being a grandmother would increase her dignified standing with the various committees on to which she had so zealously engineered a seat. There was a slight frown and a sigh as she recollected that she had not been invited to Drumrauch Hall, the Dobson residence, or seen any of her new in-laws since the day of the wedding. Even on that occasion her son's new family had given a lukewarm reception to the Fanshaw connection. But it would work out all right, she assured herself, because Reginald was such a delightful boy no one could resist his charming manner. Of course, as a youth he had made mistakes; there had been that trouble over a maid but she had obviously led him on. Anyway the problem had been easily solved by arranging that fashionable system of a 'grand tour'. He had also made a hasty return and had shown, at first, a casual interest in the Emporium which quickly left him bored as the girl assistants were plain and unresponsive and the men dull and resentful of his foolish jokes and pranks. He would have tried the brewery but, as he pointed out to his complaisant mother, he had inherited her antithesis to beer and instead he filled the cellar with expensive wines. Digging ever deeper into his pocket, Herbert tried ineffectually to reason with both mother and son. With amused condescension Reginald listened to and then ignored his father's feeble threats; while Harriet coldly pointed out that there was no need to restrict Reginald's activities as, in due course, she would inherit her father's fortune. She stressed Reginald would soon find employment commensurate with his talents and was happy to subsidise his life style with the Dobsons; he would in time have his own home, no doubt when the child arrived.

Another quick glance at the watch and Harriet pushed the bell near the fireplace and promptly after a knock and acknowledgement Olive Harman entered. It had given Harriet satisfaction to employ Olive as a washerwoman on the death of her young husband. She had applied for the post of daily help, but Harriet, when she overcame the shock of recognizing the applicant, refused that work and offered her instead two mornings of washing clothes and scrubbing the many long stone steps leading up to the house. Olive had no alternative but to accept the work to augment her meagre pension. And Harriet never failed with unallayed spite to extract every ounce of labour, every minute of time from the woman she blamed for her girlhood misfortunes. She looked into the tired face and then well noted the red wrinkled hands, damaged by water and strong soda, of the woman standing before her. What Harriet described as a morning's work began at seven o'clock and finished at two in the afternoon, allowing half an hour for a midday meal. Before handing over the week's wages of five shillings, Harriet without any preliminaries said, 'Master Reginald will continue to have his laundry done here as I need to supervise that everything is up to the standard he expects.' Everyone in the household knew it was to ensure that her son would visit her, but Olive was also aware that Mrs Fanshaw would take care that her load of washing was not lightened. Olive thought, resentfully, 'She brings me up here every week when she could, if she wished, leave my money in the kitchen with the cook.' But weekly Harriet had to witness Olive's humiliation. 'I must remind you that I require the stone steps to be scrubbed with cold water. This morning I noticed steam from the bucket as you scrubbed the steps.'

'No, you bitch,' thought Olive, 'you've never knelt on hessian on the cold stone on a bitterly cold morning up to your elbows in icy water.'

'It was such a terrible morning,' she replied.

'That is beside the point, warm water discolours the stone and Mrs Crathorne will be reprimanded if, in future, she allows you to take hot water from the kitchen – you may now go.'

Seething with anger and near to tears, Olive went downstairs. After one look at her face Mrs Crathorne said, 'At it again, is she?' and continued punching the bowl of dough. 'I've put a pot of dripping in your bag.'

It would have been a great comfort to Olive if she had known that she would never have to scrub those steps again throughout another winter.

CHAPTER 8

Monday was lamp oil day and while Inkerman Street, indeed most of Embleton Town, was lit by gas, outlying areas and surrounding farms and villages had not yet the benefit and relied on Danny Marr. Roping his tank of paraffin oil to the back of his cart he would whip up his strong pony and set off on his rounds with a 'Giddup, Boney,' as he slapped its fat sides. At the top of each street he would sound his claxon horn and women would dash out to let the pony cart through their lines of washing and, laughingly encouraged or with pretended outrage, they would, clothes pegs in their mouths, react to Danny's invitation to 'take their drawers down'. Danny would measure into cans and bottles their oil requirements while gearing his bawdy talk to the toleration level of acceptance of each customer. His near-the-knuckle, mischievous jokes would be tittered over by his aproned customers until his next weekly call.

Returning home he would, after stabling the pony, prepare for the next day and fill his cart with scouring stones, flags and paper windmills to exchange for empty jam jars, while doing a little bargaining on his way for unwanted articles of furniture, ironmongery or the clothes of the recently deceased – clothes that were often bought in one village and sold in the next.

Back in his own home the washing day was over, garments boiled, blued and starched were hanging out in the autumn breeze and lines were full of shirts from Sunday best to Jonty's pit hoggers. The cooling boiler in the back kitchen was now scrubbed and washed out. In the kitchen sink Edie poured away any pieces of hair left on the sheep's head that had lain overnight in a bucket of water and carefully slit the nostrils to remove any snot. On the table her daughter, Maisie, sulkily chopped the giant leeks, onions and a variety of root vegetables, all from Jonty's allotment. Edie put the overnight-soaked pulses, beans, peas and barley with two buckets of water, together with the sheep's head, into the boiler and stirred up the fire underneath. When the vegetables were added and cooked the thick, nourishing broth could be laded out by the panful at any time during the week and reheated quickly over the fire. At the end of the garden, filled mainly with the results of Danny's 'bits of trade' as he called them, was the stable of Boney, the pony. The stable backed usefully on to common land where, most of the year, Boney grazed contentedly. Olive Harman complained frequently to Roberto that the lamp oil shed was dangerous and the stable too close to be healthy. The paraffin oil shed was directly opposite the house across the dirt road. The shed was well worn and well bleached and a useful back rest for Danny as he sat on his hunkers preparing to annoy, irritate or entertain; the reaction depending upon his relationship with the street's inhabitants who happened to pass by. Harry Walters, head horse keeper at the Wilhelmina Colliery, came slowly past. He was a taciturn man whose life was wrapped up in the care of his ponies. His only child had been listed as missing at the Battle of the Somme and had turned his pleasant, capable wife into a confused, indecisive woman, who daily cooked and served up meals at a table always laid for three. Every Saturday she took her son's best suit from out the wardrobe and, after brushing, hung it out on the line 'in case he comes home tomorrow.' Harry would quietly wrap up the excess of food and take it down the pit for his ponies. They would nuzzle his pockets for the treats of currant buns, fruit pies and cut-and-come-again cake.

As usual Harry ignored Danny's 'How's your old nags then?' and 'Still working them ould cuddies to death then?' Harry turned into number nine and sat down to the table set for three to what had been his son's favourite tea and now for them was always smoked haddock. While his wife described her plans for making an early Christmas cake to be ready for Bill coming home, Harry Walters, as he pushed aside the half-eaten haddock, sank deeper into the misery of his own thoughts. Work was somewhere to get away from this empty shell of a woman. He loved and cared for his half-blind pit ponies, calling each by name and nursing any grazed by a tub or bruised by a bumper store. He hated the confined darkness of their lives. The ponies, at first bewildered, came to the surface for two weeks of fresh air and summer sunshine and then Harry would spend most of his time watching the delirious racing and rolling of his charges, set free in the colliery field. He always tried to ignore the pricking darts of Danny Marr but they were a constant irritation, almost he thought like a burr under the saddle would be to his ponies.

Bessy Mayhew came down the lane and tried, with a head-down nod, to placate Danny. 'How's my bonny lass then?' he jeered and Bessy with what sounded like a hiccough ran up the lane pulling her shawl tighter around her face. Danny Marr's antecedents were a mystery, for at the young age of thirteen he had found his way alone across the Irish sea and, by wit with a touch of insolence, had crossed the North of England to find odd jobs around the quayside of Embleton. God had favoured him by carrying off the parents of Edie, leaving her vulnerable to Danny's cheeky charm. His mother visited him once a year, her journey funded on the way by fortune-telling, selling blankets from a pack on her back and by a smart line in begging. To Edie's relief she refused to sleep in the house and bedded down alongside Boney in the stable, where, covered by horse blankets, she smoked her pipe, indifferent to the inflammatory nature of her bed of hay. To his children's incendiary warnings, Danny asked, 'Which one of you will give up your bed then?' Known by Danny as 'the ould wan', her annual visit was dreaded by the elder children while the twins found her a fascinating story teller.

But Roberto was a disappointment to Danny for he could not, no matter what he said, rouse a reaction in him. And today as he passed, Danny hawked up and spat out a gobbet of phlegm and 'Pick the bones out of that,' he cheerfully invited. Roberto nodded and said, 'Nice day, Danny,' as he turned into number seven. With a red, angry face Olive burst out, 'He's a disgrace to the street,' as he entered the kitchen. 'Then just ignore him,' Roberto replied, knowing that was the last thing Olive would do. There was a pot of dripping on the table and, without looking at her wrinkled, sore hands or even remembering the day, he knew where the dripping had come from. Olive also knew he would refuse dripping on his toast with the tea he had come to enjoy. Exasperated, Olive wanted to shout, 'What's wrong with a bit of dripping from Fanshaws?' He always refused any food she brought back from the Fanshaw kitchen, although it was little enough Mrs Crathorne could hide from the eagle eye of Harriet. Yet it was strange, thought Olive, Roberto had stood outside the Anglican church to watch the fashionable wedding of Reginald Fanshaw. 'I'll never get to the bottom of him,' she decided.

CHAPTER 9

E ven before her grandson was born Harriet had made elaborate preparation for the christening. She refused to allow Herbert to have his new dark suit made at her father's shop, insisting on a bespoke tailor. For herself she ordered a fine woollen turquoise suit and drove the local hat shop assistants to tears as she tried on one hat after the other to find the perfect match. Settling on a pale yellow straw decorated by a band of imitation freesias, she then scoured the area for matching accessories. At the Maternity Hospital she had been disappointed by a lack of coo's and goo's from her daughter-in-law who showed surprisingly little interest in her offspring and who seemed more anxious about her mare, who was daily expected to foal. Harriet winced as she persisted in referring to the baby as 'the brat' and only after repeated requests from Harriet rang the nurse to bring in her grandchild.

Amos stubbornly refused to buy new clothes for the christening of his great-grandson. His interest in establishing a Fanshaw line had declined over the years, due mainly to a lessening interest in Reginald as that young man's development did not come up to his expectations. Harriet, using her strong position as a married daughter, regularly descended on her father's house to interfere in its affairs. The present housekeeper retained her position by cannily sneaking to Harriet a daily diary of her father's comings and goings. She had followed the resignation of Jane Wilson, who refused the satisfaction of sacking her by handing in her notice. Harriet, incensed by the audacity, had sternly reminded Jane that she would not provide a character reference and was further inflamed when the young woman replied, 'Better wait until you're asked.' Her father had been too easy with Jane Wilson and Harriet was relieved when she departed to her home in the wilds above Hexham. Amos refused to move to a smaller house, declaring that property was money and that Harriet fully understood. She looked

39

forward to the day when the beautiful house would be hers and she could uncover the shrouded furniture and restore it to the former standards of her dead mother.

Harriet's image of the aristocracy was slowly eroded on her visit to Drumrauch Hall after the family christening of her grandson. Even during the ceremony she had noted with disappointment that Lady Dobson wore the same outfit as she had worn at the wedding and that, Harriet observed, had been less than elegant. Her excitement at seeing inside the ancestral home was sobered as she closely examined its interior. In this age of smart, modern suites she considered the shabby, centuries-old furniture as unsuitable to the prestigious standing of Sir Nathaniel Dobson. She saw portraits of gloomy, long dead ancestors spaced up the wall of the draughty wide staircase, leading to a balcony filled with paintings of equally long dead horses. The dim, cold corridors were covered with prints of fox and beagle hunts. The dead animals were less disturbing than the numerous live ones circling around her. The house seemed inhabited by a pack of labradors and cats. Harriet, who never allowed any animal in her house, kept and anxious eye, fearful of any slobberings or hairs settling on to her skirt. As each animal approached she would draw in her kid-shod feet and make small discouraging movements with her hands.

The baby had been whisked away by a determined-looking woman referred to as Nanny. The long dining room table had been cleared away and now the family, Harriet supposed, would move into the drawing room. Amelia had two brothers, both married with young children, and when Harriet had advanced with an ingratiating smile and a warm enquiry after the children the wives had replied briefly that they were at home in the nursery. She had looked forward to making the acquaintance of the Dobson family and of being able to drop snippets of information about their lives to her very small circle of friends. Instead of sitting down to an expected intimate family get-to-know-you, Lady Dobson now passed through the room without a word, dressed in an old coat tied with a safety pin and wearing wellingtons. Sir Nathaniel Dobson retreated to his study to brood over shipyard affairs and the thorns in his side – the unions. Other members drifted past now dressed in jackets and breeches smelling strongly of the stableyard. The only approach that had been made to them was from a crabbed-looking great-grandmother who, after peering intently at Harriet, dropped an inch of tobacco ash on her turquoise dress.

Reginald found his three relatives sitting together looking lost and discomfited on a large leather couch. Amos had consoled himself by frequent trips across the room to the whisky decanter and Herbert sat with half a glass of sherry beside him and longing for a pint of his own ale. Reginald came in murmuring a grinning apology; Amelia had to see a new-born foal, Nathaniel had worries about the shipyard and as he bumbled on Harriet, incensed, cut in with a cold voice, 'I would like to see my grandson.' With, 'All right, this way,' Reginald led her up three flights of stairs, past seemingly endless bedrooms with notably few bathrooms and finally knocked on the nursery door. Nanny opened the door with a shush finger to her lips. Reginald, turning on his charm, said, 'We would like to see the baby.'

'Master William is asleep, he will be brought downstairs before dinner,' and with that she carefully but firmly closed the door.

'Are you going to allow that?' demanded the frustrated Harriet.

'It's the rules, Mother. It's the way we live here. Come on, let me show you the way down.'

Struggling to keep her temper under control, Harriet sought out Lady Dobson in her garden, carefully avoiding grass and earth contact from her champagne-coloured kid shoes by keeping to the path.

'It's been a lovely day for the christening,' she said to the kneeling figure.

Her Ladyship paused with a trowel in mid-air. 'Ah yes, the christening, I suppose so,' and went on splitting dahlia roots.

In the awkward silence that followed Harriet consulted her watch and found it would be half an hour before their hired car arrived to take them home.

'I'm sorry to say goodbye but I am a Governor of St Aidan's school and I must attend a committee meeting there.'

Unimpressed, Lady Dobson continued digging and a frustrated Harriet returned to look for Reginald who, recognising the signals, had cautiously disappeared.

'We got the bloody frozen mitt in there,' said Amos as they drove home.

Still clinging to her pride in Reginald's marriage and prospects, Harriet replied, 'You could never understand the ways of the aristocracy.' As she sat back in the hired car she made up her mind that they must have their own car. Herbert said nothing, knowing she would unburden her wrath when they got home.

CHAPTER 10

R oberto was aware that his family and indeed all the inhabitants of the village of Castiglione high above the port of Naples would be wondering why he had delayed in sending for his intended bride, Maria Bonaducci. He had long since paid back with a generous interest the twenty golden sovereigns sewn into his waistcoat to fund his mission, but so far he had failed to avenge the violation of his sister Cecilia or to come within striking distance of her seducer. His father, of Sicilian extraction, was a patient man, believing that revenge must be exacted coldly, and often in replies to Roberto would remind him of the old Sicilian saying: 'Time is such a gentleman.' Everyone in Embleton believed he had made a good business for himself, now owning a smart ice-cream parlour where collier lads would take their girls for a sly courting ritual in the semi-private high-backed compartments. Here miners in their blue serge suits and white silk scarves would cool or inflame their passions with ice-cream wafers or cornets with a chocolate crumbly bar inserted. Others would prefer a glass of ice cream luridly coloured on top by a splash of scarlet syrup known as 'monkey's blood'. In winter time, straight in from the cold they would order mugs of Bovril or Oxo served with dry cream crackers at fourpence a mug. No girl above the quayside careful of her reputation would be seen in a public house where the man usually ended up after seeing his girl home. No front room courting was acceptable until the engagement ring was on the finger and then at a danger from younger members of the family bursting in unexpectedly. True, much older women were known to frequent the Jug and Bottle department where they were discreetly served through an alley window away from the front door customers. By ignoring the furtive fumblings in the box-like cabins Roberto had succeeded in establishing a flourishing trade but now he was impatient at the small profits.

Sometimes he reminded himself of the hard times when he had

scraped a living by trundling his ramshackle barrow carrying the metal canister of ice-cream made in Olive's back kitchen. Then, his customers were unconcerned about the place of production and if it had crossed their minds it would have been dismissed by the recollection that everyone knew Olive Harman was nipping clean. In summer he would work eighteen hours a day when hot weather made counting his takings a delight, but it was hard to make up for the dark winter days when sales were poor. Even on those heart-sinking days Olive made him sit down each evening to his penny notebooks and his child's early learning books. From day one Olive insisted that he learnt to speak and write the King's English or, as she told him grimly – 'Go back where you came from.' So well had he become part of the culture and environment that, seeing him in the dusk of an evening selling ice cream to home-coming miners, there was little difference between them in speech, colour or stature. The seasonal fluctuation of sales worried him and he looked for an all-round yearly trade.

The idea came to him as he passed and then returned to look into Sandy Hall's fish shop. Sandy was by dinner time well oiled and by supper time sullenly drunk as he slapped fish through the batter trough. His slipshod wife, petticoat trailing to the heel of her shoe, served fish and chips straight into the newsprint as she proffered the encrusted salt cellar and vinegar bottle to customers, headed usually by Lill buying extra vinegar with her fish supper. Roberto looked at the greasy counter, the yellowing pieces of potato clogging the chip machine and the slack coal heaped against the wall, topped with old fish boxes stacked to light the fryer fire. Passing a small warehouse halfway down the bank he noticed that it was for sale and already on his way down to Betsy Haddick's cottage his decision and plans were made. Despite Olive's disapproval and the admonition of the Priest, Roberto had never severed his relationship with Betsy. Apart from the deep sexual satisfaction, Betsy had introduced him to the ways and tales of local sea-faring folk, especially the superstitions. If men forgot their sea boots and sent back for them they must be carried in a particular way – one under each arm with the toes pointing forward. If they were carried together over the shoulder with the feet behind, the owner would be carried home drowned before night. The word 'pig' was to be shunned and if a stranger inadvertently made use of the word, ill luck could be averted by grasping the nearest piece of cold iron. With any doubtful prognosis Betsy would put her thumbs inside her doubled fists to break the spell of the evil eye. Roberto was to learn of a similar folklore of the coal mines through Jonty.

Only in the comfort of Betsy's feather bed could Roberto feel an Italian, not an alien, and had long since ceased to do penance on the flock mattress of Inkerman Street. Betsy's strong limbs were now running to fat, for with Roberto's financial donations the hard work of hawking her creel around Castletown was no longer necessary. Roberto had learnt to watch for the departing fishing boats, knowing that Sarah would be absent. Occasionally, bad weather or an unexpected heavy catch would bring her home early, when she would always ignore Roberto's presence as she had done in those early days.

Returning to Number Seven and Olive's 'I know where you've been look', he persuaded her to sit down and listen to his plans. They sat as they had done over the years with Roberto at his books and using Olive for reference as she knitted him grey stockings for week days and black stockings for Sunday. When knitting the latter she always wore a white apron to ease her eye sight with the fine black wool. Aprons, except for church, were a necessary outer garment. Those made of sacking were for wash days, yard swilling and once, to Roberto's unbelieving eyes, for scrubbing out the empty coal house floor. Others were for morning or afternoon use. Her mania for cleanliness and unceasing work had worn her to whippet leanness and her passion for scraping and saving went beyond the necessity of her prersent income. Two Christmases before he had bought her a pair of pure silk stockings, for she always wore fawn lisle cotton. She smiled that Christmas morning, showing as much pleasure as her nature would allow. Immediately she brought out her work basket and began carefully to darn the heels and toes. To Roberto's astonished question she told him the stockings would last longer and when she was finished she reached from the back kitchen shelf a screw-topped jar, dropped the stockings inside and sealed the lid. They had pride of place on her wash stand but they had never been worn.

Roberto's plans covered not only his own advancement but also for Olive it would mean freedom from the years of hardship working for Harriet Fanshaw. Freedom from scrubbing steps in icy water during the winter, from the use of harsh washing soda on her hands and from the heavy mangling of endless sheets. Roberto intended to open a clean, hygienic shop and those words acted like a starting pistol to Olive. As soon as Roberto acquired the warehouse every spare moment was spent installing the fish fryer, lime washing the walls and scouring the cement floor. At the back Roberto boarded off the preparation room. Olive still went to her two mornings at the Fanshaw house for until she was earning she took care not to lose money. Every evening the talk was about the new business venture and both agreed that it was now necessary for Maria to come to England to manage the ice-cream parlour while Roberto and Olive developed the fish business. Roberto insisted that only the best fish be cooked and sold and who better to buy wholesale and as cheaply as possible on the quayside market than Betsy, whose knowledge of fish price and quality was unequalled. They would introduce squares of clean, white paper between fish and chips and newspapers. Roberto bought and painted four square tables while Olive made red checked tablecloths. Here were the small beginnings of the restaurant he determined, one day, to open in Castletown -a restaurant selling only Italian food. Olive sniffed, for now Roberto was going too far – as if people hereabouts would eat foreign stuff like that.

CHAPTER 11

The sight of the twins' noses and those of their dogs pressed against the windows of his shop, the dogs raised on hind legs, sent Alan James into a paroxysm of rage. He had had a bad morning encounter with his wife, whose pointed nose seemed able to trace the progress of each sly cake or cream pastry from the bakery to her pocket. Certain deficiencies from cost ingredients to the cash till had roused her never dormant suspicions and following an investigation, she demanded an explanation.

'Have you been betting on the dogs or the horses?' she demanded. Unconvinced by his explanation of faulty ovens, she flounced away to retrack the production lines. The suppressed fury of Alan James came to the top when he saw two human and two canine noses pressed against his shop window. The silk stockings for the twice weekly favours from Hilda Mason caused him much subterfuge to cover under-counter selling and the by-passing of the till. Mrs James cared little for her husband but a great deal for the day's takings and her gimlet eye would have done credit to the head of the secret service. Every penny he managed by sleight of hand was used to placate his lover with expensive presents and caused Alan James much anxiety. When Hilda told him how one of his precious gifts had been soiled and endangered his anger found a focus – the Marr twins, the originators of the damage.

Sitting astride their bicycles the twins closely assessed the merits of jam tarts or maids of honour, while the slavering dogs anticipated a few begged crumbs. Although Pilot the whippet was ostensibly Jonty's dog, the brindle had been nobody or anybody's dog after being rescued as a pup by the twins, held down in a beck by a bagful of stones. He was called, for no special reason, Tyke by his rescuers. By slow degrees he had established himself from alongside Boney in the stable through the backyard to share the clippy mat in front of the fire, where he had

47

been amiably accepted by Pilot, who found a comfortable ease in the shaggy coat of his belly, and balefully by the cat. No one could ever call him an attractive dog, with his huge head and skimpy tail, his large lumbering shaggy body and his tea-plate-sized paws. Together the dogs guarded the twins on their bicycle-bound adventures and the fireplace mat from the cat. As they entered the shop Alan James cautiously ascertained that his wife was safely in the house before he launched himself from behind the counter.

'What do you want?' he demanded.

'Two jam tarts,' Joe replied.

'I don't serve the likes of you or him,' he snarled as he pointed to Jamie. 'Get out of my shop.'

Outside as they collected their bikes and their dogs the lads shared a smile; plans could be made later.

The family row between Edie and Jonty was so loud that Olive Harman would not need to hold her glass against the adjoining wall. Indeed, as Danny was not this time involved her interest was desultory. Anyway, with the open window one could almost be present in the kitchen. Jonty Marr had missed a shift as he recovered from a fight in a backyard with a husband who, returning unexpectedly, had found him trousers down in the front room on the settee with his wife. They had slugged it out man to man in the backyard and now he nursed a black eye and many bruises. His errant lover nursed much the same as she struggled to get the tea ready as a placatory gesture to her wronged husband. Opening the back door a little, Olive heard Edie shout, 'Why can't you behave decent like your brother Michael?'

Stung by his mother's condemnation on top of a hammering, Jonty lost all loyalty.

'Decent, she says, ask him where he goes every Sunday night – don't bother – I'll tell you – Clarty Clara's.'

Shocked, Edie cried, 'Michael never goes there.'

'Ask him,' Jonty said, and took his *Sporting Gazette* and bruises up to bed.

Edie crossed her breast and then her fingers, for with her superstition and religion came even handed, the former reinforced by often related dream interpretations. The stairs that Jonty now traversed had figured largely in a dream where she felt that she was doomed to lie with a broken neck. That same morning she employed a joiner to build another step to reduce the depth and was satisfied until, climbing the stairway at bedtime, she realized that the new addition brought the number of stairs to thirteen. Next morning a bemused joiner was ordered back to remove the new stair.

The local saying 'as soft as clarts' was certainly a misnomer as far as Clara was concerned, for her business affairs were carefully tabulated as an insurance policy with the names and number of visits of many local pillars of the community. Clara could be said to be more crafty than clarty. Repeated efforts to close down her establishment were made, headed by the Women's Guild and spearheaded by Adelaide Simpson, who would have had hysterics to find both her husband and son named in the book Clara so carefully kept. Every approach to the Police was met with the bland reply that there was no evidence; under pressure the expected raids found nothing incriminating in the quiet club atmosphere. Locals with sly amusement considered 'Fishing Tackle' displayed in the quayside window of the large building to be a double entendre. Innocent visitors and young boys would buy their sea bait in the fronted shop except for the careful who dug up lug worms on the beach. The same young boys usually followed their fathers' footsteps to the rear entrance when their interests turned from fishing to sex at Clarty Clara's brothel.

CHAPTER 12

Amelia pushed a booted foot into Reginald's recumbent form, 'Get up,' she said and opening a wardrobe door reached out from the rack of expensive clothes bought by his mother, his hunting clothes. Amelia, who spent more time in the stables than anywhere else, could not tolerate her husband's antipathy to hunting. He had no moral objection to either fox or beagle hunting but the truth was he was scared silly by the leaping over ditches and fences, insecure in the saddle and acutely aware of the mocking glances and cutting remarks that came his way, especially from Amelia's brothers. Irritated and humiliated, Amelia sought to goad him into her lifestyle. Her earlier attraction to the amiable, jokey Reginald had led to this ill-assorted marriage. Reginald, like his mother, could not understand this family of distanced relationships, where, in the same household everyone lived their separate lives. Lady Dobson seemed to live in a different world from her husband, her main communication was with the gardener as she, in rain or shine, shod in wellington boots, dug, weeded and planted. Harriet was deeply shocked to learn that Lady Dobson shared her morning coffee in the greenhouse with the gardener, as both pored over gardening and horticultural magazines.

Armed with expensive presents for the baby William, Harriet had determinedly forced her way into Drumrauch Hall, warily skirting the numerous animals and on these rare occasions was greeted by a semi-stare of recognition. Reginald visited his parents more often now, not only to pick up his laundry, but to complain about his wife or his brothers-in-law or to corner his mother alone to ask her for more money. He declared that everything would be all right if Amelia would join him in their own home but she refused to leave her two horses so comfortably stabled at Drumrauch Hall and where free board and lodging, with no questions asked, suited her very well. Living on his relations worried Reginald not at all but the ultimatum of a job in the shipyard worried him intensely. As he pointed out to Sir Nathaniel, he knew nothing about ships and was brusquely told any clerk could do the job he was offered. Reginald was further offended by the reminder that in the past he had not shown much acumen about brewing or shop management. His mother tried to soothe and smooth away his complaints but had gently pointed out that some earnings of his own would be welcomed by everyone. Asked about his son, Reginald replied, 'Fine, Nanny says he's fine,' and there his interest in his son, like that of his wife, ceased. In the oak-lined office with its wide windows overlooking the Tyne, Sir Nathaniel Dobson and his elder son, Martin, discussed the problems of the shipyard and foremost was the increasing number of the workers' meetings held down in the Welfare Hall. The venue particularly incensed Sir Nathaniel as his father had paid for that very building in which, according to him, the subversive unions plotted for more wages, shorter hours and better working conditions; all of which he angrily assured his son was a threat to the very existence of the shipyard and more importantly, to the Dobson family. Martin agreed as he had always agreed with his choleric father. He was perfectly content to wait in the wings, playing the subservient son until time put the family business his way. His brother had cornered the wholesale fish market and it gave Sir Nathaniel immense satisfaction and his elder son twinges of jealousy to see the fleet of vans carrying the fish to the railway station destined for Billingsgate, with others crossing the country to serve shops in inland towns. 'There is even a plaque on the wall there, commemorating his generosity.' As Sir Nathaniel had never set foot in the building he was not to know that the plaque had long since been removed and now served as an ash tray with his revered father's name now obliterated by cigarette stubs.

'If we could find a way to get rid of Albert O'Connor,' suggested Martin.

'No, he's just a balloon fellow with only an up-on-the-tub credibility, he's easily deflated, we must go after the clever one,' and with heads together they discussed ways and means, finally moving on to that other worry – Reginald Fanshaw.

'Apart from messing up the clerks with his Jack the Lad bloody jokes, the bugger's a nuisance.'

Martin nodded, 'I've had to move him from the general office, he's

51

had his hand up the skirts of some of the typists.'

Sir Nathaniel grunted and rose from his chair.

'It's time we had a look into the drawing office.'

On his way to his father-in-law's office Reginald had enjoyed the look on the chief clerk's face as he sat down ponderously on the farting cushion he had placed there and was surprised no one else in the office even looked up. Lot of dull sods, he thought. He had decided it was time for an increase in what he believed was an insulting pittance for the time he spent in the shipyard. He was particularly grieved that the board room door was closed against him. Amelia did not seem to care that he was not receiving his rightful place in the family business. Her father and those damned brothers of hers were determined to keep him out, he brooded. Finding no one in his father-in-law's office he helped himself to a large glass of gin from the hospitality cupboard and sauntered over the room to sort idly through the papers on the desk.

'Guess who was here last night?' asked Thelma Mounsey as she rolled over the bed to pinch out her Woodbine. Michael paused in the act of pulling up his trousers. Surprised, he waited, for Thelma had never before discussed her clients. He buttoned up his flies, lit two cigarettes from one match and handed one to Thelma, 'Santa Claus,' he offered.

Ignoring the sarcasm she said, 'Reginald smarmy Fanshaw, that's who.'

'A regular is he?'

'Too bloody regular for me,' replied Thelma.

As he slipped his arms through braces and slotted his leather belt through the waist tabs, he waited, for there was obviously more to come.

'Three parts drunk and loose on the lip he was. In fact,' she added with a grin, 'his mouth was the only part of him in working order. Slavering on about how the unions were in for a clout. And you are first on the list for the sack, hinny. Better watch your back on a dark night. Thought I was on to something more but he was off to sleep then. I'll bet Clara lightened his pocket when he woke up this morning.'

Michael smiled and nodded as he took his leave. He paused on the way up bank and gazed down the river where the droop-snouted cranes rested; all strangely quiet, for today was Sunday. 'Sack me,' he thought, 'I'm a move ahead of you, Sir bloody Dobson.'

CHAPTER 13

As Jonty was on early shift, before he went to bed he warned his mother not to feed Pilot because his dog was running in a whippet race the following night. Next morning Edie carefully placed the two dogs' feeding bowls high up on the pantry shelf. Their bowls were not always so special as dinner plates were often handed down from the table to be scoured clean by eager tongues. It was also to be a day of abstinence for Tyke, who had been known courteously to stand his large bulk aside from his own plate to let the slimline Pilot taste his dish. The warning was well noted by Edie, remembering the family row the day Pilot's predecessor was entered for a big race. The cat, now curled up in his fox fur, had wandered, a lost kitten, into the Marr kitchen to be confronted by, what seemed to him, a tiger-sized dog. Leaping in fright on top of a pannikin of fermenting rhubarb wine covered only by the front page of the *Sports Gazette*, it parachuted down into the wine. The dog retrieved it from the wine and, carefully trapping the soaking bundle between his paws, licked it dry. Liking this new flavour the whippet stood daintily on his back legs and slurped up a good cup full. Jonty's rage at finding his dog stretched out in front of the fire, snoring drunk, was something to behold, for he had a heavy bet on his dog, a sure thing for the first race.

October brought potato picking week when schools closed and big lads and lasses biked or walked to the surrounding farms to earn money and bring home the added bonus of a free bucket of potatoes. On this Wednesday, avoiding Edie's query why they were not out to the fields, the twins, followed by two hungry dogs, enjoyed their free morning, returning to Inkerman Street at precisely twelve o'clock. Alan James's cart was stationary there in the back street and as usual the curtains were drawn in Hilda Mason's back bedroom. The horse, yoked to a covered cart, waited patiently, glad of his weekly rest in the same spot each week. He was surprised to hear the latch being lifted at

53

the back of the van for Alan always jumped immediately on to the tail board and hurriedly drove away from his lover's house as quickly as possible. At the rear end the twins slipped a couple of sly cakes and gingerbread into their pockets and, seeing the pleading look in the eyes of the dogs, gave them a quick affirmative nod. The surprised horse felt the unusual weight that almost lifted him out of the shafts as the animals jumped into the cart and wolfed down the trays of delicacies, with Tyke's large rear paws firmly embedded in two steak pies. The dogs were called away, reluctantly leaving a churned-up mess behind in the covered cart while the twins melted away out of sight to hide in Boney's stable. They were within earshot of Alan James's shouts of rage but unable to witness the sight of a half-dressed Hilda rushing to the scene, forgetful of the many back window eyes relishing the sight of trampled confectionary being scooped out into the lane. The lads held on to the collars of the two dogs, an unnecessary precaution as they lay replete and comatose on Boney's blankets. Later they stubbornly refused to explain to Elsie the two fat stomachs heaving on the mat. Edie, dreading Jonty's homecoming, moved swiftly to lock the back door escape route and looked for the cat o' nine tails. Failing to find the leather strap, for as often as it appeared on the nail on the kitchen wall, it disappeared to be hidden in the seldom explored corners of the house, in the stable or even at Jonty's allotment. It was always a wasted tactic because Edie, short of the belt, simply resorted to a brass stair rod.

The backyards became alive at Alan James's unwise broadcasting of his courting calamity and before he returned home Mrs James had been given a full account over the counter by neighbours who masked their glee with sorrowing sentiments. The baker's wife had now quickly and satisfactorily solved the mystery of the till deficiencies, and as for him being Hilda Mason's fancy man, she could soon put a stop to that.

The last time they had had such a beating was after the hugely fat Mrs Temple had wheezed her way down to the school to report them to Mr Mitchell, the Head Master. Confrontation with the Marr family was something to be avoided at all costs, but Mr Mitchell could be relied upon to dole out a full measure of retribution. The twins had been discovered tying the hind legs of her husband's two pigs and had left the sty door open, from where the pigs proceeded to create havoc among the vegetable plot in the allotments and, despite their leg

54

handicap, the pigs laid bare patches of brussel sprouts and anything else that came their way. Mr Mitchell not only laid into Joe with his thin, skin-raising cane but gave him a double dose for his brother's part in the misadventure. Later that day, as Mrs Temple eased her fat rear over an inadequate wooden circle above the earth closet, the iron grid outside in the back lane was quickly raised and a clothes prop thumped her fat backside. The retaliation was their undoing, for Mr Temple was forced by his furious wife to visit the Marr family with the news of the twins' misdemeanours. Fortunately for all concerned, only Michael was at home and he was able to give a sympathetic ear and the assurance that punishment would be meted out. Mr Temple retreated, now satisfied that he could soothe his outraged wife. Seating the two lads on crackets, Michael demanded to hear the full story and tried hard to hide his mirth as Joe described what had happened. His humour changed when Joe showed him the scarlet weals on his backside. 'Right,' he said, 'fetch me the cat o' nine tails,' and obligingly the lads reached it down from under the fox fur and an offended cat. 'Now, Joe, you've had a hiding over the pigs and you, Jamie, will get your share over the shaming of Mrs Temple – agreed?' The twins turned to each other and with their alphabet fingers agreed that fair's fair and without hesitation Jamie dropped his trousers and bent over the sofa end. In private they agreed that their adventure had been a mistake for, with trips to the Temple backyard with potato peelings, old bread and scraps, they were always rewarded with two or three sweets each from a jar Mrs Temple kept on the boiler top and the back door was now forever firmly closed.

But this time was really serious, because Jonty had a lot of money invested in Pilot's fast legs. He was sure that tonight would see his whippet the winner of his race and a substantial amount of cash in his back pocket. By the time he returned home the full story was known down the back lane and before he had washed off the pit dirt he had both lads seized by the jacket back. Before he had even reslotted his leather belt the weals were aggravating those of the stair rods and the twins were unable to complete their week's potato picking.

CHAPTER 14

The October breeze scarcely ruffled the sluggish river as Roberto walked down bank to visit Betsy. He paused at the school to listen to children singing a roundelay:

> 'White sand and grey sand
> Who'll buy my white sand
> Who'll buy my grey sand?'

and to pause at all was not second nature to him now. From early morning to cashing up at night he never stopped to pause, his thoughts contemplating only the next day's takings. The sudden wave of emotion as he heard the children's voices caused an unfamiliar ache in his heart, that caught him unawares. He had lived out these hard years near the white sands of Northumbria and had schooled himself not to dwell on the grey, volcanic sands of his home land but the words and the sweet, young voices brought an unexpected wave of home sickness. Life was so different now, he mused. Those hungry days when he had shared an oatmeal supper with Olive, with just enough left to share at breakfast, the tea times of bread and margarine sprinkled with sugar and the meatless days were over. True, they still lived simply but the times of pinching and scraping were done and nowadays they could always rely upon a fish supper. The roundelay followed him down bank, acutely aware as he sang the words softly, that this would be his last visit to the cottage.

> 'White sand and grey sand
> 'Who'll buy my white sand
> Who'll buy my grey sand
> Who'll buy my grey sand?'

Betsy could now count herself well off as Roberto paid her well to ensure he got the best of the fresh fish landed on the quayside and expertly filleted for his fish and chip shop. It was delivered daily by Jamie Marr, who had converted Roberto's old ice cream barrow to new usefulness. That was also the term Olive used to describe the twins; they were now growing up to be useful and she added sternly, 'Learning to behave themselves, instead of roaming the streets and getting into mischief.'

Sandy Hall's dirty fish shop had disappeared due not so much to the competition of the new up bank shop with its fancy ideas of chips served on clean white paper and tables for fish suppers, but due to Mrs Hall's fall on the greasy floor, breaking a hip and Sandy's drunken mistake of putting his hand into the fat with the chips. The stomachs of many local people were not easily turned but the sight of soiled bandages slapping through the batter with their twopenny cod was more than even they could stand.

Customers from both up and down bank and even the square began to patronize, with the latter; orders collected by the general maid at the fish shop with the same name over the door as the ice cream parlour up the road. Olive took an immense pride in the fish shop, for her it was such a step up in the social scale from being Fanshaw's washer woman. Vinegar bottles gleamed and the salt cellars shone and it gave her much satisfaction to serve young couples a fish supper at her smart tables. The twins would appear nightly for a ha'pennorth of scrapings, the tasty golden scraps of batter sifted from the frying fish. Lill would souse her chips with as much vinegar as she dared to shake from the bottle and, forming a funnel until the paper was in danger of disintegration, she would cup the two edges together and drink deeply.

Olive smiled grimly as she remembered Harriet Fanshaw's reaction on the day she gave notice. As she waited for the acknowledgement of her knock, Olive took a deep breath. As usual and without any preliminaries Harriet began her spiteful criticisms.

'My silk camisoles were not properly ironed last week, you surely know that silk must be ironed damp on the wrong side – please see that they are properly ironed next week.'

Olive squared her shoulders and, bending forward to look Harriet in the eye, said, 'I won't be here next week, nor any other week. In fact this is the last time I'll ever set foot in this house. I don't know why you have vented your spite on me week after week but in future you will have to find another scapegoat.'

Aghast Harriet stood up to face Olive, 'You – you . . . such impertinence, you can't give me notice – I'm sacking you. I'll see to it you never work in Embleton again.' Inwardly she was furious, knowing not only that she could no longer humiliate Olive but also that she was losing a hard-working and – more valuable in Harriet's eyes – a cheap worker. 'People must wonder why I've let you work here at all with your doubtful reputation, for everyone knows you have that foreigner living with you.' Her moral indignation suddenly blossomed. 'Perhaps it is my duty to bring to the notice of the Moral Welfare Society, your unseemly relationship with his man.'

Olive leaned over and took her five shillings off the table. 'Why not?' she said. 'And while you're at it try taking it up with my Priest,' and gave herself the satisfaction of shutting the door with a bang. Downstairs she took out the pot of dripping that the housekeeper had placed in her bag and put it on the table. 'Give that to the next poor soul who has to scrub the steps in cold water, but my thanks to you, Mrs Crathorne, for the only kindness ever shown in this house.'

Roberto looked around the room, remembering with a pang the night he had arrived a wet, terrified stranger, led by chance to the warmth of Betsy's bed and her placid kindness. Despite her improved financial status, the room was exactly as it had been all those years ago. As he placed his feet on the fender in front of a blazing fire, his thoughts turned to Olive. Her fender – the one she had painstakingly cleaned with bath brick every Friday, labouring with a damp cloth dipped in the fine scouring powder and burnished determinedly until the steel fender gleamed like silver. The word fender troubled him – was it to ward off heat or cinders, he wondered. So much hard work she had expended over her fender and fire irons and Roberto congratulated himself when he learned how to relieve her of that drudgery. He had heard of a magical new process – electroplating – that needed only a quick rub with a soft cloth. He arranged through the co-operative store to have Olive's steel irons embellished and returned while she was out. She had been scornful of the idea, asserting that nothing could give a better shine than bath brick. They were there in gleaming splendour on her arrival. She halted in the doorway, then kneeling down drew a finger along the shining surface of the fender and, as she looked up, for the first time Roberto saw tears in Olive's eyes. Standing up she faced him and said, 'I'll wear those silk stockings at your wedding.' Then to his amazement, she went to the cupboard, brought out a blanket and carefully covered up the fender and fire irons. Seeing the looked on his face she assured him that she would uncover them on Saturdays and Sundays.

On the mantleshelf above, old Sarah's pipes were laid out in a row. One Christmas he had bought her three brand new clay pipes which she accepted with a nod and straight away broke the stems in half to accommodate her hooked nose. Opposite him, Betsy sat happily pouring out the bottle of stout he brought her into a pint pot. Over the years she had given him solace and in a way that he could not understand, a link with his homeland. Her skin and eyes were still clear, belying her forty-two years, and she was without a grey hair in the golden crown on her head – although she was now running to fat. The walking miles of hawking fish with a creel strapped to her back had kept her big framed body muscular. But now, apart from the fish shop commitments, life was easy, although no matter how early the boats came in Betsy was always there as the fish boxes were hauled from boat to quay. He remembered how glad he had been to share a fish supper with her when food had been scarce at number seven. Her laughter at his finicky ways of preparing and cooking fish had long since turned to appreciation. Betsy broke the silence, 'Will I see you sometimes, hinny?'

'Every week at the quayside with your pay but you know I cannot come here after the wedding, but I will always see you all right, Betsee.'

She nodded with a calm acceptance. 'But will you stay the night?'

Roberto stayed and their loving exceeded anything in the years gone before and finally he laid back on the bolster and sobbed.

'Don't take on so, bonny lad, I'll always be here,' Betsy said. She cradled him again in her arms crooning, 'Robbie – Robbie – ' the name she had always given him.

CHAPTER 15

As the only daughter in a houseful of brothers Maisie Marr had been less than cherished. Danny Marr would, with a loud 'lass', bang the empty salt or pepper pot on the table to indicate lack of service. Her mother accepting the more of the time and place, expected a subsidiary to her own role of cook, washer woman and cleaner, with the latter well down on the list of priorities. Brothers expected shirts ironed, shoes cleaned and food on the table; the men folk would have considered it out of place to lift a dish from the table and even more so to wash up at a sink.

The nubile Maisie, a replica of a once young Edie, escaped as often as possible to the back row of the pictures to exercise her sexual potentiality and was often seen in the semi-seclusion of the ice cream parlour with Willie O'Connor, he of the hanging jaw and wet lips which earned him the sobriquet of 'Slack Willie'. He owed his job to his father's high standing in the Boiler Maker's Union and introduction into the Marr family via Jonty and the Iron Master's Arms. The summer courtship had been swift and torrid and as Olive, glass to the wall, realized, fruitful. Edie had pondered over the best day and time to break the bad news to Danny. Each morning seemed to bring a deterring omen such as two magpies on the shed top or on another occasion Michael put a pair of new shoes on the table. Although she had hastily removed them and stepped over them three times, the uneasiness remained. Before a meal was out of the question and afterwards would depend upon the amount of pre-lunch drinking and, with the twins around, evening was also an impossibility. The twins were particularly adept at judging the alcohol influence on Danny's mood. From the end of the lane they could assess by his walk, his singing or his approach to neighbours whether to disappear out of sight or to wheedle for a penny, knowing they would with magnaminity be beerily awarded threepence.

After breakfast with the men out at work turned out to be a no better time, for Danny Marr immediately dragged Maisie from the back kitchen and with fist and belt leathered his daughter until she screamed, cowering in the corner as he exhausted his rage and strength. In her efforts to intervene Edie had been thrown on to the sofa while underneath the frightened dogs squeezed as far back as possible against the wall. His ginger hair standing peaked on his head and without dentures, he looked uncommonly like the leprechaun he so often talked about. As he turned on her Edie backed away, for diminutive as he was, the enraged Danny was a fearful sight. 'You ould bitch, why didn't you look after her?' Over Maisie's hiccoughing sobs Edie yelled, 'What had I to do – tie her to the table leg?'

Olive sat down to mull over the news – 'Well, that will set the street alight,' she thought. When Roberto called he was privileged to be the first recipient of the news and Olive's assertion that she, for one, was not surprised, for that girl, by flaunting herself, had got what she deserved. She was taken aback when Roberto rounded on her: 'It should never have been allowed to happen – her brothers should have protected her from that half-wit Willie. Neither her parents nor her brother bothered about her welfare, she has been left to run wild and for their neglect she gets a beating.' There was some truth in Olive's condemnation for Maisie never missed the opportunity to brush against him in the ice cream parlour or to accost him in the back lane, but that such a beating had been inflicted by a father on a daughter, this Roberto found deeply offensive. His anger overcame his discretion when he met Michael in the back lane returning from a union meeting. Unable to hold his tongue and without stopping to think what the consequences of his interference might be, he voiced his indignation and was shocked by Michael's reply: 'Well, she should have kept her legs crossed,' and seeing the incredible amazement on Roberto's face he added with a grin, 'Ah, don't worry, they'll be off to see Father Anthony before long. Goodnight to you.'

Roberto leaned against the back gate, his thoughts in a turmoil. He would never understand these people who could take the violation of a young girl on the one hand so viciously and on the other so lightly. As a lad he had arrived here with a desperate mission to kill the man who had seduced his sister, made an outcast of her in the eyes of the village community, and a source of humiliation to his family. Was the punishment of Maisie less than that of his sister, now entombed in a nunnery, given the title of 'Nun' but who in reality was living a life of drudgery as a lay sister? From early dawn she was expected to expiate her sin while scrubbing stone floors and undertaking forever the most menial of work. Despised, but useful, she must meekly accept these cruel deprivations for the rest of her life. As a maid in the local hotel she had fallen in love with what she thought was an English gentleman but who was no other than Reginald Fanshaw. He, warned by the management, hastily returned to England, just escaping the certain death in wait for him. On the young unmarried brothers had fallen the task to exact retribution. A place called Embleton was a long way from Castiglione but it was a place to wait for revenge. Rough as this place was, there could be no using the old ways of a shot in the dark or a knife in the back. Over the years, as he steadily prospered, Roberto watched Reginald Fanshaw, circling him as steadily as an animal patiently tracking down its prey, hearing of his extravagances, noting his weaknesses and biding his time. Both Maisie and Cecilia were the victims while the men were careless of their abuse. For the first time he began to question the ancient values of his lineage. His thoughts turned to the Marr men and he wondered hopefully if, in their own way, Maisie was already being avenged. Danny Marr had not been seen since the events of the morning, neither had Jonty, and he began to believe that even now they were inflicting punishment on the miserable Slack Willie.

Danny Marr had a beautiful tenor voice that could bring tears to the eyes of the old women supping in the back parlour of the Iron Master. With Danny drunk, the voice had a soulful timbre and even now it came from just around the corner accompanied by a regular, grating screech. They came in sight, the three men, with a rusting wheelbarrow containing the recumbent Danny loudly serenading the night and the street with the 'Rose of Tralee'. Holding one handle of the wheelbarrow was Jonty, not quite so drunk and just able to weave an uneven passage; holding on to the other side, jaw happily agape, was Willie O'Connor. Danny saluted Roberto with a raised bottle of beer and solemnly announced, 'We'll be having a wedding.'

CHAPTER 16

Callum Ogilvie, the Bank Manager, folded his hands over his enjoyable luncheon. Sitting opposite, Herbert Fanshaw recognised the signs of his falling gradient of respectability in the eyes of the manager. He was no longer offered the always to be politely refused sherry of approval as he waited uncomfortably for the anticipated tooth combing of his affairs by the Gradgrind sitting in judgement opposite. 'You have been an esteemed customer over many years Mr . . . er Fanshaw.' Even today Mr Ogilvie had never quite accustomed himself to the name change from Platt for that name at the Bank had meant prosperity for all concerned and a welcome mat to his hallowed presence. 'Your profits from the brewery are far outweighed by your family's expenditure and this has made almost a complete erosion of your capital . . . and now you want to borrow.' He was too cautious to name the extravagant spenders, but there was no need as Herbert immediately launched into a spirited defence of his wife and son. Harriet, he pleaded, was going through a difficult time, she was not well and here his voice dropped to almost a whisper, 'The change of life, you know.' Reginald was now working for his father-in-law and must be supported for a time to be in keeping with the expectations of the family Dobson. At the name of Reginald, not a flicker of expression altered the urbane face of Mr Ogilvie; that name was surfacing too often in the affairs of his less esteemed customers, but to the onlooker one could believe he had never heard of him. As it came to his lips the word 'expectations' gave Herbert a shaft of inspiration. 'My wife is, as you may know, the only child of Amos Fanshaw who is not in good health.' His voice trailed away as if he had mentioned the unmentionable.

There was no change in the Bank Manager's voice or attitude. 'In the banking world,' he pontificated, 'we deal with the here and now and not the hereafter, and I suggest you take immediate steps to deal with your family's excessive demands.' In the past Herbert had always been escorted to the door by the Manager mouthing affable pleasantries, but now there was only a dismissive bell push as his departure was watched by speculative eyes. Those same eyes lightened as the Manager rose to welcome his next customer.

'Ah, Mr Delfino, how are you – may I offer you a sherry?'

Roberto acquiesced, assuring himself that he was paying for it anyway. In the early years the Manager had scarcely noticed the dark, young man banking pennies from his ice cream barrow sales. Now Mr Ogilvie highly approved of his client, who ran two flourishing businesses and who had done well marketing stocks and shares. The Manager showed all his teeth: 'How can we help you?'

Roberto sat down and crossed his legs; being in the lower seat worried him not at all. 'I'm getting married next month.' Disregarding hearty platitudes, he continued, 'And as my future wife will be running the ice cream parlour, now is the time to expand my business interests. I want to buy a very particular property in Castletown which, I believe, is coming on to the market soon. I am in no hurry but a nod in the right direction would be welcome.'

Mr Ogilvie gave the required nod. 'What do you propose to do with the property?'

'I intend to open an Italian Restaurant,' Roberto replied.

The Manager devoted three quarters of an hour to Mr Delfino, considering the time well spent as he walked over to usher Roberto out, with his good wishes following him through the door.

Herbert dared go no further, for the ominous twitch at the side of Harriet's mouth had intensified. 'I will not have Reginald shamed in the eyes of the Dobsons. As a member of the sailing club he tells me that he feels slighted because he does not own his own boat.' Harriet had begun to talk quietly but now, as she pleated her handkerchief into precise folds, her voice began to rise. She accused Herbert of being a feeble father who could not provide for his only child. He was also a pettifogging fool who would never understand the ways of better-class people. 'You own that house in Morden Street, take the deeds to the Bank Manager and get the money. It's your house, you bought it.'

'Yes, I bought it as a home for my sister and now you want me to mortgage it for a boat for Reginald.'

'What is your sister compared to your son? Anyway, she has a safe roof over her head. We can get the deeds back when my father is dead.'

As she calmed down she could think of nothing but her handsome son, full of charm and caresses when she had finally been persuaded to make Herbert find the money. He had glowingly described the boat on offer, of how he would take her with his in-laws for sea trips and of how prestigious it was to be a boat owner.

Harriet had become increasingly irritable and restless, the phlegmatic Mrs Crathorne had long gone and such was her reputation as an employer that only the desperate gave her temporary service. Since Reginald's marriage into what she believed to be the cream of aristocracy, Harriet had ceased to visit the Fanshaw Emporium in her efforts to disclaim her trade origins. The business was now completely in the hands of Joshua Millburn, whose subservience to Harriet decreased as his security as manager emboldened him. Everything now, he suavely assured her, was handled by accountants.

'We all must move with the times, mustn't we, Mrs Fanshaw?' and he went on to assure her that the brash upstart co-operative store was no threat to the established Fanshaw Emporium. Her great consolation was to assess how long it would be before her father would do the decent thing and leave her to inherit. She noted covertly the signs of any mental or physical deterioration. Over the past ten years he had spent an increasing amount of time in those remote Northumberland parts. With a disapproving sniff she believed he was reverting to the days of his youth as a pack man. His generous dispensation of free drinks and dinners was also missed and commented upon by local dignitaries. Sadly they agreed that Amos Fanshaw had lost interest in Embleton and Castletown and its inhabitants.

CHAPTER 17

As she gave Roberto a knowing wink as if initiating him into a secret society, Edie confided that it would have to be a quiet wedding, following with a nudge – 'You know how things are.' She brightened up with the sudden thought – 'Well, it's the only way I'm likely to have any grandchildren with one son in other men's beds and the other easing himself at Clarty Clara's.'

Roberto leaned against the wall and looked down at Edie as she sat flushed, with her baking done, on the cool back door step. The row of loaves stood on end, cooling on the stone slab under the window with the round stottie cakes, the once risen rounds which, when generously spread with butter, were relished by the family. They were now arrayed against the windowsill. The Marr family were all big bread eaters, especially Jamie who never ate potatoes, not since the day he had sliced through a large boiled potato and the black slug inside it. The tantalizing smell of the new bread had often hungered Olive and Roberto in their days of privation but never had they been offered a new loaf or a tea cake. Edie knew it would not be welcome, however much it was desired. Olive's stiff pride forbade any outward recognition of her poverty and even now, although financially secure, she would accept nothing from her neighbours. Down Inkerman Street there was an easy passage over the low walls of the loan of a cup of sugar or a quarter of tea. That stopped at Number Six for, in Olive's vocabulary, 'borrowing leads to sorrowing.'

Olive still remembered with anger the day years ago, returning from the Fanshaw home cold, tired and hungry and without the little pot of dripping she regarded as incremental to her wages. The dripping was often her staple diet for breakfast and supper but Harriet Fanshaw had been particularly vigilant that day and Olive had no other means of filling the life-saving gap. Danny and Edie had been both in the yard as Olive walked her tired feet through the back gate. Danny leaned on the wall and, eyeing her slim, tired figure, called out, 'Begod, there's neither in you or on you, you could do with a good feel and a good . . .' Smothering his next remark Edie hurriedly elbowed him out of the way. 'I've a spare bit of belly port I'm cooking the now – could you use it?' Flushed and furious, Olive, as she fumbled for her door key, had turned to face the two. 'Thank you – no – I've a piece of steak to cook for my meal,' and ignoring the disbelief on Edie's face she had gone indoors and without taking off her coat, sliced a large onion and as it fried opened the window and the back door to advertise the aroma. Later she had eaten her onion sandwich, if not with enjoyment, at least with stiff satisfaction.

Roberto listened to Edie's family troubles as he had done so many times before. He had always admired Edie and the sanguine way she accepted the follies of her brood. Always she had called him a canny crack but in reality he was a canny listener. Today was farewell to living in Inkerman Street. The back rooms at the ice cream parlour were ready for his bride. Furnished, but with an economy surprising in one shortly to be a bridegroom. The hard schooling of privation in Olive's house, together with his determination to be a man of business and property, left no desire for luxuries. The kitchen behind the shop storeroom must serve as dining room and living room. The bedroom might have been a replica of Olive's back room with its large wardrobe, bed and washstand – all bought second hand, even to the linoleum on to floor. In Inkerman Street bedroom washstands were an obligatory but in reality an ornamental feature of bedrooms. People washed down in back kitchens with the luxury of a tin bath on Friday nights in front of the fire. In the cold back kitchen Roberto had installed a bath, covered by a wooden lid hinged to serve as a work table. The cross so often flashed over by the lighthouse beams, Olive had given him and it now hung over the marital bed. The photograph of Maria, the daughter of his father's life-long friend, lay in his breast pocket. In the glowing testimonials from home she had been described as a good girl, who would undertake her wifely and religious duties conscientiously. He often looked at the photo, at the pale, serious face with its large dark eyes, and wondered about the girl who would be the mother of his children. Roberto knew he should have gone personally to Italy to marry, but he had pleaded that he was unable to leave his business affairs and consoled himself with the knowledge that he was paying for the bride's aunt to accompany the motherless girl to England. He smothered the agonizing truth that he could not return to Italy until his sister had been avenged. He had not seen Betsy since the last passionate night of farewell and avoided the quayside by sending her weekly fish money by Jamie Marr.

With a start Roberto tuned in on Edie's monologue. 'There was a share out of free boots at the school yesterday. I sent our Joe to school in the oldest pair I could find – his toes were sticking out but that old sod of a schoolmaster, Mr Mitchell, wouldn't give him a pair. Do you know they are clipping a little hole in the back of the uppers so that their mothers can't pawn them? Can you believe that!'

Roberto interrupted the indignant Edie and her endless monologue by saying, 'Want to hear a secret, Edie?'

She stopped in mid flow, her mouth a round 'O'.

'Maria, my fiancée, is due to arrive on Monday.'

Flattered by the confidence Edie nodded her head sagely. 'I know how to keep my mouth shut – there's a saying here, discretion is the better part of value.'

Roberto nodded, smiling, 'I've got to collect the last of my things from Olive's but I'll be around – look after yourself, Edie.'

'And you, bonny lad,' she replied.

Reliable as ever, Olive had his clothes stacked neatly on the table. Angry with herself for the conflicting emotions that disturbed her, she reassured herself that it was time she had the house on her own. She took the wooden mushroom out of the sock she had been darning and, folding it with the other, laid the pair neatly on top of the pile. As Roberto came through the door she said, 'Would you like a cup of tea?' and together they sat down at the table with the tea things between them. Neither knew what to say, Roberto wanting to express so much and Olive unable to, because of the lump in her throat. Upstairs in Roberto's vacated room another single bed had been installed for Maria's aunt. Pillow cases, sheets and bedspreads were snowy white and without a crease. Olive was to be hostess to the two women and was conscious of the interest and envy in the street. She kept all the tantalizing details to herself, although she knew that Edie Marr, full of self importance, had told the neighbours of the day they were expected. 'Well, we thought she would never get here' was the not unexpected retort. Olive looked over at the man who had changed and filled her life and who had slept under her roof for the last time. 'He's a good looking man,' she decided; on the short side, like most of the men around here, but with a fine head of jet black hair, wary dark eyes and an olive skin that looked as though he had lived all his life in the sun. He would make a fine mate for the girl in the photograph. Roberto, looking across the table, knew that any expression of thanks or sorrow would be unwelcome or perhaps greeted with caustic severity. Olive had never divulged her age but he guessed about fifty. There were a few grey hairs and fine wrinkles but the harshness of those early years had left little mark.

'Will you go down to the quayside, with me to meet Maria and Zia?'

'Certainly,' she replied as she laid some brown paper and string on top of his pile of clothes. 'You had better be getting along, it's time I was off to light the fires in the shop. Wrap up, it's turning cold outside,' and she walked out of the back door.

CHAPTER 18

The Lady Amelia Dobson's two brothers fulfilled the tradition of carrying out their own life styles and touching family life on the fringe as lightly as possible. The late autumn to early spring hunting calendar was the only bond between them. The younger of the two brothers, Tobias, entered the attic room above his office to peer through his brass telescope way down the river to watch the docking and unloading of the early morning catch. In this way he could secretly keep a check on the landings from his fleet of boats. He lit the popping gas heater and turned to the window to watch and count the boxes being swung ashore by men joints frozen from an icy night's work. Idly, he watched the crew men slowly making their way from the quayside to disappear into the narrow streets. Suddenly, he noticed something on the quayside and carefully adjusting the telescope, he was surprised to see a familiar car parked outside the Fishing Tackle; well, he's not there to buy tackle that's for sure, he mused. The car was the newly bought acquisition by Reginald. It had taken hysterics on the part of his mother and the deepening gloom of his father to finance the car, bought as a status symbol to uphold his fading credibility with the Dobson family. Even though he had squealed to a halt in front of the portico at Drumrauch Hall, no one had seemed sufficiently interested to come out to admire the car. Tobias made a note of the time and date in a book and when later the column was full he deemed it time to consult his father.

Sir Nathaniel was choleric with temper. Having planned to sack Michael Marr he had entered the meeting with the unions prepared to coerce Albert O'Connor, the father of Slack Willie. Instead, he found himself facing Michael Marr across the table who coldly informed him that he had been voted in the new secretary to the union and was replacing the retiring Albert O'Connor. At every twist and turn of the agenda he found himself coolly questioned and blocked. Refusing a large whisky, Michael pressed on with his line by line examination of

70

the agenda. The air fairly bristled with hostility and Sir Nathaniel realized with fury that he now had an adversary such as he had never encountered before. Heavy with meaning was the underlying threat of a strike that could bring the shipyard to a halt. He realized he would need to negotiate with this man annual renewals for pay, uses and shorter working hours. If the threat of a strike became a surety the expected Government order for two new battleships would go either to the Clyde or Belfast. The essential climb down brought bile to his throat as he recognised a new leader well versed and well read in law and union history. The puzzled Sir Nathanial wondered how this sudden jump from the easily manipulated Albert O'Connor to this hard-fronted Marr had come about. Over the last few years he had noticed a more intelligent approach to negotiation and was aware of the stronger back up of Michael Marr. Mindful of the threat, he had decided to sack Marr but he had been forestalled. As only his son knew of the dismissal plan, he could only assume that luck had been on the side of Marr. But luck had little to do with it for Michael had lobbied against the limited Albert, while shrewd workers recognised in him an adept and powerful leader.

It was not a good time for Tobias to unload his discovery of the frequent and often overnight visits by Reginald to Clarty Clara's. Sir Nathanial had not been over concerned when Amelia had married Reginald, for indifference was a long held tradition in the Dobson heritage. His irritation at the juvenile behaviour of Reginald was shrugged off, but that his daughter was shared by seamen's trollops demanded action. And Amelia's reaction was surprising. Yes, Reginald's evening absences had not gone unnoticed nor had his claims to be at his mother's home been believed. Her placid acceptance of the news could be explained by the fact that her own attentions were now fixed on the hunt whipper-in, a tall athletic man who was as good a judge of horse flesh as he was of women. When Reginald returned from the shipyard Amelia curtly told him that his clothes had been moved to a room at the back of the house and from now on her bedroom door would be locked. He raged downstairs to confront his father-in-law in his study. After the day he had undergone, Sir Nathanial was in no mood for conciliation. Reginald was given a list of his improprieties and told either he distanced himself from Amelia or that he left Drumrauch Hall and relinquished his rights to see his son. In the back bedroom overlooking the stables Reginald sat on the edge of the bed with his head in his hands. The most awful contemplation of the future was that his mother should know of his disgrace. Her pride in his marriage and connections was the lever he used to obtain money from his father. However uncomfortable and humiliating his position in the house, he knew he must stay at Drumrauch, for the ace card left to him was the little boy now taking his first steps in the nursery at the top of the house.

CHAPTER 19

For the first time since her own wedding Edie's thoughts turned to her wardrobe. With neither fashion knowledge nor the inclination to what she believed was fancy clothes, she prevaricated until the last moment. This was ever her way. Throughout her life she believed any problem was better shelved and it was with something of panic that she realized, as the wedding day became imminent, that as the bride's mother she would be closely examined and her outfit meticulously scrutinized. Her spreading girth ruled out any dress worn on the summer occasions of yesteryear. As she stood in the front room which had also served as Maisie's bedroom since decency forbade her bedroom-sharing with the twins upstairs, Edie's eyes rested on the oak chest full of her late mother's clothes. Unlike the rest of the house, the front room retained an aura of the days when it had been treasured and its contents beautifully polished. Just now the lovely old sideboard was less than adorned by a full chamber pot, the contents on their eventual way by the backyard and Jonty's allotment bucket. Had she known the origin of a sideboard was to house chamber pots installed to ease the bladders of card-playing gentry, it would have been of little interest to Edie. Maisie's single bed in the corner was squeezed between a walnut cabinet full of fine china and the oak chest, its brass fittings now dulled by neglect. Olive would not have been surprised but would have ached to see such a front room desecration.

Edie opened the chest and the smell of camphor brought tears to her eyes as she moved the tissue paper that had lain undisturbed for years. The pre-Danny Marr days came back in a flood of memory as she examined the fine quality of the yesterday clothes. From among the wool and cambric she drew out a dark blue silk dress and, as she held it against her, realized she had inherited exactly her mother's mature figure. The dress fell in graceful folds to just above the carpet slippers that were Edie's habitual footwear. Suddenly she kicked off

73

the slippers and rummaging in the dark, tall wardrobe brought out the fine leather shoes she had worn to her wedding. The heel inches gave her a long forgotten dignity as she placed the dress on the hanger.

Maisie was to move from her single bed in the front room to a double bed in the O'Connor front room. While Jonty was willing to drink with Willie, neither brother was prepared to share living space with him; especially now, as there was a growing coolness between the families following Michael's appointment as union secretary. Albert O'Connor was still unsure how it came about, for he was still unaware of the quiet undermining that had taken place. The sudden transmission from being the back-slapped, megaphone-holding worker's mouth to suddenly being presented with an overall retirement requirement had him bewildered. The possibility of being voted out of his long held position had been inconceivable and his bewilderment turned into a slow hatred of the family about to be related to him by marriage.

Edie leaned over the table to count the pies, cakes and sandwiches prepared for the wedding. Maisie was packing the food into long trays borrowed from the Welfare Hall. While few had received a formal invitation to the wedding ceremony and reception, all of the street expected to be invited to a drink and a dance in the evening; none were to be disappointed. The men had done their share by stacking up crates of beer at the end of the hall and had cautiously hidden bottles of whisky under the sheet-covered table, to be judiciously doled out to the favoured and to those reckoned to be able to carry it without disgrace. Michael had impressed upon Jonty that they both carried the onerous task of keeping their father acceptably drunk. Panting with exertion, Edie was about to sit down when the light from the kitchen window darkened. 'Dear God, not before the wedding,' she cried, as she recognized the shawl-covered head of her mother-in-law. Sorcha Marr had unknowingly arrived the day before her grandaughter's wedding and even now was casting an interested eye over the array of food. With a sinking heart Edie remembered she had brought on the bad luck by spilling a bag of salt at the baking. Ignoring the resigned look on Edie's face and the hostility of Maisie, who just knew the old woman would spoil her day, she demanded, 'Is there a drop of tay in the pot for I'm fair parched?' Edie poured out a large pot of strong tea, sweetened liberally by tinned condensed milk.

'Maisie is to be married the morrer.'

'Well, Holy Mary be praised, I've come meself at the right time.' Dropping the large pack from her back she drew up Danny's large armchair to the fire, causing distressed yelps from the dogs as the heavy chair legs moved them off the mat. 'Begod, it's good to see a fire,' she said as she folded far back several sweat-stained skirt layers, exposing her strong thighs to the heat and knee-length stockings gartered with string. Hastily, Maisie began to move the food into the back kitchen, muttering to her mother that the smell of her would knock you down. Old Mrs Marr, although the Mrs was a courtesy title, received a conflicting welcome from the rest of the family. The twins gave a delighted yell and impervious to her strong body odour sat down beside this fascinating story teller. Michael with barely a look of recognition took his books from the high shelf beside the fireplace and disappeared to his bedroom. Jonty, his teeth showing a white smile in his coal-dusted face, said, 'You old devil, where have you sprung from?' and Danny, singing, went under the stairs to bring out bottles of stout.

With all of Inkerman Street knowing of her condition, Maisie had forfeited the right to a virginal white bridal gown. Many before had forfeited the same right, but the question of a swelling figure, or the broadcast by a family row, carefully concealed the aberration, with a white silk or satin gown. Father Anthony Howard eyed the wedding congregation as he awaited the bride. Their eyes, he knew, would be focused on the midriff of the bride as they tried to assess how far she was 'gone'. From face to face his eyes slid over the waiting throng, remembering their fears, hopes and anxieties temporarily left in the confessional box. Without fear he could look at Olive Harman, now neatly sitting, for the old dangerous attraction had been channelled into another direction. With a sad heart tug he was glad that life was easier for her now and it certainly showed in a more contented visage; he was glad he had introduced her to a better life through Roberto Delfino.

At first he did not recognize the dignified figure of Edie as she walked down the aisle to her favoured place on the left-hand front row. Her only purchase for the wedding ceremony had been a small light blue hat which complemented the lovely silk gown so sleekly fitting. Across the aisle was the waiting Willie and Father Anthony recalled with distaste his slobbering with wet lips over the communion cup. Willie had gleefully broadcast the news of his approaching fatherhood, convinced that at last he had achieved something worthwhile. One would think he had invented impregnation. Even from this distance the elder Mrs Marr advertised her presence and the Priest was grateful that Agnes Cowen had followed her, that morning, into the confessional box with floor cloth and polish. The sudden organ peal caused him to look up to see Maisie proceeding down the aisle on the arm of her father. Danny's hair was slathered in brilliantine, which only just held down his spiky ginger crown, and Maisie had not outraged public opinion, by appearing in a pale blue dress. Her fair hair shone under the translucent veil and Father Anthony thought, as Roberto had before him, 'What a waste on Willie O'Connor.' Like a child at a birthday party, Willie sat alongside his best man and got up to greet his bride while his family rose as a glum rearguard.

To all but Agnes Cowen, Father Anthony was known as an abstemious man, for he never accepted a drink apart from the bridal toast. Many of his parishioners looked upon this as a shortcoming. In his study at night among the consolation of his books, he drank steadily alone and only Agnes heard as she lay in bed the sound of the wooden cover being lifted and the subsequent clink of a dropped bottle down the garden well. With her rosary in hand she prayed in her silent room as the mole moved up and down.

Apart from the wedding selected few, the Welfare Hall soon filled with Inkerman Street neighbours, ship yard workers and miners. Men, who tossed red hot rivets as easily as they tossed pennies at pitch and toss, stood glass in hand with Jonty's coal face marrers. A group stood in the corner laughing at Stan Wilson from number fourteen. The elderly bachelor, well known for his meanness and always the prototype for every miserly joke, ate as though he had fasted for weeks. Holding an umbrella between his knees, he made determined grabs at every passing plateful. His early attempts at courting had been flouted by the girls he escorted up to the pay desk in the picture hall queue with the earnest exhortation, 'Get your money ready, there's going to be a scrush.'

Olive sat apart, her mouth drawn as thin as the blade on the Marr's bread knife, stiffly holding a small glass of sherry as the fiddler and pianist set feet tapping. She determined that Roberto's wedding would be in a different class to this, as she eyed the full and empty beer glasses either in hand or parked on window sills. But Roberto as usual was busy with his books, although he had promised to look in later. As glasses were emptied and refilled the pianist thumped harder to be heard as the noise escalated and the floor reverberated to the clump of heavy boots and solid bodies. The twins, unnaturally neat and with stockings firmly gartered below their knees instead of lying layered around their ankles, acted as waiters and were especially solicitous of their grandmother, who sat drunkenly crooning in an unknown tongue with a *cordon sanitaire* around her.

Suddenly Olive found her glass put to one side and she was pulled to her feet by Danny Marr. Hugged close to his face and clamped by an arm around her waist, tight as a vice, she found herself waltzing and unable to escape. She had primly noticed, over the evening, his careless flirting with the women, most of whom shoved him off and left in peals of laughter. Now as she struggled not to enjoy the swaying intoxication of the dance, Danny whispered, 'Just let yourself go, darlin'.' Immediately Olive pulled away, declaring it was time she went home and ran to the door, passing a surprised Roberto at the entrance.

Stan Wilson struggled to his feet clutching his umbrella and, flushed with food and drink, decided to make his way home. He was followed outside by Jonty and his cronies. On the steps of the Welfare Hall they grabbed his umbrella with a 'looks like rain' and they opened it over Stan Wilson who was showered by cake and sandwiches. Snatching at a falling pie he made off, followed by drunken laughter. Then on the steps they formed an escort party to the bridal pair as they were bawdily serenaded on their way to the O'Connor home.

CHAPTER 20

Michael knew there was a plant at the union meetings. Motions agreed and carried in the Welfare Hall were known to Sir Nathanial Dobson before he had time to utilize them to the worker's advantage. By carefully side-stepping trouble and using his considerable knowledge of rules and practices he had worked himself up to a strong position of power. With the elimination of Albert O'Connor, whose policy was not only to invite trouble, but to go out and drag it in, he was now considered of some importance and even the local Labour Member of Parliament for Castletown courted him assiduously. Although he still shared a bed in the back bedroom with Jonty and paid his mother well for bed and board, Michael withdrew more and more from his family. Now he had a small office up bank with the bust of Lenin transferred from his bedroom and now conspicuously displayed on his desk. When he acquired an office telephone Edie regarded her elder son with awe. Even with Percy Metcalfe, his second in command, Michael was reticent, knowing from his own practices that it was politic to watch the man behind you already measuring up for your shoes. Percy was given only selected information yet often found himself first in the firing line. Michael believed that unquestioning loyalty was useful and admirable but that it came only from the ignorant, who could easily be manipulated to the ballot box. Mr Mitchell, the schoolmaster, now became interested in his former pupil, Michael, and recalled that in class he had been a strange lad for he always wrote with an arm curved over the top of his desk, thus shielding his note book from other pupils.

Since Robert Marshall of South Shields had built his first iron ship, the Tyne had prospered but now, in the postwar depression, times were hard. There was a division among the men, the desperate with large families and short means who would strike for a sixpenny increase and the caffy-hearted who would accept any conditions to keep their jobs. Strong union principles did not prevent him from a deep pride in the vessels built on the Tyne and he relished the phrase by Daniel Defoe, written in 1427, 'They build ships here to perfection – I mean as to strength and firmness and to bear the sea.'

Albert O'Connor would always be greeted in the Iron Master Arms with a co-worker affection and Percy Metcalfe had inherited some of that easy association with members; a fact that Michael had not overlooked. Michael was given respect as a man who could recite former cases of intimidation or exploitation as easily and profoundly as a lawyer. He would quote verbatim the 1871 strike, when after three weeks, the employers were forced to agree to a nine-hour day: a dispute simmering since 1866 and known as the 'nine hours' with four hours on Saturday.

Doris, the cleaning woman on Sir Nathanial Dobson's office corridor, eased her bunions by stretching her legs out under the table on a red leather stool. 'Over here, Michael,' she called. He frowned at the familiarity of a vaguely recognised woman and reluctantly walked over with his glass. 'How can I help you?'

'Nay, lad, it's how can I help you,' and she moved an empty glass over the table.

Michael, making nods of recognition, walked through to the bar and returned with a half pint of beer.

'I reckon it's worth a large gin,' Doris said pointedly. Realizing nothing more was forthcoming at present, she sighed and said, 'There's a fellow you know very well who stays behind in the locker room after his mates have gone home. I seen him often leaving Sir Dobson's office when I clean in the evening.'

Michael's thoughts focused sharply and, meeting Doris's eyes over her spectacles, walked again from the snug through to the bar, to return with a double gin. Placing it in front of Doris he leaned forward expectantly. Doris took a sip and murmured, 'That's better.' Unable to play out the charade any longer she whispered in his ear, 'You know him, that Chris Simpson.'

Michael certainly did; a man who regularly attended Union meetings and who paid a flattering attention to his every word.

Answering the back door, Chris Simpson jumped back as he saw the group of grim-faced workmates headed by Percy Metcalfe who said, 'You've got a bit explaining to do.' Chris caught the glimpse of a shot gun and quickly slammed and locked the door, thus confirming their suspicions. By the time the men had rounded the street end Chris was out by the front door and, passing the rows of houses, sprinted across the park with the men spurred on by anger, rapidly overtaking. Three of the men had now headed him off by leaping over backyard walls and now surrounded, in desperation he leaped at the bottom branch of a large tree and given strength through fear, clambered up the oak tree. Heaving and panting the men circled the tree and called him to come down and face them like a man. Chris Simpson's answer was to clamber further up the tree. Finally a voice called, 'I'll get the bugger down,' and a shot was discharged up the tree. Screaming, Chris Simpson let go his hold and fell to the ground, adding a broken leg to the gunshot wounds in his backside. After Michael Marr's bedside visit, Simpson stubbornly refused, despite Police pressure, to name names or to prefer charges and within weeks of leaving hospital had, with his family, left the area. It was considered a satisfactory conclusion, especially for Michael who, even if charges had been brought, had not been at the scene of the wounding. He was not over concerned that charges might have been brought against Percy Metcalfe for, as he smiled to himself, why keep a dog and bark yourself.

CHAPTER 21

Olive, looking out of the window, hesitated purse in hand. She had promised Roberto to go to Alan James shop to pay for the decoration of the bride cake. She had baked the cake herself and now it was down in the shop being decorated, for everyone agreed that Alan was a dab hand at that. It would have to be collected on the wedding morning by Roberto for Alan James was banned, by order of his wife, from Inkerman Street but, as many people knew, it had not put a stop to his illicit tryst with Hilda Mason.

While Edie was well known to keep a good table and that bread and cakes were her forte, all the street accepted that Olive's fruit cakes made from a family recipe were unbeatable. The Christmas ritual of 'tasting the cake' was ingrained in local custom. Neighbour might be scarcely speaking to neighbour but neither would have the ill manners to refuse the customary invitation to taste the cake and drink a glass of port or ginger wine. Roberto had always, with fascination, watched the October preparation of the Christmas cake. The careful washing of dried fruit, afterwards spread thinly on to clean cloths and dried on the fender before the fire. The spices, fresh butter and eggs filled the room with a bountiful aroma, unusual in Olive's kitchen. She would stand back and regard the hand-blended mixture with an artist's eye to decide on the depth of coloured richness. Taking a large, old tablespoon from the kitchen drawer she would caramelize spoonfuls of sugar over the open fire and add them to the mixture until it reached the satisfying depth of colour, adding cream last of all. Drawing the ashes from under the oven, she would place the cake, bound in several layers of brown paper and tied with string, into the oven above a shallow tray of water. The oven she would judge to be ready by the heat on her face from the open oven door. Then she would sit nodding in her chair until the early hours of the morning; rising stiffly to stir the cooling embers of fire and take out the cake tin. It stood on the back kitchen table for twenty-four hours before she unwrapped the crackling paper and wound the string into a neat ball. With a thin knitting needle, Olive pierced the crust and poured in rum to soak. Finally, wrapped in a linen tea towel, the cake was placed in an air-tight tin, covered by a clean sacking cloth and placed high on a cool shelf until early December. Rumour had it that cakes baked to that same recipe had, by Olive's mother, been further wrapped in oil cloth and buried in the cool garden soil until Christmas. Questioned as to its authenticity, Olive would neither affirm or deny, declaring she would not give them the satisfaction. Even Olive had to succumb to the Christmas obligation but was careful to accept the invitation to taste when she was sure Danny would be absent. She would sit uncomfortably noting the dust on the bulbous legs of the dresser and the confusion of dishes pushed to the back of the table. In return Edie would be equally on edge as she watched her reflection in the shining fender of Olive's hearth. After they had wished each other polite compliments on the cake, the wine and the season they would return to the acceptable standards of their own home, a neighbourly duty thankfully over for another year.

Olive's hesitation was due to the presence of Danny sitting hunched back to his shed in the lane. Earlier, the sound of raised voices and the crash of pottery against her chimney wall made her wary of stepping into trouble. Previously, Danny had expressed an unjustified opinion of Edie's cooking in the classic style of Inkerman Street, by heaving his dinner, plate and all against the fire back. Now hungry but unable to climb down and return to the house, he sat vengeful on his hunkers waiting for a victim and the pub opening time. There was something more than puckish in his attitude, for it held an element of malevolence. The local council granted him yearly permission to scythe any grass from the roadside and Bonny's winter fodder was secure. This morning's gleanings now stood in a heap over the fence with his long hay fork leaning against it.

The twins had escaped the parental row and were now relishing the despised stew, Joe with a hill-sized heap of potato and Jamie with half a loaf of bread. Their grandmother sat at the fireside with the pot in her lap, spooning up the remainder of the stew. Michael called in to pick up a wanted book, took one breath inside the kitchen and hurriedly departed upstairs. 'Did I ever tell you about that old wan Murphy,

God love him, him that lived near Sinningtons bog and died alone?' The lads hastily scooped up the last of their dinner and took a seat at each end of the fender, looking expectantly towards the old woman. 'Well, he passed on,' and here she crossed herself with the stem of her pipe, 'and was never found for a day. When I come to lay him out the ould soul had died with knees up to his chest. When I tried to straighten him out his head came up to the back of mine with one hell of a thump and nearly knocked me out. Begod, I needed a glass full after that.' Howling with laughter the twins telegraphed each other their appreciation of the tale while Edie called reprovingly from the back, 'That's enough now.' But the old lady was already wheezing a laugh at another remembrance. 'His sister, now there was a quare one, married to a fellow she hated. Fought every day and most of the night and what did she do when he died?' The question was left in the air as a rumbling cough released a gobbet to be spat hissing on to the fire bars. Recovering her breath she chuckled and repeated the question. 'What did she do? She went to the churchyard every Friday night and pissed on his grave.' Edie, dish cloth in hand, came through the kitchen door. 'Out you lads,' and as the giggling pair ran out into the backyard the old woman laid down her pipe and settled back to sleep in the armchair.

Charlotte Brown came around the corner wearing her black funeral clothes and elastic-sided boots. Every night she marked out the lately deceased from the evening paper and noted any forthcoming funeral of which she could claim even the remotest relationship or acquaintance. Her green eyes, protruding like the glass alley stoppers in lemonade bottles, would light up to calculate the ages of the departed and pat herself with satisfaction at having outlived them. Struggling to the graveside on her very bowed legs, she would add her own benediction to those gathered by profound pronouncements, 'He was always good to his mother,' or 'She never said a wrong word against anybody.' The judgements were tailored to the sex, age and moral acceptance of the mourners. Today, smarting from the way she had been elbowed out from a funeral tea by determined relatives, she was not pleased to encounter Danny Marr. 'Been up to the graveyard, have you?' he taunted. 'At your age you could have saved shoe leather by staying there.'

Charlotte glared pop-eyed. 'Pity you've nothing better to do than upset decent people.'

Danny retaliated to her huffy back, 'Them bow legs of yours couldn't stop a pig in a passage.'

To ease his knees Danny stood up and eyed Vinegar Lill who was glad to escape with only the gibe of, 'Chuck the vinegar, Lill, it's giving you a neck like a hen's leg.' Danny leaned against the shed and as Harry Walters passed he gave him a brown-toothed grin. 'Is it haddock for tea again, Harry?' he called. Without a word Harry swung round cold faced and, seizing the hay fork, lunged at the tormentor. The fork collared and pinned Danny to the shed wall with less than a quarter inch to spare each side of his neck. There was a heart-stopping silence when nothing was heard but the singing twang of the prongs of the embedded fork as they vibrated against the wooden wall. The silence was finally broken as Lill slid to the ground in a faint, her vinegar bottle shattered on the hard road. Hilda Mason began to scream as vinegar and splinters of glass hit her legs and treasured stockings. Michael rushed downstairs and out of the house to see the departing back of Harry Walters and the white face of his father struggling to release the fork. He propped Lill against the wall while Hilda, now sobbing, dabbed at her legs, and placing his foot against the shed wall jerked out the fork. Danny, colour returning, began to rage threats, but Michael pulled him round. 'You asked for that, you annoying old bugger. It's a wonder you weren't killed. Stop shouting for the Pollis because nobody in this street would stand up for you in court.'

Olive from her back kitchen window had witnessed the whole scene and now held on to the kitchen sink, whitened knuckles showing through her clenched grip.

CHAPTER 22

On a cold November morning, little white wavelets slapped spitefully against the river bank, at least it was a clear morning with no fog, Olive reckoned, as she buttoned up her second-best coat. Her shivers were overcome by the warm thought that it was the first time since childhood that she had owned a second-best coat. Its newly bought senior was now hanging in her wardrobe, to be worn at the wedding and covered by a sheet would be fine for best in winter. Roberto stood beside her resplendent in a dark great coat, that she had carefully brushed. He looked anxiously at his watch and then way down the river, hoping to catch sight of the incoming ship. Jamie shivered in the background and he would be warmer if he pulled up his stockings, thought Olive, and anyway it was time those Marr lads were put into long trousers. Still, he looked fairly respectable as he stood by the newly scrubbed fish barrow, ready to push the newcomer's luggage up the hill. Roberto looked around at the wooden dolly, creel on her back and a monument to the quayside fisherwomen. He remembered the two men who had terrified him as they approached with a glinting knife, only to cut a sliver of wood each to put in their hat bands to assure a safe return to their home town. Many chipped edges were evidence of their simple faith and hope.

Suddenly there was a rush of movement on the quayside as the ship silently but swiftly came into view. Amid the noise of docking, Olive stepped into the background leaving Roberto at the foot of the gangway. She eyed the descending passengers closely, looking for the two Italian women. Suddenly a short, stout woman, dressed completely in black, flew to Roberto, hugging and kissing him. Olive looked uneasily about to see if anyone was watching this unseemly display of affection. With relief she realized that the young girl quietly emerging from behind the woman and being awkwardly kissed by Roberto, was the bride to be. Maria. She had a nice figure, judged Olive, but there was an unhealthy sallowness to her complexion. Talking excitedly, at least the older woman was, to Roberto, he led them to meet Olive, who politely held out a gloved hand. The two older women eyed each other curiously and Olive wondered uneasily how she could put up with this woman, gazing at her with black currant eyes, living in her house until after the wedding. The woman was using a phrase that she would repeat continually as she complained of the cold and that Olive was to learn by heart. '*Fa molto freddo.*' The girl said slowly, 'How do you do?' with a pause between each syllable. As Roberto's prospective bride, the girl was not up to Olive's expectations. Maria's long, dull brown coat, topped by a head shawl, looked poor and shabby and her shoes were clumsy; except for the colour she was a dressed replica of her aunt.

Jamie silently loaded the bass boxes and parcels tied with rope on to the barrow. Olive was aware of Roberto's discomfiture as he extricated from the torrent of Italian, and for her benefit, the information that Maria had been very sea sick during the voyage. Suddenly the older woman thrust a large box into Olive's arms and she gasped at the overpowering smell. 'What is it?' she demanded of Roberto. Awkwardly, he explained that it was a cheese made especially in Castiglione but he suspected that the warm cabin, on the sea voyage, had not been beneficial. 'It's a present for you,' he said, begging with his eyes for her to accept it. 'Thank you,' she said but there was a frown on the face of the aunt at the reluctant acceptance. Olive fought the urge to throw the box in the river, but instead held tightly on to the string, while trying to keep the large parcel away from contaminating her skirt.

Olive had enjoyed the feeling of power as she withheld information about her forthcoming visitors. Her secrecy had added to the expectations of the Inkerman inhabitants, whose ideas of the Italian people were coloured by picture hall images of handsome women with large gold earrings and many-tiered, swirling, vividly coloured skirts. Some misconceptions might have occurred between signorinas and senoritas, gipsies and peasants, but they were all in one suspicious category – foreigners. Olive knew very well that neighbours would be sure of her visitors being shown through the front door and that they would already be making reception preparations. Mats that previously been dadded against back walls were now brought out for front wall treatment. Vinegar Lill decided on window cleaning, although the cold, moisture-heavy air made any shine impossible. Hilda Mason, with higher echelon ideas, decided to weed her garden where, in November, weather prevented any growth, weed or otherwise. Any triumph by Olive was, like the expectations of the street, to be shattered. As they passed front doors the cleaning activities increased to a frenzy and the party followed by Jamie and his fish barrow encountered covert but photographic glances. Looks and gestures were followed by murmured undercurrents and the consensus of opinion, travelling down over the hedges, was that she was dowdy looking and dowly with it. Hilda, eyeing the visitor's apparel, sniffed and decided she wouldn't wash the floor with the things they wore. Olive, disappointed and feeling let down in front of her neighbours, opened her front door and led the party along the passage into the kitchen. The aunt took one look around the large cold kitchen with its tiny fire and pointedly took out a woollen shawl to wrap around her shoulders, bleating. '*Fa molto freddo.*' It was Roberto's turn to feel frustrated, for surely, he thought, on this special occasion Olive should have opened her front room to welcome his compatriot and his bride-to-be or at least have had a decent fire to warm them. Feeling his disappointment, Olive's colour was high as she seized some of their luggage and gestured for the two women to go up to their room. As she entered the bedroom the aunt gave a piercing scream which brought Roberto bounding up the stairs. The aunt was crossing herself as she pointed to the wall, recrossing and repeating the performance. Where the cross had hung for so many years, nightly illuminated by the lighthouse beams, the cross shape was clearly visible on the faded wallpaper. Holding her by the arm, Roberto, with some irritability, explained the situation, promising to show her the original in the home he had prepared for his bride.

Olive stamped her way angrily downstairs. The prospect of sharing her home with that weedy-looking lass and the woman Roberto kept calling Zia brought her to boiling point. The smell from the cardboard box assaulted her nostrils as she lifted it at arm's length. Going into the back kitchen she placed it on the table and opened the window wide to the cold November rain. To show her disapproval she lifted the two wine bottles Roberto had previously bought and placed them on a high shelf. Wine in November, she stormed – people only have a glass of wine at Christmas. Then the voice of Danny Marr came loud and clear through the open window. 'There's an awful stink from Olive's house – smells like a whore's handbag.' Olive slammed down the window and trembling she turned to face Roberto. 'Either that cheese goes or they do and if they go – it goes with them – your decision.'

CHAPTER 23

F ather Anthony Howard stirred in his armchair and as the empty tumbler fell from the arm of his chair frowned as he tried to remember whether it was three or four full glasses he had drunk. He smiled as he turned out the light and fumbled for the door, for the night would be kind. As he lay in bed something troubled him, there was something he had to remember – that was it, the arrangements for Roberto Delfino's wedding. Both Maria and her aunt had been to confession. Once the latter realized that he understood Italian her heart-lifting joy had percolated through the iron grill of the confessional. The volubility had increased until he had repeatedly to say '*Calma, calma.*' The girl puzzled him for he had expected '*una ragazza prospera*' as a bride for Roberto, and this meek unresponsive girl, with her whispered confession, was a disenchantment. True, the girl had lost some of her pallor but she seemed to be attached, limpet like, to the side of her aunt. The Priest wanted the occasion to be very special, for Roberto was a worthy and respected supporter of the church, but the flourish of the High Nuptial Mass could be wasted on this insignificant foreign bride. As he fell asleep he did not hear the slippered Agnes Cowen stepping quietly downstairs and as she measured the whisky left in the bottle the mole slid further down in grey desperation

Zia Lobosco, aunt to Maria on her mother's side, was unimpressed by the reception to Embleton, its inhabitants or the area. The Victorian edifice of the church she found uninspiring and the statue of Our Lady plain and unadorned. She and Maria were punctual every morning at Mass, waylaying Father Anthony after the service with a torrent of Italian. Her relationship with Olive had deteriorated into a state of armed neutrality. Olive resented her visitor's determination to make herself comfortable by methods hitherto unknown in Number Seven. At first she had heated bricks in the oven, coolly purloined from Danny Marr's gateway, and placed them, towel-wrapped, between

Olive's pristine white sheets. Then Roberto, evidently under some pressure, hesitantly introduced stoneware, pudding-shaped hot water bottles which were filled every night by Zia and held accusingly to her breast as she made a bad-tempered way to bed. Olive, who had never succumbed to such a weakness, exclaimed sourly, 'Work keeps you warm.'

She resented the officious appropriation of her home more and more each day. Her fish suppers brought piping hot from the shop were cautiously approached, with the crisp batter shunted to the edge of the plate and chips ferreted and forked as though they were slugs. Surreptitious peeps into the back bedroom had upset Olive, for the room, formerly kept meticulously tidy, now resembled a jumble sale. The visitors seemed to have ignored the freshly papered drawers, with little lavender bags discreetly cornered, and their clothes were in a scattered, untidy mess. Two boxes stood in the corner still tightly roped.

When Danny had cheerfully ventured a cheerful, 'How do,' to the formidable Zia he had been met with a gale of language that could have been from anywhere in the world, but the body language was unmistakable. Zia launched from a, 'What are you staring at?' to an overall pronouncement on the climate, people and country to which she had been unfortunate enough to shepherd her niece. Lost for words, which did not often happen, Danny retreated to the kitchen and as he retrieved his dentures from their murky depths, told himself, 'That one has a face like a well-used chopping board and a tongue that could clip clouts.' Zia's unfortunate habit of stopping by each gate to examine the contents of the yard did not endear her to the families in Inkerman Street. Olive passed on to Roberto the neighbourhood comments, together with her daily resentment of the liberties taken in her own house. Zia had no hesitation in inspecting drawers and cupboards and Olive took the key of her front room to hide in the fish shop, for she told herself she wouldn't put it past that besom to poke her nose in there. Zia's original animosity stemmed from the rejection of her gift of the cheese, so carefully carried from Castiglione. Roberto had partially placated Zia by promising to find suitable storage until the wedding when, he lied, it would be probably appreciated. Father Anthony had agreed to store the offending cheese in an outhouse, much to the indignation of Agnes Cowen who contemplated dropping it down the well but was afraid it would attract attention to the other contents down there. Olive was ill-tempered, she felt her street credibility had slumped; instead of respect, she was pitied for being lumbered with people who behaved oddly, although she tried to hide her disappointment from Roberto. The girl also defeated her expectations for she showed little interest in Roberto's early learning books. Her concern for Maria was tempered by the belief that it was high time that girl stood up for herself and showed a bit of gumption. Holding her hand Roberto had asked Maria to work hard at learning English, explaining how he had overcome his lack of learning, language and knowledge of his adopted country. He would spread a pound, shillings and pence on the table and as if in a game, would give her little sums to add and subtract. Sometimes with impatience he felt like leaving the table for her progress was so slow, her mistakes so many and her enthusiasm difficult to arouse. Her large, dark, pleading eyes would fill with tears as the forbidding responsibilities of the prospect of the ice-cream parlour weighed heavily. Under the watchful eye of Zia, who sat with feet on Olive's shining fender, liberally stoking the fire with Olive's precious stock of coal, Roberto tried a tender courtship. Gently he would tease her about her mistakes, trying to evoke a smile, and then assure her that everything would be all right. 'But I see so little of you,' she murmured sadly.

'I know – I know,' he said. 'But I'm very busy just now.'

CHAPTER 24

Roberto was indeed very busy and his business dealings had not gone unnoticed. Joshua Milburn had followed, with curious attention, the building operations next door to the Emporium. As manager he ran things very much his own way during the frequent absences of Amos Fanshaw and since Harriet had washed her hands of trade associations. She could not equate as trade the selling of ships to that of flannel drawers and haberdashery. The first encompassed worldwide dealings, with visitations from exotic foreigners from distant lands, and the other only humble housewifery purchases. She was surprised and alarmed by the visit of Joshua Milburn, his tongue as sleek as his brilliantined hair. He informed her, although he hastened to add he was not quite sure, someone had bought the property next door to turn it into an Italian restaurant. The property in question had formerly been a bookshop and had been on the market due to the death of its owner. Other properties in the same street consisted of offices belonging to solicitors, estate offices and a Masonic Hall. The idea of a greasy foreign restaurant in Selby Street was anathema to Harriet and immediately using her latest status symbol, the telephone, she demanded Reginald look into the matter.

Declaring his mother needed him on urgent family business, he was able to absent himself from his despised office job. Harriet, shrill with anxiety, pointed out how disastrous it would be to have valued customers in such close contact with a down-grade eating house. Valued customers were uppermost in her mind, less important customers she cared less about; they should, she believed, be dealing at the Co-operative store. She called on Reginald's duty as a son to deal with this outrage, protesting that her husband was no help, as he stubbornly held that the Emporium was none of his business and her father was seldom at home, preferring to wander around the wilds of Northumberland. Reginald sat calmly admiring the polished elegance of his fine leather shoes, then looked up and said, 'Perhaps we should consider whether Grandfather would be better off in a home, it could be a nice country home where he would be well looked after.'

There was an interested flash of acknowledgement between mother and son and Harriet lowered her eyes, aware of the exciting glow the prospect had given her.

'Well, maybe it's time he retired, he seems quite happy at some farmhouse where he stays. We will have to think it over and you know, Reginald,' she said in a self-pitying voice, 'I am not at all well these days.'

Reginald rose and hugged his mother. 'Well, I'm your son and what else should I do but look after my dear mother and take worries off her shoulders.'

Reginald enjoyed his lunch, generously libated before and after, at the Sailing Club and happily aware of a wallet well lined by a grateful mother, drove to Selby Street. He opened a door and entered into a mêlée of activity. Joiners and painters were busy at the end of a large room. At a desk in a quieter corner a man was bent over papers. Reginald immediately moved into his jolly-along approach.

'I'm interested in what's going on here. I hear some Eyetie has bought the place.' He grinned pleasantly.

The dark head came up slowly and Reginald looked into cold, plum-dark eyes.

'What is your interest?'

'Well, if your boss is around, I'd like a word.'

'I am the owner of this property and I am an Italian.'

'Oh, well, I didn't know, only heard some foreigner . . .'

'I am also a naturalized British citizen.'

'I had better introduce myself.'

'There is no need for that, I know very well who you are, Mr Reginald Fanshaw. If you have any problems concerning the adjoining properties please communicate through the regular channels.'

His anger and the rumbling repercussions of a heavy lunch brought the sweat out on Reginald's brow.

'Have you planning permission for this change of premises?'

'That is my business.'

'Your workmen may have damaged our wall,' he began to bluster.

'Through the regular channels I said and I believe I make myself plain.'

Reginald turned and charged through the door. As he unlocked his car door he looked up at a signwriter working from the top of a ladder. He was carefully finishing off the final 'O', of a name. Reginald felt an uneasy clench in his stomach as he read the name of Delfino written in gold leaf on a brown background.

Roberto gazed through the window at Reginald looking up at the signwriter. 'Look well, Mr Fanshaw, for the name is Delfino – surely you remember Cecilia Delfino?' He hurried through the double doors where the joiner was fixing kick plates and into the kitchen. Luigi Taroni was examining the quality of the pans he was unpacking from a crate on the floor. He knocked the base of the pan with his knuckles. 'Not bad, eh?' and smiled. Luigi had brought, by the excellence of his cooking, quite a lot of business to the Royal Hotel before Roberto had convinced him that there were new opportunities awaiting his forte – Italian cooking. He had worked his way from Taormina in Sicily to Castletown followed by an accommodating wife and a houseful of children. Now in middle age he bounced his barrel shape from stove to chopping board. Already he was dredging up recipes learnt in his youth and his enthusiasm even surprised Roberto. Luigi had been deeply honoured when Roberto asked him to be best man at his wedding. In truth, the fact was that when Roberto looked around him, he realized he had no other friend to fill the role. Work had encompassed his whole life since he arrived in England and had left him on a bare plateau devoid of emotional ties. Zia had been delighted to make the acquaintance of the Taroni family and to Olive's relief, Roberto now drove her daily to Castletown where she happily merged into a houseful of noise, children, wine and rapid Italian. She entertained Luigi's wife with scalding interpretations of the habits of Olive and her neighbours. Maria was left behind to her plodding English exercises and timid introductions by Roberto, to the ice-cream parlour.

CHAPTER 25

Sorcha Marr disappeared as unannounced as she came. Apart from a hollow depression in the hay in Boney's stable there was no sign that she had ever visited. The night before, she and Danny had enjoyed an evening of reminiscences and she awoke in him fading memories of his birthplace. Danny had begun the evening's entertainment with his well-known act of giving a massive fart in the back kitchen while opening the back door to call to an empty yard, 'Come in,' followed by a run up the stairs making lessening noisy emissions on every stair. This remarkable feat would produce admiration and whoops of laughter from the twins but the humour was long since lost on his elder sons, who would murmur, 'Silly bugger,' into their evening newspaper or *Sporting Gazette*. The grandmother and Danny, swopping bottles and soulful songs, ended their mutual enjoyment when the old lady tapped out her pipe and declared it was time for all decent folk to be abed. As she swayed down the yard her son broadcast an admiring question, 'Isn't she a wonder, that ould wan?' He looked mistily down the yard and piously hoped that God would be good to her. With the grandmother gone the air in the kitchen was sweeter and as Jonty remarked, it would be a relief to old Boney. But Boney only laid his head on the stall partition and gazed at the depression on the hay. Certainly the twins missed her and the raw, earthy telling of her tales; not only the twins but the anti-social cat who would descend nightly to curl up in the capacious depths of her upturned petticoats (a gesture he never made to anyone else in the family), while triumphantly glaring defiance at the deposed dogs.

Jamie had given up his small-time pickings as bookie's runner to Bacon Jack for he had grown too big to evade the sharper eye of the shipyard's new gate watchman. He was now a useful go-between for Betsy and the fish shop and able to haul fish daily up bank from

Betsy's filleting shed to the fish shop, where he would sluice down his barrow. Both Joe and he looked forward to the summer and Joe's school leaving. Their undecided dream choices lay between Captain of the *Queen Mary* or engine driver of the *Flying Scotsman*. Evenings were busy with the Meccano swopping of parts of the several bicycle skeletons out in the yard, if the weather was fine, or in everybody's way on the mat in front of the fire. They had outgrown the indignity of having their blond hair tooth-combed every Friday night on to brown paper spread over the crackets. If there was an infestation at the school both lads would count the lice, or as they affectionately called them, 'dickies,' as they cracked them under a thumb, adding their separate scores as carefully as a darts player. Now, as weekly their arms shot further out from their cuffs, they were delighted to be given long trousers. That they were shortened cast-offs and inherited from Michael did not lessen their pride in this symbol of manhood. They laughed at Edie's father's photograph taken when he was three and dressed in a frock. But Edie admonished them for it was well known that evil spirits would steal little boys away, so mothers dressed them in frocks to conceal their sex. The lads were now taller than their mother, identically alike and, with their blond hair and dark grey eyes, looked like developing into handsome young men, that is, if one could overlook the disturbing yellow flash in their eyes. Olive nodded approvingly as she watched them bent over their old bicycles. They were now becoming useful, although it was a shame that dumb lad would never be any good except for hauling a barrow load of fish from the quayside, just as well the other one was normal. Careless of anyone else's opinion of them, the twins believed they could achieve anything and of this they assured each other in their secret language.

CHAPTER 26

Considering that it was the first week in December, the weather was considerate, cold, but a sparkling clear morning under an unblemished blue sky. As Roberto transported trays of cakes and pies from Alan James shop and finally the wedding cake, he looked forward to the future with Maria. The restaurant was thriving and against all dire predictions local people came, at first curious and then with anticipation to enjoy the new experience of Italian cookery. Soon he and Maria would settle down to enjoy, he hoped, as happy and fruitful a marriage as Luigi and his wife with their tumbling brood. Although the curtains in the back bedroom were firmly closed to the back lane gaze, he respected Olive's wishes not to run the risk of seeing the bride before the ceremony. In fact, nobody except Zia saw the bride that morning, not even Olive. Through a narrow opening of the door, Zia made her demands clearly heard, coffee, toasted bread, hot water and extra towels. Tight lipped, Olive thanked heaven that Zia would soon be on her way back to Italy. Maria settled in the flat over the ice-cream parlour and she would know the blessed relief of having her house to herself. Earlier she had retreated to her front room, emerging to lock the door carefully behind her. Hesitating, for it was her habit to curve the little mat against the door (to stop any dust getting in), today she laid the mat flat upon the floor. She checked the big square table in the kitchen, every inch covered by pies, cakes and sandwiches, the latter covered with upturned plates, and finally laid a slightly dampened, large white sheet over all. A trestle table, again cloth covered, held the many cups and saucers Roberto had brought from his restaurant. In the back kitchen he had arranged, very much against Olive's will, bottles of wine, spirits and glasses. This wedding was to be decently celebrated, she insisted, not like that stagey bank fair of the Marr wedding. Anyone wanting to wish good luck to the bridal pair would be welcome to return to the house and a food plate and expected to make their departure after a decent interval.

Apart from the Luigi Taroni family and Zia, Roberto had no relations and few friends in his adopted country. Luigi's eldest daughter, a rather exuberant fifteen-year-old, was to be bridesmaid. Olive had no living relatives, acquaintances – yes – but no friends, so a house reception was acceptable. 'Don't go to the expense of hiring a hall and feeding half the town,' she advised Roberto. Father Anthony was to be a special guest. After the ceremony there was to be a quick trip to the photographer, for Zia had insisted on this proof to take back to Castiglione. After Zia and Maria's less than spectacular introduction into Inkerman Street, Olive believed there would be little interest in the wedding ceremony. With their expectations shattered, the neighbours had shown little curiosity in the foreigners. That it was to be a house reception rather than a hall, to be followed by a dance, satisfied Olive that she would be in control, and that there would be no carryings-on. The general feeling of disappointment felt by the street inhabitants led everyone to forecast a shabby wedding. Roberto had arranged for a car to collect Olive, to be followed at a respectable distance by the bridal car. Roberto, Luigi and his family had assembled in the new flat. As Olive entered the church and made her obeisance, she was surprised to see such a large number in the congregation. Sitting in the prestigious front pew, Olive wondered sourly how many of these had ever set foot in a Catholic Church before. Then grudgingly she admitted that Roberto was a popular man, both well known and respected in the business area of the town. She smoothed down her new coat, looking anxiously at the pew edge and at the hassock for any rough surfaces that might snag her silk stockings. Drawing on those precious stockings with care had given her such a feeling of pleasure that she had hastily snapped on her suspenders.

Olive looked over at Roberto sitting quietly beside Luigi and felt proud of the years she had shared with him. They had battled through hard, dark winters, short of everything except a determined will to survive and win. 'If I'd had a son I'd have wanted him to be like Roberto,' she thought and felt a strange constriction in her throat and unbidden tears in her eyes. 'You are a sentimental fool,' she told herself, crying like the mother of the groom, and turned to look at Agnes Cowen stealing officiously up and down the aisle – would she never get something done to her face! Olive had already noted Betsy

Mayhew – poor soul, it would take a miracle to do anything about hers. Edie Marr had smiled and nodded to her, happy to be recognized as she sat beside the heavily pregnant Maisie.

There was a wave of movement as the organist ceased his soothing murmuring to break into the Bride's March from *Lohengrin*. Roberto had wanted Widor's *Toccata*, the request almost giving the organist a heart attack. He wailed that he had never played anything except the Bride's March at a wedding and where in Embleton would he find a copy of the music!

As she stood up, Olive felt another small irritation that Mendelssohn's Wedding March had been scorned by Roberto. Steadfastly looking ahead, Olive became aware of a surge of interest behind her, yet her glance did not waver and she did not turn until the bride was alongside, when she was too overcome to return Maria's shy smile. Never had the Church of the Sacred Heart seen such a beautiful bride: not in shiny satin nor dulled silk, but regally in a gown of pure white velvet which fanned out behind her. The bodice and train were encrusted with pearls, nestling among a delicate silver thread design of flowers and leaves. Her short veil was held in place by a coronet, a row of pearls interspersed with silver leaves, and as the pale sun shone through the high window Maria appeared luminous in its gentle warmth.

Roberto, both pride and amazement in his eyes, looked fleetingly away from his bride to Olive and their glance met in delighted approval. Maria had passed down through the awe-struck admiration of the congregation on the arm of her aunt and Olive had to admit that Zia looked handsome in a pearl grey woollen suit, with her dark hair piled majestically around a fine gold band. So that was the secret of the two unopened boxes among the untidy confusion in the back room – it was the wedding finery and what finery! Before she turned her mind to the wedding service, Olive smiled to herself – 'I too, can have my secrets.'

CHAPTER 27

Father Anthony blessed the house and the wedding party as they entered the long passage from the front door and as Roberto hurried to open the kitchen door, Olive intervened, 'Today we will receive your wedding guests in the front room.' Removing a possessive arm from his bride Roberto opened the room door. Used to the stark utility rooms of Number seven, the colour and beauty took his breath away. Two fine gilt chairs upholstered in red velvet stood under the window against a background of plum-dark curtains and a matching sofa covered with silken cushions stood against the opposite wall. A beautiful oriental carpet, glowing with blues, greens and red, covered the floor. On the walls were gilt-framed pictures of exotic hand-painted flowers and exquisite Japanese garden scenes. Chinese bowls stood on the heavily carved seaman's chest, the one he realized that must have held the warm clothes he wore on his first night in Olive's house. Delicately carved figurines in porcelain and alabaster filled the mantlepiece and wall cabinet. From a warm glowing fire, tongues of light reflected their age-old beauty. This was Olive's heritage from a long-dead, sea-going father and husband and Roberto, open mouthed, wondered where all these treasures had come from and how had they been transported. No wonder Olive kept her front room curtains closed and the door locked. All Zia could say was, *'Mamma mia,'* as she and Maria took their seats in the gilded chairs, feeling like royalty. This, thought Zia, is how all weddings must be celebrated in this country, and she registered a growing respect for Olive.

As nearest neighbours Edie and Maisie were the first guests to follow the wedding party, sturdily elbowing precedence. Edie had bought a pair of towels as a wedding present from the Co-operative store, but, as she gazed at the wonderfully dressed bride, she changed her mind and her present. Pushing the towels in a drawer she unlocked her mother's china cabinet and choosing a fine Royal Doulton tea pot, she carefully wrapped it in tissue paper and hurried to present herself and the present with Maisie in tow. As the news went down the back lane there was an influx of eager visitors, their shoes examined by Olive with anxiety.

They came in a shuffling line, a decorous drink in their hands to give their best wishes to the bridal pair. But all were overwhelmed by the luxury of the front room. Almost forgetting their manners in the absorbing interest of the Aladdin's cave, they congratulated the pair, at the same time noting that Roberto had to stand beside the bride while that strange aunt occupied the other sumptuous chair. But they gave Zia a guarded smile and doubled back to fill their plates and exchange amazed comments with their neighbours at what they had seen in the front room. This, they agreed, must be how all weddings are conducted in Italy and came away gratified that they had been part of a resplendent occasion.

Their small gifts were carried into the kitchen and stacked on the green cupboard shelves, as if their humble origins would be further demeaned by the opulence of the front room treasures. Betsy Mayhew, shawl in hand and covering the side of her face as though she had toothache, offered a small, brown butter dish as she wished them happiness and good health, inwardly praying that they would never have any scarred children. Vinegar Lill handed over two water glasses obtained through a free pickling vinegar offer, while Hilda Mason brought a set of crotched circles, heavy with blue beads, answering the puzzled glances with the genteel explanation, to cover jugs from the flies. Harry Walters came with his wife and placed a lucky brass horse shoe in Maria's lap. His wife begged to be excused as she needed to get the smoked haddock cooked in case her son arrived. Harry gently elbowed her out of the room to make way for Stan Wilson, who brought nothing but good wishes and a burning desire to get back to the food in the kitchen, the same he had earnestly looked over on his way in. Olive had pointedly deprived him of his umbrella, but he made the best of it over a piled high plate. Other inhabitants of the street came and went and finally, as the outgoing Charlotte Brown skimmed the door posts with her bow legs, Olive breathed a sigh of relief and anticipated the pleasure of a quiet cup of tea on her own when the bridal party left her house. At that moment she sat worrying about the effect of the traffic over her sitting room carpet, when Jamie

Marr came, with a shy smile he indicated the front room and Olive nodded. He entered, smiled at the bride, offered a box to Roberto and silently left the room. Roberto opened the small box and took out a lovely model of a schooner. On the side was a newly painted name – BETSEE.

'Who is that from?' demanded Zia.

'Just from an old friend who cannot be here today,' Roberto replied quietly. He placed the little model back in the box and closed the lid firmly.

CHAPTER 28

Knowing that she was the centre of surprise, envy and admiration, Olive held her head up high and walked as though on stilts from house to fish shop and back. She was conscious of the interest in her front room treasures and took a delight in foiling their efforts to peer through the window by drawing the curtains even closer than before. She had expected to be relieved to see the back of Zia but Maria's loud outburst of weeping as she parted from her aunt on the quayside made Olive realize the difficulties ahead. As she sat with her cup of tea, the emptiness of the house closed in on her and matched the feeling of emptiness inside. She realized sadly that the relief of having the house to herself left her with a vague unsatisfied feeling that even the energy expended in clearing up after the wedding could not satisfy.

Maria and Zia had clung to each other, hugging and crying out loud while impatient crew members urged Zia on board. Olive shifted uncomfortably as Roberto broke their sobbing embrace and she noticed with annoyance that Betsy Haddick, on her way up from the filleting shed, had walked slowly past watching Roberto as he tried to calm the two women. Thank heaven he has finished with her, Olive thought crossly and irritably, if Maria knew who was behind her, she would have something to cry about.

Her foreboding about Maria was not ill judged. The early months of the year were cold and wet and Maria caught one cold after another. With Zia gone, her home-sickness and depression increased. Roberto engaged Luigi's daughter, Marina, to help her run the ice-cream parlour. Looking pale and drawn, Maria stood behind the counter, anxious not to make mistakes with the money and timid of these strange people who stared at her so curiously. Each night she strove to learn the few new words on the list Roberto made out for her but usually she was too tired and unhappy to care. After Roberto's experience of the warm, comfortable embraces of Betsy, his love life with Maria was

103

disappointing. Although himself a well-disciplined Catholic, Maria's nightly prayers under the votive lamp and her devout crossing with murmured prayers before sex, had a chilling effect on him. He tried to excuse her lack of response as due to her youth, her virgin status at the marriage bed and her strict upbringing. In spite of this reasonable approach, after intercourse he would leave her angrily as she cried into her pillow. His days were full, driving between Embleton and Castleton, and as he became increasingly absorbed in the success of his restaurant and fish shop, he expected a similar drive in the ice-cream parlour. Olive tried to ease his disappointment by pointing out that he should know the limitations the Northern weather imposed upon the sale of ice cream. Each night he counted the takings, a frown upon his face made Maria dread his unspoken criticism. She began to go to bed as soon as the parlour closed to will herself back to the family warmth she had left behind. Only that evening Roberto had said curtly, 'Who in our home village owns a car, apart from the Padrone? You don't appreciate how lucky you are.' Zia had spoken to her with admiration of a certain Mussolini who would bring new colonies and greatness to Italy, but all Maria longed for was her extended family enjoying summer evenings in the piazza.

She had turned to Olive for comfort but there was an awkwardness in their relationship. Olive's response to her fits of crying was to clear Maria's sink of dirty dishes and point out the Northern way to soap, blue and starch the washing. On her short visits Olive would exhort her to emulate Roberto, who had so easily become adjusted to the ways of the North-East, but her advice to settle down left Maria more despondent than ever before.

The warmer weather and the softer up-river breezes brought an improvement in Maria's health. She still, with longing, awaited the postman with letters from home, but she ceased to cry on the days when none were delivered. Roberto and Luigi were delighted when they were able to announce in the local paper that Friday, Saturday and Sunday evening meals were only available for advanced bookings. Curiosity had turned into appreciation and many locals would now pride themselves on forking spaghetti correctly, nodding sagely to proclaim it 'al dente'. Knowing the regions of Roberto's imported wines became imperative and the wise solemnly sipped and discussed the varying merits of the wine with Cecil, the gangling wine waiter, the son of Luigi. Cecil, known in the restaurant as Cesare, had been born in England and had never been to Italy but he was sensible enough not to say so and was careful to copy his father's broken English. Roberto decided, if he could find another Italian chef of Luigi's calibre and dedication, he would cross the Tyne and open up a new area.

CHAPTER 29

Harriet's twitchings and sleepless wanderings about the house lessened when she heard of her father's death. Not so much concern at the death of her father, although there was some irritation that he had died way beyond Hexham, as the nuisance of bringing the body home, for what she decided must be a funeral of distinction. With a gigantic upsurge of energy she descended on her father's big house in the square. Covers were whipped off the furniture, windows opened and a swiftly engaged army of cleaners were hired to sweep and polish every room in preparation for guests to the funeral feast. Impatiently, she urged Reginald to see to the dismal arrangements of bringing the body of Amos back to Embleton. Reginald's arrangements were as scant as his respect for his grandfather and he hurriedly turned over his responsibility to the undertaker. Harriet's demands for a solid oak coffin with the finest brass handles were idly relayed, together with the specific details of a horse-drawn, not a new-fangled motor hearse. The flowers and the funeral meats and drink were her diligent obligation. When the shut-faced undertaker returned from Northumberland after taking coffin measurements, he discreetly failed to mention anything except murmured costs to Reginald, working in the time-held belief that those who do the ordering do the paying.

The elaborate announcement in the local papers, extolling the life and work of the deceased Amos Fanshaw, woke local dignitaries into a flurry of calls upon the broken-hearted daughter and an eager acceptance to the funeral and to Harriet's diplomatic murmur, 'Afterwards at the house.' Glowing in the warm acceptance of the Mayor's assured presence in the cortège, Harriet ordered herself the deepest of mourning with a veil copied from that worn by Royalty. Sir Nathaniel Dobson and sons grudgingly agreed to attend, acknowledging more respect for the deceased than for the rest of his family. In the clubs and bars old tales were dredged up of the young Amos, from his sharp dealing days to the suspect relinquishing of the town, back to the pedlar days of his youth. Joshua Milburn had large notices pasted on to the shop windows announcing the closure on the day of the funeral. He instructed all male staff to wear black ties forthwith and the females black blouses to be supplied at cost. After all, they were getting a day off work. With oily deference, he ensured that his efforts came to the nodding satisfaction of Harriet. He further assured her that he personally would vouch for the attendance at the church of every employee. On that fine Saturday morning Harriet looked with approval on the weather. Good weather meant good attendance and she was determined that the whole town would remember for years to come the funeral of her father, the late Amos Fanshaw, founder of the elegant glass-fronted Fanshaw Emporium. Finally, dressed in deep black morning clothes, she watched, tapping her fingers on the window sill, as the four black horses with nodding plumes drew up the hearse in front of her father's house, the house she intended to make her own to ensure Reginald's place in society. She beckoned Herbert to her side, pointed out the Mayor's coach preceded by that of Sir Nathaniel Dobson, now centred between his sons. Her own car was intended for herself, Herbert, Reginald and Amelia. Her anger had surged when at the last minute Reginald explained that Amelia had to take a newly foaled mare for servicing. Shocked, Harriet exclaimed shrilly had her daughter-in-law no life outside the stable. But Reginald, handsome in his dark suit had held her hand and soothingly begged that he would see that everything went all right. Harriet made a dignified veiled descent to the waiting cortège, encouraged by the long line of following cars stretching as far back as the eye could see.

Almost as she stepped into the car she noticed behind Sir Nathaniel's car a small car containing a woman and a young man. 'Who is that?' she hissed to Reginald, over the head of Herbert, as she hesitated with one raised foot. Reginald glanced along the line of waiting cars and urged, 'Never mind, Mother.' The car and its occupants infuriated Harriet. To have unknown mourners at the head of the column worried her in case some jumped-up employee, was seeking to get his name in the local paper. As she sat in stiff-backed splendour, and as the cortège moved away, she decided there would be a slice off the undertaker's bill for allowing this cross blunder in protocol.

CHAPTER 30

Edie had finally given way to Joe's pleading for cinder toffee and now the twins eagerly watched the pan as she stirred in the bicarbonate of soda, causing a brown whoosh as the sticky liquid turned to brittle crackling. Edie spooned it into a tray of cold water and the boys were immediately touching the cooling toffee and sucking their hot fingers. As soon as finger and tongue could bear it, they sucked and cracked the delicious nutty-flavoured toffee. With an admonishment, 'Leave some for another day,' Edie held the tin tray over her head; to avoid marauding hands she placed the toffee tin on the high pantry shelf. The laughing lads wheeled out their old bicycles for the ride down Canny Hill bank to their morning job to stay guard for the pitch and toss men.

The reined-in black horses with a dignified plod traversed down Church Lane to pass the intersection with Canny Hill bank. In the chief mourners car the Fanshaw family were engrossed in their own thoughts. Mother and son were reckoning in their improved social and financial status. Alongside, Herbert sat in the corner, aware of the pain in his tired chest and along his arm. He had long since ceased to look for love, comfort or solace from the wife of his threadbare marriage. Since the birth of his son every warm approach had been repulsed with whalebone severity. The delicate scent of wild roses came through the open car window, a relief, he thought, from the over-powering smell of the many floral wreaths stacked in his father-in-law's hall. At least the old man they were burying had made his money, gone his own way and done exactly what he wanted. Sadly he looked at Reginald, his son, who through his mother had seen him only as a well-lined pocket to be dipped into for every fancied whim.

Although the trio were engrossed in thought – Reginald planning a good night out to shake off this gloomy burial business, perhaps topping it off with a visit to Clarty Clara's, Harriet already choosing new curtains for her father's house – it was Herbert who first saw the laughing lads free-wheeling pell-mell down Canny Hill bank. Before he could call out in alarm the pain gripped him and he never saw the twin crash head first through the side glass panel of the hearse. The boy lay in his gushing blood, his head inside the hearse. The bicycle lay a crumpled heap beneath him. His young blood flooded over the coffin as his body hung down over the side of the hearse. The thudding shock had halted the horses who now began to move restlessly as they smelt the blood. With the sawing to-and-fro movement of the hearse wheels, the body collapsed over the bicycle frame.

The funeral cortège had halted, those near the scene in shock, the remainder in silent curiosity. In the seemingly endless silence the horrified funeral director stumbled out of the car and stared at the wide, jagged gash cutting through half of the neck. As, white faced, he clutched at the ornamental lamp on the hearse, he became aware of the sky-reaching screams from the chief mourner's car. In the corner, being violently sick, was Reginald while Harriet, wild faced, screeched as she shook the unresponsive body of Herbert Fanshaw, demanding that he get out and do something. Failing to get any answer she drummed her heels on the floor of the cab as the screeches wore down to a moaning sob.

Sir Nathanial Dobson got out of his car and ignoring the rigid undertaker and his stricken staff, took off the white silk scarf from around his neck and bending over staunched the unbearable wound. He shrugged off his fine Melton overcoat and with his two sons, gently on to it, laid the boy's body. Tobias covered the face with his fine linen handkerchief. As the murmured horror spread from car to car, some, led by the Mayor, hastily disassociated themselves from the catastrophe and headed back to town. Nathanial Dobson opened the car door, looked at the two helpless heaps on the one seat and at Reginald, sour in his vomit, on the other. 'The boy is dead and I'm taking him home,' he said curtly. As he watched, still gulping bile, Reginald saw the Dobson brothers laying the body on the back seat of their father's car. 'What have I to do about my grandfather's funeral?' wailed Reginald. 'Get him buried,' came the sharp reply as Sir Nathanial shut the door. He then put his head into the small car now in the gap where the Mayor's car had been. There was a nodded assent from two heads. 'Get in with these people and see to the funeral,' and Reginald stumbled out, crying now, and sat in the stranger's car. He watched as Martin Dobson jumped behind the wheel of the chief mourner's car and drove sharply off with Harriet Fanshaw in shock beside the dead body of her husband.

The Dobson chauffeur, as impassive as if he were driving to a family picnic instead of conveying a dishevelled boss holding on to a dead boy in the back seat, pulled out of line and, upon instructions, turned the car up Canny Hill bank and towards Inkerman Street.

CHAPTER 31

The Reverend Guy Flintoff glanced into the vestry mirror and reassured himself that he was impeccably dressed for the auspicious funeral of the worthy Amos Fanshaw. Idly he wondered if there would be a church beneficiary from the will of the same, for rumour had it that the deceased was a wealthy man. He glanced at a copy of the church service, elaborately printed and with a deep black edge of mourning. He knew he was called upon to give a memorable performance, for Mrs Harriet would be picking on the slightest error. It was not as if she had been a long-time member of his congregation, having in recent years denounced her former church as not 'High enough.' In fact, Harriet had been, as her parents before her, brought up in the Methodist Chapel, but her religious ambitions had risen with her financial status, beginning with her church wedding to Herbert Platt.

The open grave had been lined with young, green boughs and the excavated raw earth covered with a green felt cloth. Mr Jordan sat poised, high up on the organ stool where he practised each evening, seeing in his mind's eye, 'The funeral music was played by Mr Simeon Jordan, B. Mus., L.R.A.M.,' in the evening newspaper report. He expected that the black and white ratification of his impressive musical qualifications, as it had in the past, would encourage fond mothers to enrol their offspring for piano or organ lessons. The number of pupils had lately decreased considerably since that unfortunate business of the Clayton lad. Fortunately the mother, frightened by the panoply of law, had withdrawn the charges, but Simeon Jordan had detected an uneasiness among the hovering mothers during practice time.

The Reverend Guy Flintoff passed down the aisle where, just inside the outer door, were the tall boxes where long-dead Victorian worshippers had placed their top hats. At the porch door he waited, gazing solemnly at the lych gate, for the cortège. He was disturbed to see a B.S.A. motor bike skid to the church door, the disturbed gravel skirting the wheels. The funeral director, top hat jammed on his head, the black braids horizontal in the air stream skid, hurriedly shut off the engine. Bert Whittaker had dealt with few unpleasant burials in his family business; most people, their lower orifices well plugged, were decently interred. His father had once told him of a deceased man, some weeks at the height of summer in a lonely cottage, who had been quickly shovelled, a heaving mass, into a quick-lime based coffin and hastily covered with iodized wadding. His own sombre pall bearers had once had their uniform dark suits ruined from a body that had died filled with water. The offensive liquid had leaked on to their shoulders, despite an inch-thick base of fine wood shavings. Still shaken by the horrific death at Canny Hill bank, he pushed his commandeered motor bike against the church wall and hastily outlining the events of the morning, begged the vicar to forgo all the unnecessary ritual, read the burial service and inter the body. As the Vicar tried hard to assimilate the astounding news, the hearse arrived at anything but a funeral pace. The restless, foam-flecked horses pulled up the hearse, revealing the shattered window and the blood-splattered coffin before the Vicar's unbelieving eyes. Where was the Mayor, Sir Nathanial Dobson and the chief mourners? Automatically he mouthed the receiving words as the vomit-stained Reginald, supported by two people he had never seen before, lined up behind the coffin. Joshua Milburn, Manager of Fanshaw Emporium, equally non-plussed, with questioning sharp eyes led his bus load of black-tie and black-bloused employees waiting at the church gate to follow the three mourners.

Mr Simeon Jordan waited in vain on his organ stool for the signal to start the music. Later, he decided, he would pop round the corner to tell the young boy how naughty he was to smoke a cigarette while pumping the organ; even though the boy had sought to hide his sin by cautiously puffing the smoke up the open lips of the organ pipe tubes.

There was to be no sound of music for the funeral of Amos Fanshaw, only the sound of feet as the service was briefly read.

CHAPTER 32

L ooking out from the back bedroom window Michael Marr thought he must be having an hallucination. For one moment he believed his Union's chief adversary, Sir Nathanial Dobson, was standing at the backyard gate. Sir Nathanial had halted the car away from Number eight and on foot prepared to break the shattering news to the Marr family. Edie, preparing the Saturday fry-up dinner, had been surprised by the head-long rush of Jamie and the dogs into the kitchen where they had huddled together on the broken-down couch. As she moved forward to ask where was Joe, she too halted unbelieving. For there was the well-known figure of the shipyard owner fumbling with the latch gate. Behind her Michael came rushing down the stairs and then halted a moment, drawing breath, before he opened the back door and walked down the yard. The breeze gently ruffled the silver hair of the one and the thick, dark hair of the other.

'I'm sorry to bring you bad news.'

'What bad news?' He was always bloody bad news.

'There has been a terrible accident. The lad killed is, I understand, your brother.'

Michael glanced back through the window and noted the left-side yellow triangle in the staring eyes. 'It's Joe – what's happened?'

Briefly Sir Nathanial told him of the ghastly accident and motioned him to the car standing in the back lane, where already neighbours were making shuffling approaches.

'It's Nathanial's car.' 'Accident.' 'One of the twins.' 'Which one?' 'Don't know.'

As the whispers were circulating Danny Marr, leading Boney, came round the top corner of the street. Dropping the reins he ran to be alongside Michael, while Boney, restless to be in his nearby stable, began to move forward. Danny turned his head to yell a peremptory 'Whoa,' and then looked to Michael, uncomprehending. Michael pressed his father's shoulder, 'There's been an accident – Joe's dead.' Sir Nathanial, his son Tobias and the chauffeur were lined up like statues as the pair approached the still figure covered on the back seat. As Michael turned back the coat lapel and gazed, speechless with horror, the voice of Sir Nathanial broke the silence, 'Someone had better warn his mother.' In a daze Michael nodded as his father sank back on his hunkers against his shed, great sobs tearing at his throat. Edie was already at the gate, her mind jumping to the conclusion that Michael had again got into trouble with the shipyard owner. Michael saw the leaping alarm in her eyes at the sight of the sobbing Danny and moving swiftly, turned her back into the house. As the chauffeur stared steadily at the brick wall, Sir Nathanial and his son gathered up their horrendous burden. They carried it into the house the shabby shoes tapping each other as if the wearer were still alive. Michael led them into the front room and Joe was laid on his sister's vacated bed. With murmured expressions of sorrow they walked past the fright-frozen Edie. The pair then hesitated and looked a question to Michael. He glanced at Jamie's rapidly moving fingers and said calmly, 'He's talking to Joe.' Sir Nathanial cleared his throat, 'Really,' and concluded uncomfortably that Michael Marr's mind had been unhinged by the awful calamity. Out in the yard the two Dobsons came face to face with the bizarre figure of Sorcha Marr. In spite of all the terrible happenings that they had witnessed the two men could barely repress a smile at the pickled-walnut-coloured face, pipe in mouth and a shapeless felt hat on its head.

'Morning to you, sar,' said Sorcha, recognizing gentry, although confused by the setting. As she watched the departing backs of the Dobsons and waited until the car backed down the lane, she dropped her bundle and made the unnecessary remark, 'Begod, there's trouble here.' She walked over to Danny and said sternly, 'There's a horse to be unyoked there,' and turned into the house. For the first time in his life Michael was glad to see his old grandmother as helplessly he held his stricken mother.

Olive had stared from her back window at the coat-covered package carried in by no less than the Dobson men. She recovered from her speculations with a jolt as Sorcha's voice came through the doorway. 'Have you a decent bit of linen to tear up for a bandage?' Uninvited Sorcha stepped through the doorway as Olive backed into the kitchen.

A few sentences made her forget the unwelcome smell and sent her rushing upstairs for a clean, worn sheet.

'Holy Mother of God, but I pick my times to visit. Last time it was the wedding and now I'm here to lay out the body of my grandson.' Sorcha picked up the sheet and with a nod of thanks went out, shutting the back door. Even in shock Olive automatically re-opened the door to air the room.

CHAPTER 33

The words of the Office were almost drowned as the sobbing voice of Danny Marr alternatively railed against and then begged forgiveness from God. Father Antony, finally murmuring a 'conquiscat in pace,' felt he would rather have stayed with the still, waxen-faced corpse beside the keening Sorcha, than the assembled Marr family. The bitter tight lips of Michael contained his grief and his scorn of the rites of the Church. Although he had attended Maisie's wedding, and would also follow Joe from church to grave, it was only as a mark of respect he felt due to his family. Jonty soothed and supported the heart-broken, now silent Edie, her face puffed and swollen from weeping. Father Antony glanced uneasily at Jamie, fingers still shaping what the family said were his conversations with Joe. He felt he should condemn such a weird interpretation, but in the tense cross-winds of grief he knew that anyone in that room, after one wrong word, could turn and rend him. It was a mad household, he told himself as he overdid his nightly drinking. He had suggested tamely to the Marrs, as he watched the unnerving behaviour of Jamie, that perhaps the lad might be helped by becoming an altar boy. In the silence that followed Michael challenged coldly, 'Why don't you ask him yourself?' Father Antony refilled his glass and opened a newly obtained book on the Vatican, hoping to erase the memory of his visit. Agnes Cowen looked at her bedside clock and moved silently downstairs, agitating the grey mole as she prayed. Too late to wake him now, she thought, and gently took off his boots. Carefully, she unclipped his collar – that symbol of priesthood. She tucked the empty bottle under her arm, unbolted the back door and dropped the bottle down the well.

Jamie, after seeing his brother impaled on the jagged glass of the hearse, had fled on his bicycle with the dogs back to the corner of the couch. He scarcely moved from there, where he held his silent communications, except when he slid down to the mat and slept

116

between the dogs.

It took only a short while for Olive to recover from Sorcha's visit to spur her to do the decent neighbours. Duty stepping into the back lane, she beckoned Charlotte Brown from the uneasy movement of the gathered neighbours. A few words in her ear sent Charlotte eagerly on the errand as fast as her bow legs could roll her to the Co-operative, where, briefed by Olive, she ordered the hired funeral pack of two sheets, one pillow case and two purple ribbons for the bed head, to be delivered immediately to Number eight, Inkerman Street. With composed dignity Charlotte informed the drapery attendants of the circumstances of the death, impressing upon them that she was fully empowered to hire the linen and guarantee its safe return after the funeral. She was heartened by the knowledge that this participation ensured her a special place at the funeral and the subsequent tea. It was Olive who stepped in to arrange practical details, for daughter Maisie was heavily pregnant and son-in-law Slack Willie could be relied upon doing everything, as his father-in-law always said, 'Arse first.' Olive took fish suppers to the house for those who could eat, sent word to Betsy Haddick to get someone to bring up the fish, for even in the midst of this sorrowing confusion, Roberto's business must not be neglected.

Roberto brought food from his restaurant, but the men-folk looked carefully at something called Pizza, at slithering stuff called Pasta, and pushed it to the back of the table. For the first time in their lives they were having to eat bought bread which, while privately acknowledging the necessity, they agreed had neither tack nor taste. Edie, who had been persuaded to take to her bed, her tea having been previously laced with whisky, fell into an exhausted sleep. The size of the funeral surprised everyone. It seemed that the tragic death of the young lad had touched the troubled heart of the town. There was really no need for the bidder, that black-coated messenger, as he knocked steadily on street doors. There was always an answering quiet nod of awareness from the occupant of the house. Street collections for floral wreaths were generously contributed to and there was even a handsome wreath from the pitch and toss men. The coffin of Joseph Marr was placed where, in life, he had never been considered worthy of being an altar boy.

Jamie had never left the house since the day of the accident until this day of the funeral. Father Antony noticed anxiously, as he conducted the service, the quiet finger movements as Jamie stared at the coffin. Later it was Jonty who realized that he was missing and quietly he wheeled out his bicycle to search the town. There was no sense in alarming his still dazed mother and if by chance she noticed his absence from the sofa she would assume they were out together. After an hour's fruitless search, it was then he remembered – he knew – and turned his machine towards Canny Hill bank, where the lads had watched for the pitch and toss men and where as youngsters they had bowled their pace eggs.

Jamie was there, sitting on the bank side at the corner where Joe had died. Jonty laid his bicycle on the grass and sat down beside the stricken, white-faced boy. It seemed a long time before he noticed a single tear glistening on his brother's face. Drawing him gently into his warm, comforting arms Jonty held the lad as a sobbing wail heralded a torrent of tears, breaking as if a dam had burst. The tears soaked his shirt and it seemed as though the young heart was breaking. Jonty held him even tighter and, stroking Jamie's fair tousled head, he said tenderly, 'Now then, bugger lugs.' Time passed unnoticed as the sobbing storm quietened and in the long silence the only sound was the joyous singing of a blackbird. Suddenly Jamie stirred and as Jonty prepared to pick up his bicycle, said, 'Let's go home.'

Jonty sat down again heavily. 'What did you say?'

'We'll away home, Joe's gone now.'

CHAPTER 34

Charlotte Brown, that expert in all things funereal, had been less impressed by the Street's absorption in a miraculous intervention than by the size and quality of the funeral tea held in the Welfare Hall. To be buried with ham was to her the accolade of putting a body to rest. Vying her intake with that of Stan Wilson, on whose umbrella she kept a stern eye, she enjoyed her place at table, a just reward she felt for her timely visit to the Co-operative Store to obtain the funeral bed linen. By a convoluted cross reference she passed down the table, a claimed relationship with Edie's mother, on her father's side. This did not stop the earnest application, hers or anyone else's, to the plate pies, sandwiches and cakes. The Priest had scarcely closed with a '*In nomine Patris, et Filii, et spiritus sancti,*' before she embarked upon her graveside rhetoric. Joseph Marr, she claimed, had been too angelic for this world and The Good Lord had taken him to a better place.

Olive Harman pooh-poohed what the street was calling a miracle. It was the shock of Joe's death, she insisted, and because he had always been dependent on his brother – well, now he is his own man. Unlike many people, particularly in Inkerman Street, Betsy had no such feelings of awe, only of delight as Jamie appeared with his fish barrow at the door of the filleting shed. Lumbering heavily, Betsy clasped him in her arms with a 'By, lad, it's good to get you back.' Jamie, his face pressed against a wet, oilskin-covered chest, wasn't in a position to say anything. Finally he emerged from the capacious bosom to rub fish scales off his cheeks. 'Where's the fish then?' he said, and there was a hint of a smile on his face.

Inkerman Street returned to its day and night life; occasionally Joe Marr would be remembered in a fine appraisal of his youth and character. Easily misdemeanors were forgotten or glossed over as Joe's memory was clouded with saintliness.

Roberto, calling for the late night takings at the fish shop, noticed the tired droop of Olive's shoulders and promptly offered Jamie a full-time job to work with Olive in the shop. He explained he wanted him to light the fryer fire, peel and pull the heavy iron grid that chipped the potatoes, all to be incorporated with his original fish delivery responsibilities. Jamie listened and nodded. Olive was relieved and grateful for Roberto's thoughtfulness. She had to admit that the twice daily sessions at the fish shop, with only a Sunday break, were beginning to tire her. Roberto would have liked the fish shop open on Sunday evenings but knew there would be little business. The standard Sunday night supper in every house was invariably a huge fry-up of the dinner-time vegetables topped by cold meat. Jamie's work proved worthy of Olive's standards. He rarely spoke and then only in monosyllables; he never used words where gestures would suffice. In her own mind Olive's first regret had been that the twin who could talk should have died, feeling that dumb Jamie could never make his way in the world. Now, she admitted to herself, she had been wrong. Jamie was quick and thorough in everything he did. She was surprised to find how much he had learned from Betsy about the quality and pricing of fish. Soon she allowed him to count with her the day's takings and initiated him into her own simple, but accurate book-keeping methods. At the end of the first week Jamie took home his twenty-one shillings wage. When the week had gone well, his father in jovial mood, would cry out to Edie, 'Hold out your pinny,' and Edie would lift the hem of her overall while Danny tossed the housekeeping into it. There was only Edie at home when Jamie stood, shyly in the doorway and said, 'Hold up your pinny, Ma.' As he tossed over his wages tears ran down Edie's face. 'Here's your pocket money, son,' and she handed him half a crown. Smiling through her tears she said, 'Joe will never be dead while you're here, Jamie.'

CHAPTER 35

The stiffly starched breast of the Matron had never been known to crease but it came near to crack when a sister called her to inform that a hysterical woman, punching a dead man in a foul-smelling funeral car, had drawn up outside the cottage hospital. When the Matron discovered that the strange ensemble had been driven there by the son of Sir Nathanial Dobson there was a swift alteration from disapproval and downright disdain to one of determined intervention. After all, Sir Nathanial was Chairman of the Hospital Governors. Her swelling dignity deflated to one of servility as she rushed to the assistance of Tobias Dobson. Very shortly, all he asked for was that a taxi be ordered for him, he added the names of the car occupants and assumed that someone would pick up the funeral car. Discouraging further conversation, much to the disappointment of the Matron, he stood at the Hospital entrance awaiting rescue from a distasteful situation. From the funeral car, Harriet, frothing at the mouth, still hoarsely screaming for Herbert to do something, was prised away from his body. The scratched face of her husband was decently covered and removed out of sight.

Reginald Fanshaw had never had to face up to a difficult situation throughout his life, as always his doting mother had soothed and smoothed out life's thorny problems for him. Now, with his grandfather ignominiously buried, his father dead and his mother heavily sedated, with pathetic sobbing he begged for advice from his father-in-law. Sir Nathanial gazed stonily at the handsome face and gave the same advice as before, 'Get your father buried,' but this time he added, 'Quietly, there has been enough unpleasantness.' To the subdued announcement of his father's death was added, 'Funeral private'. It was five days later before Harriet Fanshaw was well enough to face reality. As she pleated perfectly shaped half-inch pleats in the hospital bed sheets, she demanded the newspaper reports of Amos Fanshaw's funeral. Reginald hovered around her bed as she read desperately, trying to find words to tell her that she was a widow, but Harriet absorbed in the newspaper never asked about Herbert.

'There were some lovely wreaths, Mother sent for Grandfather's funeral.' He produced a bag of wreath cards. 'Would you like to read these?'

Harriet responded bitterly, 'With nobody at the graveside to see them – what good are they?' and she tossed the bagful into the waste bin. Reginald tried another topic. 'The reverend Guy Flintoff would like to call to see you, Mother, and he wondered if he could be of any help.'

'No. I don't want to see him.' Somehow he too was embroiled in the shameful fiasco and Harriet was venomous to shed some of the blame. Ignoring Reginald, Harriet with a lowering brow read the large headlines, 'Tragic death of a young boy.' There were full paragraphs, in detail, of the horrific events, followed in second place by the much lesser coverage of the death and interment of her father. Many, headed by the Mayor, had judiciously contacted the newspaper office to ensure that they were not associated with a half funeral, nor to broadcast their sudden exodus from the scene of the disaster. In the newspaper account the list of mourners was non existent, except for the naming of his grandson at the graveside. Further explanations of absences were made smoothly superfluous by the announcement of Harriet's illness, brought on by the unfortunate death of her husband coming so sadly on top of the death of her father. Apart from the long and genuine tributes in trade magazines, Herbert's death attracted little comment. His funeral coincided with the finding of a decapitated body on the railway lines. As the dead female had long been known to be involved with a local baker, the newsmen swarmed around Alan James' shop. The life and death of Amos Fanshaw was relegated to the inside bottom left page and truly mourned only by his sister.

Harriet was furious at such an ignominious end. What had been planned as the dignified interment of a notable public figure had ended in shameful disarray. Her father, she stormed, had been shovelled into his grave all because of an accident caused by a young ruffian.

'The boy is also dead,' Reginald said, warily watching the pleating fingers and the rising colour.

Like a hiss of steam she poured out a torrent of words. 'Yes, from

Inkerman Street. I've read that. And living next door to that harlot Olive Harman. She has troubled me since I was a girl – yet I kept her from starving by giving her work. And now from the same street more trouble. My poor father's coffin to be covered in blood and nobody there of consequence to see him buried. Who was at the graveside with you?'

'Just a couple of strangers.'

'Who were they, and what were they doing at the funeral?'

'I don't know. Sir Nathanial asked them to look after me, remember I was in a state too. He took the boy's body home.'

Ignoring the last remark, Harriet concentrated. 'Were they in the car behind the Mayor?'

'I think so.'

While Harriet's mind ranged around friends or acquaintances who had presumed to occupy an unwarranted place, Reginald blurted out, 'And father's dead and buried.'

'I know, I know, now there's only you and me, son,' and the tears of self pity rolled down both of their faces.

'There's a lot to be settled as soon as you are well enough. You understand, the reading of Grandfather's will and also Dad's.'

Harriet dabbed at her eyes and, sitting up, said suddenly, 'Have you contacted the lawyers?'

'They contacted me, but we agreed to postpone the reading of the wills until you are better able to deal with things.'

'Tell that nurse I want my clothes.'

CHAPTER 36

Although they lived in the same avenue, the two solicitors had offices at different ends of the town. The windows of Messrs Heslop, Heslop & Fairburn commanded an eastern view of the Tyne while Messrs Pickering, Pickering & Shepherd looked westward. Each senior partner cogitated and then in a gentlemanly manner, through discreetly worded letters, circled each other like two aged tortoises. Each held the plums of will knowledge to himself as each one tried to puncture the hard shell of professionalism of the other. For Amos Fanshaw had had his will drawn up by Heslop, Heslop & Fairburn while Herbert Fanshaw had favoured Pickering, Pickering & Shepherd. Each knew that he was handling a minefield of problems while both, unperturbed, considered the meeting with Harriet. Both men were well used to the greedy and grasping hiding their avarice behind their veils as speculative eyes shifted from one suspect beneficiary to the other; men usually sat very still contemplating the far distant view through the window. The worst of humanity often sat with white knuckled tautness in their fine leather chairs; the stupid, the feckless, the mean and the vengeful. Very rarely an unexpected reward for a care or a kindness would bring a mild surprise to their eyes, but it was usually, they cynically reminded themselves, when death was on the doorstep of the will maker. In this case there was the added complication of precedence. Was the will of the father who had died first to be read before that of the husband? Much time and clients' money was satisfactorily wrapped up before both agreed, while attaching involved repudiation clauses, to allow Harriet to decide as she was the spouse of one and the daughter of the other. This momentous decision was something that even Slack Willie could have worked out. Harriet made a crisp decision – 'Your father's will first and the other one later. He was always whingeing about money. I had a terrible time extracting money from him for the essential things that

124

we both needed. First thing we will do – we will sell the brewery. I never liked being associated with beer.'

The senior Mr Pickering laid down his spectacles at the end of reading the simple will. Raising his hooded eyelids he looked from the hard face of Harriet to the carelessly lounging figure of Reginald, who asked, 'Put it plainly, how much has he left?'

Ezekial Pickering began by explaining that the brewery had declined in value over the years, partly because of the grave economic situation when people needed to buy more important items than beer and partly . . .

Here Harriet interrupted. 'We know all that, it's wasting our time, we don't need to be told.'

Ezekial Pickering ignored the interruption and resumed his sentence, '. . . because there should have been money set aside for new vats and more modern machinery, but the profits were always drained away by large expenditure on other things.' There was a faint hint of satisfaction in his voice as, facing the two, he said, 'The late Mr Fanshaw was about to be made bankrupt. His affairs are already in the hands of the receivers and the bank will forclose on the mortgage.'

By now Reginald was as bolt upright as his mother, who was carefully pleating a handkerchief on her lap. In a choking voice Harriet said, 'You mean the mortgage on his sister's house.'

'No, Mrs Fanshaw, my late client gave the deeds of that house to his sister, Miss Platt, some years ago.'

'Which house is mortgaged?' hissed Harriet.

'His own house, Mrs Fanshaw, the house in which you live.' Ezekial Pickering continued smoothly, 'I understand he took out the mortgage at the time to cover some debts and to buy a boat.'

Harriet jumped up and clutched the back of the chair. 'Do you mean to say we have nothing – that we are paupers?' Her voice rose to a screech.'

With a sour look at the lawyer Reginald took his mother by the arm. 'You've got it wrong – there must be something left.'

The lawyer shook his head slowly. 'These are the facts and I'd advise you not to move or sell any possessions in the house until all is cleared up.'

Fury rose like a bitter pain. 'Some bloody lawyer you are to let the old man get into this flaming mess.'

Ezekial Pickering began to enjoy himself. 'I knew your father for many years when the Platt brewery was a thriving business. I knew him personally as a man of moderation, who spent little on the pleasures of this world – a man I esteemed.' The lawyer withdrew into his shell, feeling that for the first time in his life he had said too much. As they went to the door Reginald called back, 'Don't bother to send the bill, you won't bloody well get paid.' Ezekial Pickering made a gentle movement of his hands – he had already taken care of that.

They drove back in silence. Harriet flung off her coat and hat in the hallway and pushed her way into the drawing room. Anxiously Reginald followed. 'Now, Mother, take it calmly and don't upset yourself.' Harriet couldn't get the words out quick enough. For God's sake why had she married such a beer-swilling fool. She had given him a fine son and the best years of her life and what had she been left with? The public shame of bankruptcy, left penniless without a roof over her head. 'What can I do – what can I do?' she moaned as she paced back and forward across the carpet. Reginald shuffled anxiously; he had always hated his mother's tantrums and longed to be away from the disturbing scene. Had he not been through enough trouble with those two ghastly funerals? Unhappily, he told himself that he must stay in the house, not so much to be a comfort to his mother, but through dread of facing his Dobson-in-laws with the news of the Fanshaw financial disaster. Reginald felt deeply sorry for himself. Life had always been so pleasant; now just when a fellow should be enjoying himself he was beset by deaths, hysteria and no money. Fat lot the bloody Dobsons would care. His handsome face was petulant as he filled his whisky glass and tried to ignore the raging torrent of words. 'Perhaps,' he thought, 'I will threaten to take young William away from them if they cold shoulder me. That would give them something to think about.' Of course he had no intention of carrying out the threat, but the thought of the power he could wield cheered him up. How could he look after a young child? A nice enough youngster – a bit on the quiet side, he thought, but then he had never had time really to get to know him. 'But I can threaten those Dobson buggers, especially Amelia, if they try to put me down.'

'Oh, shut up, Mother,' and Harriet subsided into a chair and began pleating the table cloth. 'You would think we were done for – there's Grandfather's house and money waiting.'

'Yes, you are right. Will you make an appointment for me as soon as possible – and, Reginald dear, will you stay here with me?'

'Of course, Mother. Where are the sleeping pills the Doctor gave you?' Thankfully he watched her going up the stairs. 'I'll give her an hour for the pills to work and then I'll slip out to Clarty Clara's.'

CHAPTER 37

Riding her new mare, Patches, in the early morning sunlight, Amelia felt an urgent call of nature. Behind the bushes covered with diamond bright cobwebs, she pulled up her jodhpurs and saw a young man standing beside her horse. Cautiously she peered through the bushes; she circled the stranger, who seemed to be interested in the harnessing tackle. She watched as he smoothed the nose of her mettlesome mare, talking gently as Patches nudged nearer. Amelia stepped out of the bush coverage. 'That's my horse you're handling,' as she appraised the blond young man, shirt neck open, velveting the ears of the now quiet mare.

'Well, I didn't think a saddled horse would be a bloody stray.'

Amelia looked at his thatch of blond hair, latticed by the shifting sunlight. 'You are trespassing.'

'Not this side of the hedge, bonny lass, but maybe we are both out of bounds.'

Amelia stood beside her horse waiting for the cupped hands. With no movement forthcoming she turned around to the laughing face of Jonty Marr. 'There's a tree stump over there – help yourself.' As she straddled her horse he stared at the strained jodhpurs and slowly traced a finger down her leg. 'See you next Saturday,' he called as she rode off. Picking up his bicycle he leaned on the saddle to watch her out of sight. On the following Saturday morning there was a misty drizzle as Jonty waited under the tree for shelter. As she swung off her saddle Amelia asked, 'Who are you?'

'The name's Jonty Marr – christened Jonathan, but I've never heard anybody call me that; except that old sod of a schoolmaster. I don't need to ask who you are. Your face is in the papers often enough. Only in the best ones, mind you,' and he laughed. 'Come on, we are getting wet, there's a beaters' hut over there.' With Amelia leading Patches, Jonty went ahead and flattened the barbed wire with his heavy boots.

The horse walked daintily over the wire and carefully through the hedge.

Amelia took off her jacket and sat down upon a dusty, wide, low shelf. 'Do you know what I've come for?'

'Why aye, I very well know and you've picked the right man,' and Jonty unbuckled his belt. He had tumbled many beds in Embleton, usually married ones, with willing, even eager partners but his stolen Saturday mornings took on a spicy excitement. Amelia brought blankets and pillows and as the long mornings, like their passion, waned, they would lie together smoking and talking. 'I noticed when we first met how you gentled Patches, are you fond of animals?'

'Well, I've never owned a horse, but the old man has a pony called Boney, who is anything but. I see plenty of ponies down the pit. A chap called Harry Walters looks after them – now there's a bloke who loves animals. A neighbour of ours, he once frightened the shit out of our old feller by pronging him with a pitch fork on to the back of the garden shed. But Harry, he would empty his big pockets and feed fancy bits to each cuddy.' Jonty went on to describe Harry's life. 'Tied to a daft wife who never knows if it's Christmas or Easter, an empty shell living only for the return of a dead son. Harry's pit clothes hang behind the kitchen door and the whole house smells of horses.'

Amelia giggled, 'Sounds like home.'

'Well, that's my world,' said Jonty and he pulled her down to nuzzle her breasts.

She slid down and brown eyes looked steadily into grey. 'I like it better than mine.' Later, lying in his arms, Amelia asked, 'Have you ever heard of *Lady Chatterley's Lover*?'

'No, who's he?'

'I'll lend you the book.'

Shoving aside class barriers, they found they could talk easily to each other, laughing over their different life styles.

'Your brother Michael is nobody's favourite at Drumrauch.'

'I know, but I heard tell of how your Dad brought my brother's body home. I've told Michael he can't be that bad. Michael is a Union boss.'

Amelia nodded at the well-known information.

'Funny that, he never minded heights when he worked in the shipyards, but he's scared of the pit. Me, nobody gets me up a height.'

Suddenly he changed the subject. 'You've got a bairn, haven't you?'

'Yes, William's almost three now and sitting well on his pony.'

Jonty lay arms locked behind his head as he watched Amelia screwing out her red lipstick. 'That looks like a billy goat's pestle,' he remarked.

Amelia smiled as she continued making up her face.

Looking carefully at her, Jonty said, 'It's Felton autumn fair next Saturday, let's take young William.'

Amelia looked round in surprise and then dropped her make up into her bag. 'He's never been out without Nanny.'

'Shove Nanny, we'll take him.'

'I suppose I could borrow the car.'

'To hell with the car – we'll go by bus. Meet me last stop out of town at two o'clock.'

CHAPTER 38

The reading of Amos Fanshaw's will was destined to take place in the dung-coloured office of James Heslop, Heslop & Fairburn with its Eastern view of the silver tides of the Tyne. Harriet, with aid of medicine administered with a soothing bedside manner, felt able to face and to handle her father's will reading. As she dressed carefully and waited impatiently for Reginald, she re-ran the bitterness she felt towards her now dead husband. Clearly she remembered asking him for money to buy a boat for Reginald and pressing that he should mortgage his sister's home, pending her inheritance from her father. And what had he done! Mortgaged their own home, feeding the surplus money to allay brewery debts. It was not the house in Morden Street that had been mortgaged, but their own home. What should she do? Pay off the mortgage on this house with her coming inheritance or move to her father's lovely Georgian house upbank; the house in the square that she had always coveted. She despised her present home, declaring it had been bought by Herbert with beer money. Equally she scorned the corner end-terraced house Herbert had bought for his sister. She told herself the Georgian house in the square was where she belonged.

Mr James Heslop, senior partner of Heslop & Fairburn, courteously escorted Harriet to her seat. With a quick turn of her head she noted with amazement a woman and a young man already seated. The decorum of her forbidding black debarred her from demanding that strangers should be excluded from the reading of the will. Suddenly she remembered the pair in the car in front of the Mayor – Reginald said he had been helped by two strangers. Her indignation was hard to conceal – obviously they were claiming some remuneration. But how dare they trespass upon the intimate details of a will reading and why had the senior Mr Heslop allowed it? She would take care they didn't get a penny. Reginald, equally puzzled, with a nod gave an

131

awkward recognition of their graveside association.

Without preamble James Heslop senior began, 'This is the Last Will and Testament . . .' Harriet dragged her outraged glare from the quiet composure of the plump little woman, with her hands in her lap covered by black gloves and her sensible country shoes peeping out from under a dark-coloured shirt. Harriet frowned as she tried to recall – somewhere she had seen this woman – she shook her head and gave up trying to remember. 'All my goods and possessions to my wife, Jane Fanshaw, with the exception of the deeds of my farm, to my son Amos Fanshaw junior.' Odd words and half sentences were registering and receding as Harriet sat transfixed. 'The house in the square of Embleton to my daughter Harriet as she always desired the same. The Fanshaw Emporium to my grandson Reginald Fanshaw in the hope that he will at last make something of his life. A thousand pounds to be entailed for my great-grandson William Fanshaw . . .'

Words seemed to be battering the brain of Harriet. Jane Fanshaw, surely they had got it wrong. It should be Harriet Fanshaw – worldly goods to my wife – no, that should have been my daughter. The searing truth caused Harriet to shake. Jane Wilson, the maid she had sacked when she had noticed the glint of interest in her father's eye. The old fool had followed that girl into Northumberland. That explained his long and frequent absences and, great heavens – he had fathered a son on a woman young enough to be his daughter. The factual situation had also been realized by Reginald as, white with anger, he rose and pointed at the young man so calmly seated. 'God Almighty, he's my bloody uncle.'

'Certainly,' said Mr Heslop. 'Mr Amos Fanshaw junior is the legitimate son of your grandfather and,' he announced suavely, 'your mother's half brother.'

'Jane – Jane Wilson, the scheming bitch,' jerked Harriet's thoughts. 'I sacked her from my father's house,' and turning on the quiet figure she screamed, 'You got the old fool's money by the world's oldest trick – you got yourself pregnant.'

Jane Fanshaw rose simultaneously with her son. 'Your father and me had twenty good years together, living the life he loved in the only place he wanted to be. There is nothing more we want out of Embleton.'

'No, because you've got his money and a farm.'

'We have both worked for the farm, my son and me – you have the

132

house and your son the business.'

As the true implications of the will sank in, Reginald faced his future with horror. He was saddled with the responsibility of a business he despised and a penniless mother to be kept out of the proceeds. The young man was almost the same height as his mother and for the first time Harriet and Reginald looked him full in the face. There was no doubting the paternity, for Amos Fanshaw lived on. His son took his mother gently by the elbow, saying, 'Our business is finished here. Mr Heslop will see to the details. Come on, Mother, I've got to be back for the milking.'

At the doorway a thud made them turn round to see Mr Heslop and Reginald raising the fainting form of Harriet off the floor. Amos Fanshaw junior holding his mother's arm, shut the door quietly behind him.

The firm insistence of Mr Callum Ogilvie, bank manager, forced on them the reality of their situation. Reginald and his mother, their hopes of inherited affluence shattered by the discovery of Amos's fertile second marriage, shared embittered accusations between themselves and anyone else on whom they could spit their venom. Harriet tossed and turned in her bed at night, feverishly rejecting one plan after another. Every day she visited the big house in the square, muttering as she fingered the lovely old furniture. Mr Ogilvie had made it plain that she must vacate her present home. She knew they were all laughing at her, she heard their voices quite plainly in the night. And leading them on was that girl in the pale green dress. A silk dress shot with silver, a May Day crown upon her head.

CHAPTER 39

B ill Chambers, the gamekeeper, his cap flattened and folded in a omelette shape, had asked for a meeting with Sir Nathanial. Bill could move and disappear with the melting skill of an Indian. But with Patches quietly cropping the grass outside the hut, no tracking was needed. He knew very well who was one of the hut occupants. Right from the beginning he had watched the meetings of Amelia and Jonty, carefully checking the bedding after they had departed. With a secret smile he gloated over the thought of informing on Jonty, who had once reflectively, eyed his wife. But he had to handle this carefully – this was the boss's daughter. With an unsurpassed innocent expression, he explained that someone was using the beaters' hut. Once he had caught a glimpse of the trespasser who, apparently, was there every Saturday morning. Wouldn't like to be sure, but it seemed like a collier lad; might be wrong, he depreciated, but he looked like a Marr lad from Inkerman Street. Her father quickly put two and two together. Amelia had been missing every Saturday morning; out with her horse but not at the hunt. He recalled the raised eyebrows when her absence was noted. With years of negotiation behind him Sir Nathanial could cut the crust. 'Thank you, Chambers,' he said crisply, 'leave this one with me,' which Bill Chambers rightly interpreted as 'keep your nose out and your mouth shut,' and he slyly waited developments.

It was not only the deeply satisfying sex, nor the tantalizing class differences that intrigued Amelia and Jonty, although the differing attitudes within their family relationships were a revelation to both of them. Amelia recalled that stolen afternoon at the fair, where William, wrestled from the confines of the nursery, had been perched high on Jonty's shoulders, plied with roundabouts which Jonty called shuggie boats, and with chocolate ice-cream, to be satisfyingly sick behind the caravans. Amelia was engulfed with a strange feeling as she watched Jonty carefully wiping William's face and helping him to pee behind the hedge. The infant had enjoyed the kaleidoscope of noise and smells and was exhilarated by the lights and movement. Sitting on the hobby horses, cradled in Jonty's arms, he clapped his hands as they circled the garish figures tapping the drums and beating silver bells. Amelia watched them going round and round and wondered why she was crying. Her pit laddie, his blue coal-scarred hands circling her son, had reached private depths that she did not know existed. Grimly she thought of that partly daft Reginald who had caught her in a giddy whirl of adolescent skittering, and of the meaningless whipper-in episode. Thankfully he had moved to Southern Kennels before the relationship became unbearable. Looking at Jonty laughing into the ecstatic face of the youngster, Amelia realized that she was for the first time hopelessly and deeply in love. Lying in each other's arms with a Valor Oil stove heating the hut they explored the bodies, minds and experiences of each other. Amelia was fascinated by Jonty's tales of his family; of after a few jars of ale, dancing his mother around the kitchen accompanied by the delighted barking dogs and of their cat spitting defiance from the depth of the old fox fur. For Jonty had inherited the hypnotic story telling style of his grandmother, Sorcha. There was a 'tell me more' look in her face as he described Danny's late night drunken solos; of how he chopped the sticks to light the morning fire, under the stairs where he kept a large axe. There he would sing soulful ballads such as 'Pale Hands I Loved Beside The Shalimar', interspersed with the thud of iron on wood. When the singing ceased and the snores began, either of his two elder sons would hoist him over a shoulder and carry him up to bed. 'One of these days he'll chop his bloody leg off,' laughed Jonty. He went on to describe his father's farting expertise at the back door and up the stairs. The twins, and he nodded, were creased by the performance and then he would be silent; lighting up a cigarette and staring at the wood-slatted roof. Now she knew he was remembering Joe. He would begin to tell her of their mischievous capers and then stop suddenly. The first speech of the long dumb Jamie was something that he found hard to come to terms with. The eerie sensation of a voice coming apparently from the grave was to Jonty as miraculous as anything handed down from the Bible. Quickly he would move on to describe his allotment, talking with pride of the size and freshness of the potstuff he took home for the set pot broth. 'You and my mother would make a great pair, she loves her garden.'

'Maybe, but I'll bet she doesn't empty the piss pots for fertilizer – mind you, there's nothing to beat the weekend's water.'

Amelia wiped away tears of laughter. 'Tell me about Maisie's husband.'

'Oh him – Slack Willie. Well, mainly he keeps his hands in his pockets – it's a wonder he doesn't damage his nose.' Reflectively Jonty resumed, 'It's hardly likely, he seldom moves – only his elbow so he canna fall down. You've never mentioned your grandmother.'

'Oh, my grandmother, she's a dotty old soul, smokes like a chimney and steals tins of food from the kitchen to hide under her bed. She still thinks there's a war on and she drives the cook mad. She's a queer old stick.'

'You should meet mine – Granny Sorcha,' said Jonty. He broke the long silence. 'I saw your husband in town last week, looking daft in them shit keppers.'

'The Prince of Wales wears plus fours and Reginald always follows his fashions.'

'What are you going to do about him, Amelia?'

Amelia rolled over, the red mica light from the Valor stove giving a glow to her snuff brown hair.

'Him.' Amelia dismissed him with a click of her fingers. 'He's out of my life. I have enough money from my grandfather. He had this funny idea that, with so many spinsters left over from the war and apparently I was such an ugly kid and would never marry, I'd better be provided for. Well, I did marry and look what I got.'

'What will you do with the money?'

'Breed Cleveland Bays. I love them.'

'Me, I'd rather have Shires.'

'Why?'

'Well, it's a change from pit ponies.'

'Jonty, I've grown up. I want to leave Drumrauch Hall.'

'What about young William?'

'I haven't thought that one out.'

'Well, it's time you bloody well did. Are you going to leave him to that arse-faced nanny, what's her name, Dora Benson, and that sodding Reginald? He's yours, remember.'

Amelia sat up, surprised by the anger in Jonty's voice, and then she

136

smiled as though engrossed in a wonderful thought. 'Of course I'll take him with me, he sits his pony wonderfully well.'

'Oh aye,' echoed Jonty sarcastically, 'he sits his pony wonderfully well.'

CHAPTER 40

Betsy Haddick moved her heavy body uneasily in the bed, aware of a stomach discomfort. 'Must have been them kippers I had for supper,' she mused, but kippers had never disagreed with her before. Judging by the light showing under her too short curtains, it would soon be time to meet the early morning fishing fleet and never in her life had she been late for that. Pushing herself upright in the cupboard, or what her mother called the desk bed, she decided to take a dose of liver salts, before she made her tea. Each time the pain came and went she believed the trouble was settling down. She finished the filleting by eleven o'clock and was glad to hand the fish over to Jamie. 'I'm away home, I've got the bellyache.' Jamie watched her walking slowly up the stone stairs that led to the rabbit warren of fishermen's cottages. Betsy, despite her big frame, never walked slowly up the steps; years of fish hawking had given her strong muscular legs. This morning Jamie noted uneasily that she stopped to hold on to the iron railings. He slowly rested the handrails of his barrow, with its wooden props, on the ground and was about to bound up the steps after her, when Betsy straightened up and climbed to the top of the steps. Relieved, Jamie trundled his barrow load of fish up the bank road to the fish shop.

Her neighbour, Chrissy Blackburn, watched Betsy's slow progress along the street. 'What's up, Betsy?'

'Have you owt for the colic? I've a cruel bellyache.'

'The kettle's boiled, I'll bring you a cup of ginger tea.'

When Chrissy, pot in hand, opened the door she saw Betsy hanging on to the post of the cupboard bed. Chrissy set the pot of ginger tea on the table.

'It's not colic you've got, lass, you're in labour.'

Betsy clutched her stomach. 'Good God Almighty, are you sure?'

'So sure,' said Chrissy grimly, 'I'm away to fetch the handywoman.

138

Nobody knows better than me, I've had six of me own.'

The pain spasm passed over and Betsy sat down thankfully in the chair to drink her ginger tea. To have fallen wrong after all these years! Betsy shook her head unbelievingly. 'I thought I was barren.' But right enough there were those strange movements she had dismissed as wind. 'Wait till me Ma knows she is going to be a Granny.' Betsy gave a rueful laugh. 'You gave me a farewell present all right, Robbie.' But her laugh was cut short by a twisting pain.

Chrissy Blackburn, shawl over her head, ran through the narrow streets to Bella Makepiece's cottage. 'You're wanted, Bella, can you come to the Haddicks' house?'

'Is it the old woman?'

'No, it's Betsy, she's in labour.'

Pausing, poker in hand from riddling ashes out of the fire back, Bella shook her head in disbelief. 'Betsy's never that way!' She continued easing up the coals with the poker and then said thoughtfully, 'Although mind, with her size, it would never show.' She took a clean apron from the drawer. 'Late forties, isn't she, and a first one? At that age it will be hard on her. I'd rather have them young, after one or two they come as easy as shelling peas. Is her Ma there?'

'No, she's away with the fishing but back tonight, mind. By God, wait 'til she sees what the tide's brought in. There's that new Nurse Jopling, but she lives on the other side of town. Shall I send one of my lads for her?'

'Plenty of time, plenty of time,' Bella dismissed the proposal with the wave of a strong, lean hand. 'We don't want her hanging around afore she's needed. Tell Betsy I'll be along as soon as I've set me man's tea.'

Bella Makepiece was a tall woman, very capable of attending births or death beds. In that small, closely knit fishing community, she was one who, after sharing the most intimate moments in a family's life, would never broadcast their limitations of bedding or pantry. Her own shortcoming was the scorn in which she held the district nurse. Bella and her mother before her, until the new arrival, had been the unquestioned authority on all matters to do with the entering and leaving of this world. Proud old women would quietly draw Bella aside to confide in her, in which drawer were two clean linen sheets. Bella also knew there would also be a carefully hoarded ten shillings, left between the sheets, for the laying out fee.

Bella knew all the ties of friendship and relationship around the neighbourhood; who to send for to take the washing or do the family's baking. Children would be sent out to play in charge of the eldest and told which family friend or relation to go to for their meal. If Da, the man of the house, was at home, he would be told, firmly, to go down to the allotment or to the pub until the birthing was over; and thankfully he would escape from this woman's work. Bella was expert at knotting a strong towel over the bed rail for a labouring woman to pull on, or to improvise where ideas or household articles were in short supply or non-existent. As she put on her apron in Betsy's cottage, she noted the wet-stained skirt, so the waters had broken and it would be a dry, hard labour.

'Right, Betsy. Let's have you into a clean shift,' and she helped the sweating, restless woman into a dry night gown. 'Have you any clean newspapers, Betsy?'

'There's a pile in the back, Jamie brings them from the fish shop.' The words ended in a shriek as she pulled on the knotted towel ends. The towel was fastened over a wooden slat above Betsy's head. Bella looked thoughtful. 'She's a powerful lass, hope she doesn't bring it down.' She nodded to a long-held confirmation that there was nothing like a strong brass bed head for a labouring woman. Bella placed the wad of unfolded newspapers on the table and, pulling out the bottom drawer of a chest, she emptied the contents on to a pile in the corner. Opening another drawer she found a blanket and a white shawl. She lined the drawer with the blanket and laid the shawl to warm on the fender. Realizing the pains were coming quicker and stronger as Betsy pulled at the towel, creaking the whole of the bed, Bella knocked on the fire back with the poker. Chrissy Blackburn appeared almost before she had time to put the poker down.

'Better get your lad off for the nurse,' she said reluctantly.

The importance of his mission put wings on the bicycle pedals of Chrissy's Jimmy. Answering the door the nurse's landlady read the grubby pencilled note.

'Tell them the nurse is called away at the other side of Embleton; she'll come as soon as she gets back.' Mrs Adelaide Williams made her announcement with the air of one who handled affairs of state. Then she shut the door on the lad in the ragged Jersey and trousers.

140

Bella sponged down Betsy's sweating, straining body, assuring her that everything was all right and, 'You've got to expect a longish time with your first.' But she was quietly worried at the long labour and considered sending for the doctor if that damned nurse didn't hurry up. She also knew that neither Betsy nor her mother were on the threepence a week Doctor's panel, with the added optional indulgence of an extra penny a week for the cottage hospital. Never having had a day's illness in their lives, such a financial commitment was considered unnecessary. Anyway, that doctor was a hard case; her neighbour's man had gone to him complaining of depression and swearing that for two pins he would do away with himself. The Doctor had calmly turned back the lapel of his coat and offered the man two pins.

Bella was glad when Chrissy offered to stay with her, for she too, was feeling the exhaustion of the long day in the warm kitchen. Betsy's cries were quieter now but no less agonizing to hear. She was getting near the end of her tether and Bella in an unguarded moment wished that nurse would get herself here. The door opened, but it was not the nurse but old Sarah, her seal-skin coat still glistening with fish scales, her pipe in her mouth and a bass bag of fish in her hand. The situation did not need much explaining. Betsy was heaving on the bed, her rich colour gone except for a few tiny red veins standing out on her now white cheeks. Her lovely hair was sweat matted and looked a dull, tawny colour.

'I've had her all ways,' Bella explained. 'But I canna fetch it.'

Sarah put her bag of fish on the window sill. 'Get her up,' she demanded as she reached for the big chamber pot from behind the curtain. Then, 'Kneel over,' she said and the moaning Betsy straddled the chamber pot.

'Hod her up,' and the two neighbours obediently held her until their arms ached with the weight. Sarah brought her jug from the back room and poured half a cupful. 'Drink,' she commanded and, as her mother tipped up the cup, Betsy, half dead with fatigue, swallowed the rum.

'Now come on,' she ordered.

'Must be a lazy lad,' Chrissy offered helpfully as she eased her own aching back. Betsy gave a last despairing pant and the child slid out into the waiting hands of Sarah, cupped together near the bottom of the chamber pot, as if it had never meant to cause any trouble at all.

'I said it was a lazy lad,' Chrissy grinned triumphantly as she stretched her weary arms.

'Aye, by God, and he's fathered himself,' said old Sarah, she waved her pipe and looked closely into the tiny facial replica of Roberto Delfino.

CHAPTER 41

Nurse Jopling pedalled with firm feet towards her lodgings, planning as she rode along her evening's activities. There was that new Weldon's print dress pattern she intended to cut out. She knew her landlady did not approve of her, hands and knees and the pattern pieces spread out on the sitting room floor, fearing a carpet cut out with the pattern. The landlady had also the added worry of stray pins puncturing the delicate paws of her beloved Siamese cat. Euphoric with duty performed, Nurse Jopling returned from the birth of a baby daughter into a family previously blessed with two sons. She sighed, pedalling hard against the wind, if only all children could be born into such a satisfactory family. A cluster of aunts in the kitchen had used her brief spells from the bedroom to produce, from under layers of tissue paper, hand embroidered cot covers, crotched baby boots, frilled bibs and small tatted pillow covers. This was the first girl child born into that family for over thirty years, they said, and she had shared in the family adulation of the infant. Coyly refusing a celebratory sherry she made her way home to a scones and tea cake tea time.

'Where is neuk end?' she asked as she handled the piece of paper carefully smoothed out previously by her landlady. Mrs Adelaide Williams managed her home and her lodgers' affairs with the same diligence with which she undertook the leadership of the Chapel Women's Guild. Now a widow, with her indulged son engulfed in city life, she was free to enlighten her lodger about sins and vice so abundant in Embleton. 'Neuk end,' she pontificated, 'is common talk for "corner end". It's in a small street leading off the quayside stone steps.' Moving nearer to Nurse Jopling's eager ears, she resumed, 'That Haddick woman is a well-known bad character on the quayside for her carryings on with that Italian chap, Delfino. I remember the day that him, a Catholic, walked into our Guild meeting in the Chapel.' Time had not appeased the outrage felt by Adelaide Williams at the desecration of her personal temple and she proceeded to give a less than factual account of that day many years ago. The combination of the circumstances brought a downturn of Nurse Jopling's mouth and a disapproving shake of the head. 'Well, I will go there after I've had my tea. After all this Betsy Haddick is not officially on my books.'

As she cycled past Number eight Inkerman Street, the nurse recalled a recent birth there. That too had been a girl child, born in her grandmother's house. She hadn't liked the young father-to-be; hanging around, mouth open, and trying to peep into the room where his wife was in labour. It wasn't decent, having a man around at a time like that. Even the miners observed proper behaviour and waited to be invited back at the proper time. 'I suppose,' she meditated, 'that even in these desperate times childbirth can still be called a happy event.' The look of awe and delight on the faces of the numerous children sharing an overcrowded house as they shuffled around their mother's bed, taking turns to gaze at the newcomer, made even Nurse Jopling smile. Old great-grandmothers would back up the chorus of wonder with, 'God never sends a mouth but what he sends something to put in it,' as another mouth was added to the already strained family finances.

It was dark as she wheeled her bicycle down bank, eager hands pointing her onward to Neuk End. She leaned her machine against the wall and lifted her Lysol-smelling obstetric bag off the rear. The sudden atmospheric change was a nasal shock as, stepping out of the clean salty night air, she was assailed by the stuffy heat and the strong combined smell of fish, rum and sweat. Bella Makepiece looked up triumphantly. 'We've managed all right, he's here and a fine lad as well.' The nurse cast a condemning eye over the cluttered drawer contents heaped carelessly in the corner; at old Sarah, still in her seal-skin coat smoking her pipe, at the other two women tea cups beside them and at the shawled baby asleep in Bella's lap. Pointedly, she moved an old dish containing the afterbirth and some stained newspapers into the back kitchen, where she washed her hands. Returning, she said stiffly, 'I will see to the mother.'

'Oh, I've washed her down an' all.' The allied smug looks of Chrissy and Bella were too much.

'That binder is too tight.'

'When you've bound as many cords as I have, you'll have room to judge.'

Betsy, acting the peacemaker, smiled weakly. 'Well, it's good of you to come, nurse, but we're all right now.'

Nurse Jopling pummelled the bed and made a halter collar shape of two pillows. Trying to ignore the united animosity, the nurse turned to Sarah. 'Are you the grandmother?' Sarah removed the pipe from her mouth and nodded. Determinedly the nurse took the child from its woollen cocoon and placed it in a linen bag suspended from a weight recorder. To Betsy, the only pleasant-faced individual in the room, she announced, 'Eight pounds six ounces.'

The child in its disturbed suspension began to yell and Bella with an accusing, 'Look what you've done now,' look, wrapped the child in its woollen folds and laid it in the drawer. Asserting her professionalism the nurse announced sharply to Betsy, 'I'll be around tomorrow morning to wash you down and bath the baby.'

At the comfort of her landlady's fireside Nurse Jopling detailed the grim circumstances she had had to put up with. Mrs Williams stroked her purring cat and sadly shook her head, knowing that all her previous condemnations were once again confirmed.

145

CHAPTER 42

After breakfast Roberto lit his first Gold Flake cigarette of the day. One of the joys of being in his own home was that he could smoke whenever he wanted to. Olive had barred cigarette smoking in her house and Roberto had been forced to smoke either in the yard or to slip into the Marr household where the Marr men lit up continuously from each other's Woodbines. He eased his thumb into the top of his trousers with difficulty and had to admit to his thickening girth. The result of the combined cooking of meals by Zia and Maria and the frequent meals at the restaurant were self evident. But today Roberto shrugged such a detail aside, for his happiness was overwhelming. He had seen the 'For Sale' notices at Harriet's house and also at her father's, but something else had filled a pleasurable cup. His greatest wish and desire had been granted. He stepped out of the Delfino's Ice-Cream Parlour and stopped to watch half a dozen children playing Hitchy Dabber' on the chalked squares along the pavement. He would take care that his child had better playthings than an empty boot polish tin to be hitched along the pavement by scuffed and worn-out old boots. Across the pavement two little girls sat arranging pretty coloured pieces of broken pottery that they called 'boodies'. With intense concentration they arranged the reds, blues and yellows in a circle on the ground.

The thought of Maria's pregnancy sent a curl of delight through his body. Desperately he had waited for this confirmation that a child was on the way and for once business was not uppermost in his mind. He hoped for a son – no, for sons and daughters, a family he would be proud to take back to his homeland and when the time came, to introduce them to their adoring relatives. And Maria had never looked better, apart from a morning sickness. 'She's settling down now,' he told himself; although she over indulged in a calendar of numerous religious feast days. Later he would call on Father Antony and give a

146

donation to the church as thanks for his answered prayers. He felt he did his duty by attending a weekly confession and Mass and that Maria's assiduous attendances made up for any further claims on his time. On this Saturday, as on every other, he carried Olive and Jamie's wage packets and he carried also, for Olive's ear alone, the news about the baby. For once his delight and pride had ousted the daily appreciation of his mounting bank balance and his substantial increasing investments.

Edie hailed him with pleasure before he reached Olive's back gate. 'Eeh, I'm pleased to see you, come in and see our Maisie's baby.' Edie, in her usual attire of cross-over pinafore and carpet slippers, turned to lead the way into the kitchen expecting no refusal. Lying in Maisie's lap it was certainly a beautiful child, with honey-coloured down and long, dark golden lashes fringed on a sleeping face. Roberto placed half a crown in its small hand and wished it the usual health, wealth and happiness, while wondering how such a beautiful little creature could have been fathered by Slack Willie. Maisie had come home to be confined and seemed reluctant to return to the O'Connor household. Olive told him that there was war on between the two families over that Union business and Danny had taunted Albert O'Connor so much that they had come to blows at the back of the Ironmasters Arms.'

Happiness flooded Edie's face as she took the baby and rocked it in her arms. This grand bairn was definitely the finest ever seen in Inkerman Street, or all of Embleton for that matter. This little creature would ease some of her heartache over the death of Joe, he thought. The baby began to cry and Edie hoisted it up on to her cushion of a shoulder and patting its back, said professionally, 'Wind.' Danny appeared from the back kitchen where he had been washing himself. 'Give that bairn a ham bone,' he advised, a broad grin on his face. Confidentially he turned to Roberto. 'What some folks would give for a little lass like that, eh.' Without waiting for the expected confirmation he explored his still damp ear with a spent matchstick. As he examined a glistening wax globule he declared, 'There's none of the O'Connor in that bairn, she's all Marr,' and it would have been dangerous to contradict.

Promising to call again, Roberto made his way out, followed by Edie who whispered by the back door, 'There's a bit of trouble on.' Carried away by his liking for Edie and forgetting caution he softly

147

told her his news, regretting it the moment the words were out of his mouth. Her round face shining, Edie began a torrent of words of congratulation. Hastily he shushed her and begged it would be kept secret for a while. Adjusting her expression to conspiratorial solemnity she assured him that her father had always said, 'Two can keep a secret if only one knows.' As he backed out of the yard Edie yelled the time of day of the baby's christening adding, 'You'll be welcome.'

At Number seven, without preliminaries, Olive said, 'I heard her asking you to the christening.'

'Well, you will be going too, I hope.'

'I suppose so,' and she added with a sniff, 'Do you know what they are calling it?'

'No.'

'Doreen Edith. Well, the Edith is all right, it's both her mother and her grandmother's name, but that Doreen. It's after some film star that Maisie goes to see at the pictures.'

Roberto bursting with his own news, could wait no longer.

'Listen, Olive, I've some good news. Maria's expecting in the summer.' He waited expectantly for Olive's expressions of delight and congratulations, but Olive's face hardened.

'Did you tell her first?'

'Well, look, it's like this, I intended to tell you first but I got carried away in Edie's after seeing Maisie's baby.'

Stung by not being the first to know, Olive said bitterly, 'It will be in everybody's mouth by tea time.'

'But you must be pleased about the baby.'

'Well, you're married, it's to be expected,' she said coldly.

Roberto felt angry and rebuffed as he placed the pay envelope where he always did, on the mantlepiece. Olive put on her coat, saying it was time she was down at the shop. They walked down the hill in silence; the one consumed by jealous hurt and the other confused and crestfallen.

Both were jerked out of their thoughts when they found the shop door locked. By this time of the day Jamie, the dependable, always had the fires going, the fat heating, potatoes chipped and a tidy shop awaiting customers. As they looked at each other in puzzlement, Jamie appeared, sweating and panting as he pushed his barrow load. With the abrupt short sentences he always used, he blurted, 'Betsy's not there. Took bad yesterday. Had to get what fish I could on the quay. Filleted it myself.' Jamie was not used to praise and he certainly did not get any for his efforts and initiative. He unlocked the door to Olive's command, 'Let's get on with it.'

Roberto, to neither in particular, said in bewilderment, 'Betsy never ails anything,' and Olive as usual, when Betsy's name was mentioned, said nothing, only knotted her apron firmly around her waist. Roberto followed Jamie through into the back preparation. He halted Jamie as he was emptying a sack of potatoes.

'Did she say what was wrong?'

'Only that she had a bellyache.'

CHAPTER 43

When Jonty opened the door of the hut he almost dropped the can of paraffin that he was carrying. Sir Nathanial Dobson sat on the edge of the bunk bed, his hands folded over a shooting stick and his chin on his hands.

'Good morning, I don't think we have met.'

'No, but we nearly did when you brought my brother's body home.' Instantly he regretted the words spoken, fearing he had given Sir Nathanial the impression that he was under an obligation to him, or in some way subservient.

'Do you smoke?' offering his gold cigarette case.

'Yes,' and Jonty, deliberately drawing out his packet of Woodbines, lit up and replaced the packet in his pocket. The old man snapped his case shut and did likewise. Despite Jonty's action, Sir Nathanial saw no fear, spite or malice on the open face of Jonathan Marr.

'I know your brother Michael.'

'I'll bet you do,' and there was a glimpse of a smile on both their faces.

'I don't intend to prolong this discussion because I do not want to embarrass my daughter. I just want you to know that I am aware of what is going on here. Perhaps this is not the best place for you to meet with Amelia.' With a whimsical look he added, 'It takes my gamekeeper's mind off his job.'

'I'll get that bugger, Bill Chambers,' Jonty quickly decided.

Looking the elder man straight in the eye, Jonty replied, 'We come here because it suits us. We make no secret of it, anybody passing could see the horse outside. Not that many would pass this way. That would be trespassing on your property,' he said disarmingly.

'Well, Amelia cantering off down the woods instead of joining the Saturday hunt has caused some comment and raised eyebrows.'

'Now then, we could always put a notice in the paper.'

'He's a cheeky young devil,' Sir Nathanial decided as he eased himself off the bunk. Jonty could have kicked himself for opening the door to Sir Nathanial who, as he walked out, remarked that it looked like rain. Later that night, while unfastening his collar studs, he wandered into Lady Dobson's bedroom.

'Did you know that Amelia is having an affair with a miner?'

'How old is he?'

'I mean a miner with an "e".'

'Does Reginald know?'

'If he doesn't, he soon will; I'd bet on it.'

After calling Reginald into his office, Amelia's father was sure that his son-in-law did not yet know of his wife's involvement with a collier. Time to move he thought. Amelia had confronted him immediately after hearing of his meeting with Jonty and had made it quite plain that this was no hedgerow affair.

'I want a divorce and I intend to marry Jonty Marr.' As soon as she said it a quick shaft of fear unnerved her, for she wasn't sure that Jonty had marriage uppermost in his mind. He had always avoided the subject and if true to his reputation, he was unlikely to marry anyone. But marriage or not, this was the man she wanted and Amelia always got what she wanted.

Reginald regarded his father-in-law with curiosity tinged with fear. There was a finality in the older man's face that worried him. Without altering his chair position, Sir Nathanial began to speak. 'It is better that I discuss this matter here with you than at home. I must tell you that my daughter is filing for a divorce and it will be pleasanter for all concerned if you leave Drumrauch Hall as soon as possible. Now that you have your grandfather's business there is no point in working here any longer. You have long complained that the work you do is a menial job and I'm sure you would be better employed in building up the Fanshaw Emporium. From what I hear it is in sad need of attention. Please clear your desk by tonight.'

Reginald sat in stunned silence. This was the will readings all over again. Everything was falling on top of him – so many different and terrifying problems looming suddenly on to his previous comfortable lifestyle. Divorce; pointedly told to leave the shipyard and worst of all forced to vacate Drumrauch Hall, for he had enjoyed the life and prestigious address. Indignation jolted him out of his seat. Yelling

151

over the desk he shouted, 'She can't divorce me, she has no grounds for a divorce. It's all your fault, you've persuaded her to do this – you and your bloody sons. But I'll fight it, there is nothing that she can bring against me.'

'Sit down,' and then it was made cuttingly cold and very clear that Amelia had every right to a divorce. From his desk drawer his father-in-law drew out a paper listing all known visits to Clarty Clara's, so painstakingly recorded by his son Tobias. He made it clear that Tobias was willing to testify in court to the numerous brothel visits. Reginald, flushed with fury, reared up: 'Tobias – I'll get a revenge on him.' Who was Tobias anyway? Despite his upper-class background he was no better than a sodding fishmonger.

Reginald for the first time in his life was finding out the misery of a sleepless night of worry. All his life he had laid his petulance and his troubles into the receptive lap of his mother. And now she was his problem. He had always ignored his maiden aunt, Polly Platt, his father's only sister, but suddenly he had nowhere else to turn. He descended on the little house in Morden Street exuding his easy charm. He begged his aunt to look after his mother who, he declared, was losing her mind over the death of her father and her husband. The elderly Miss Polly Platt was no fool and looking her nephew straight in the eye, she laid down her terms. She would take Harriet in for one month only until Reginald found a home for the two of them. After all, she pointed out, Harriet still had that grand property, her father's house to sell. Certainly she had agreed to sell, said Reginald eagerly, concealing the trouble his mother was causing in the selling of the house. A keen prospective buyer, while inspecting the house, had been frightened off by a screaming woman ordering him out of the house, shouting that he was a burglar come to rob the place. Although Reginald took the door keys away from her, Harriet haunted the gardens shouting abuse and banging on the windows each time she saw a prospective buyer inside with the estate agents. She was quietened only by the sleeping tablets that the Doctor had prescribed and which Reginald encouraged her to take. The Doctor refused Reginald's request to assign his mother to an asylum, saying firmly that Harriet's condition was temporary and caused by the recent family tragedies.

Although Reginald had been excluded from Amelia's bedroom and pointedly given a room overlooking the stables, life at Drumrauch was still comfortable. His meals, tray laden, were brought to him and his rooms cleaned as before. He told himself that he preferred taking his meals that way, rather than sharing the communal board with the frozen-faced Dobsons, who talked of nothing else but trade, horses and dogs. He had his own liquor cabinet and recently had taken to popping into the nursery, where he always had a welcome tea and a sympathetic hearing from Nanny Benson. It was only when he thought of Tobias Dobson's treachery that he became desperate for revenge against the Dobson family. Well, there was his brother-in-law's wife and he wondered if Celia would be worth a tickle. When they had met her eyes seemed to follow him around the room. Such strange eyes, dark, watchful and very steady, if rather unnerving.

The last thing Reginald wanted was to share a house with his mother and he had every intention of leaving her with his Aunt Polly. He was quite sure that he could rely on her not to turn his mother out on to the street. After all, he reasoned, Aunt Polly had done very well out of the brewery money; for his father had provided better for his sister than he had for his son. While Harriet was temporarily shelved and reluctantly on probation, Miss Polly Platt resented the imperious manner of her sister-in-law, particularly the intrusion she had made into her erstwhile comfortable life. Always so clean and particular, Harriet had now lost interest in her clothes and her hairdresser. She had to be forced to wash and the irate Polly counted the days until Reginald took his mother off her hands. From his comfortable room, Reginald moaned into the darkness, bitterness corroding his throat as he mulled over, time and again, the perfidious conduct of his brother-in-law. Above all was the sickening thought that he was being booted out from the prestigious Drumrauch Hall by Amelia's father.

CHAPTER 44

Dora Benson, William's nanny, was broad of face and flat of foot. From the age of fourteen she had worked as a nursemaid and then as nanny to a succession of children. Now at the age of fifty-four she was satisfyingly comfortable, living in the Dobson household. And it was a family of which she highly approved. Here she was queen of her own domain, the family did not interfere and her only charge, William, was a quiet boy who gave little trouble. Her last post had been a nightmare, with three children under six years of age to look after and an interfering mother who believed her offspring should be free to express themselves. Throwing paint on the nursery walls and stuffing her starched caps down the lavatory went unpunished. Her attempts at slipper chastisement had brought down the wrath of the parents upon her bonneted head. Thankfully she had reached this haven of comfort where the child was escorted down before dinner for a few absentminded pats and nodded back again to the nursery. Exercise was taken in the grounds of the hall where Dora could sit working at her crotchet while, solemnly, the child explored a wide world of plant and animal life. The sturdy three-year-old was always attracted by movement as a relief from the stationary conditions in the nursery. Dora carefully tried to steer the boy away from his grandmother working in the garden, as he usually came back annoyingly dirty from the potting sheds or greenhouses. Unless his mother came to give him a riding lesson, William was solely in her stultifying care.

But now there was a worrying development, for Amelia, without a word of explanation had suddenly begun to whisk the boy away, usually on Saturdays. The first time William had come back, rather sticky and burbling over and over the words, 'Jonty,' and 'Shuggie boats'. Each time he spoke the words William giggled happily. The puzzled Dora wondered where he had picked up such common words.

Before these outings he had seemed indifferent to his mother's visits, but lately he ran to get his coat when his mother appeared at the nursery door. Dora was pulled two ways. While she enjoyed the extra free time to herself she felt, uneasily, that her position was being undermined. Her security was threatened. All her working life she had scraped and saved. With uniform provided she needed only one outdoor outfit to visit her church, where her needlework expertise was warmly appreciated. As a devout member of the Church of England she gave full support to the Reverend Guy Flintoff; especially after that dreadful funeral. As if it were not enough for such a sensitive man as her Vicar to have to bury a man in a blood-covered coffin, there had been the added business involving the organist Simeon Jordan, and a choir boy. Dora Benson banked every spare shilling against the day when she would no longer be needed by the family. For when the boy was packed off to boarding school she would be forced to live with her irritating sister. The removal of William for undisclosed outings brought that dreaded day nearer.

The cook and Nanny Benson respected each other as paramount each in her own domain; each advocating the need to keep the other servants firmly in their place. Although Cook visited the nursery for her afternoon 'sit down', Dora would have considered it beneath her dignity to have a gossipy talk in the kitchen. In the nursery Dora could always assert her slight superiority of position by relating stories, sprinkled with Honourables, and the upper class houses in which she had worked. Over cups of tea they would discuss the affairs of the other staff and the Dobson family; the former with indignation, giving examples of 'Stepping out of place,' and the latter in conspiratorial whispers. Nanny had only one underling, a large, shy village girl called Ruby, who lived for her paperback romances and her weekly magazine *The Red Letter*. William enjoyed Nanny's day off, for Ruby sat him on her knee and told him all about her family and the people who lived in the village. She was also very generous with homemade toffee. Nanny told Cook that, unless Ruby was carefully watched, she would have her head in a magazine. Cook reciprocated with her usual complaints about Lady Fanshaw's mother constantly stealing food from her pantry that had to be retrieved from under the old lady's bed.

'I've complained to her Ladyship time and again but she doesn't listen.'

'She would if it were seeds or flowers being pinched,' and the two heads nodded over the teapot.

Inevitably they would conclude by discussing the marital discord of Amelia and Reginald. Both were firmly on the side of the estranged husband. Such a charming man with such good manners, they told each other.

At first Reginald sought Nanny's favours because she was so good with the needle. He found a willing substitute to his mother Harriet, for soon Dora was darning his socks, replacing shirt buttons and finally doing his laundry. If it crossed Dora's mind that something more tangible than the lavish praise and effusive 'Thank you,' should come her way, she put it to one side. With tears in his wide blue eyes he would, holding her hand, confide of his loneliness and despair at being spurned by the family. Bursting with pride at such confidences she would dispense snippets of interest to Cook, with the tea.

Today Cook hugged to herself her startling news as she puffed her way up to the nursery. Before the tea was out of the pot she edged her chair nearer to Dora.

'You'll never guess,' she said excitedly.

And into Dora's incredulous ears she poured out the story circulating in the kitchen. Miss Amelia, a lady, was carrying on with Jonty Marr from Inkerman Street. The child's repetition of the words, 'Jonty,' and 'Shuggie boats,' came to Dora's mind immediately. So that's where she was off to with William; to meet that common man. While she was shocked at such behaviour, she was also annoyed that she had not previously put two and two together and could thus have forestalled Cook bringing her the news.

Dora was horrified at this breach of class boundaries. As they mulled over the news, they agreed that it had been known for young male scions to fumble the maids but for a lady to, 'You know what,' in a hut with a miner, that was beyond all decency. Poor Mr Reginald, Dora wailed, married to a hussy like that. The teapot had long gone cold and the Cook departed when Dora decided that it was her duty as a Christian woman to inform Mr Reginald of his wife's infidelity. When he appeared with a disarming smile and a bag of laundry, Dora was unable to contain herself.

'Mr Reginald, I've heard something shocking today and my heart tells me that there's something you must know.' Here she clasped her capacious bosom. His reaction to her news not only surprised but confounded her. For what looked like a smiling triumph shone on his face and, with a 'See to these,' he dropped the bag and left her. That reaction, she thought angrily, was not to be expected from a deceived husband. Cheated out of her role as a comforter, crossly she pushed the bag of washing to one side.

CHAPTER 45

Roberto stood alone in Betsy's filleting shed. In leather pockets over the sink were three flenching knives, honed razor sharp. The fish quay was deserted, with only two men in the marketing shed hosing down the concrete floor. With the morning's business over there was an emptiness along the riverside. Uncertain what to do, Roberto tried to turn off a dripping tap blipping maddeningly over the marble slab. As predictable as the tides upon the river, Betsy had never let him down and as his worry deepened he concluded that, whatever had caused her to leave her work, it must have been something serious. Although he missed her warm comforting body and unquestioning patience with his unannounced visits, he had not approached Betsy since his marriage. While he felt uneasy and reluctant to go down to Neuk End, he also felt an urgent need to find out what had happened to her. For the first time he realised how dependent he was upon her expert fish supply to his fish shop and restaurant. A preliminary move was made by approaching the two men swilling down the market shed. They knew the Delfino fellow all right and why Betsy was absent from the quayside; for one of them was Chrissy Blackburn's husband. Chrissy, whose back and arms still ached from her part in Betsy's harrowing labour had, safe in her secure wedlock, expressed her feelings about the poor little bastard next door. Without pause or altering the force flow of the hose-piped water, they silently shook their heads to Roberto's questions.

The euphoria over his forthcoming fatherhood was wearing a little thin as business problems occupied his mind. He was planning to move into the wholesale business in opposition to Tobias Dobson; he needed Jamie Marr as a van driver and Betsy's unequalled expertise on fish price and quality. He decided that he would need extra staff, for Betsy must now go into a managerial role – a far cry from hawking fish in a creel around Castletown. With every step towards Neuk End warm, yet wild, feelings engulfed him. The big, red-headed woman who had rescued him, a terrified youth, out of the storm of a winter's night into her bed, had given him shelter and comfort and was in some indefinable way a link with his homeland. Over the years he had escaped from the spartan existence in Olive's cold house to the warmth of Betsy's untidy fireside. Her uncomplaining acceptance of the end of their physical relationship had left him with feelings of guilt. Why hadn't she attacked or threatened him? Those who knew her would say she wasn't very bright or she would have skinned him like a rabbit. Sometimes in a quiet reverie he would pick up the little painted model schooner and smile at its name, 'Betsee'.

He didn't knock at the door. A knock, heralding a stranger, would have startled them. The accepted procedure in the fishing community was to open the door and call unnecessarily, 'I see you're in.' His first glance took in Sarah Haddick, hand cradling her short pipe, a pint pot at her side and Betsy sitting opposite. She had a crotched shawl around her legs, for Betsy had no intention of conforming to a ten days' lying-in time. With her strength returning from the agony of the child's birth she was already up and out to bed. To Roberto's amazement there was a large, newly resplendent perambulator under the window.

'Robbie, it's good to see you,' and the tears flooded down Betsy's unusually pale cheeks. Roberto stepped towards her and almost took her in his arms but the sardonic look in old Sarah's face stopped him.

'We're all glad to see you, hinny, especially your son,' and she pointed the stem of her pipe in the direction of the baby carriage. In the small kitchen it took only three steps for Roberto to look down upon a facsimile of himself. When he did he had to hold on to the pram handle to steady himself. The thatch of black hair, the olive skin and the bone structure of the face was as Italian as if the child had been born in Castiglione instead of on the cold banks of the Tyne. He touched the pram covers as if he could not believe the sleeping baby was really there.

'The pram's a present from his Granny,' said Sarah with the smear of a smile on her face. Roberto sat down in a chair and almost immediately got up again to look at the child.

'Here, you could do with this,' and Sarah pushed a pot over to him.

Roberto automatically drank the contents. Tea laced with rum, the very drink that Betsy had given him on that terrible first night when he had set foot in this cottage. And it tasted just as vile.

'Why didn't you tell me, Betsy?'

'It was sprung on me, lad. I thought I had the colic,' but she was the only one to laugh. Thoughts flashed through his mind – what would Maria say! Would she need to know? Would anyone tell her? Olive Harman would be disgusted, for her disdain of Betsy remained undiminished over the years. So many happenings in the space of one morning. Earlier he had been gloating over Reginald Fanshaw's downfall, preening himself over Maria's pregnancy and here, unbelievably, he had a son.

'Betsee, I'll look after you,' he blurted out.

'Better wait until you're asked,' interrupted Sarah.

'I don't want anything, Robbie, just my wages. I'll be back down in the shed in no time. How are you managing?'

'Jamie's doing his best. But, Betsee, you can't stay here with the child.'

'Why not? It was good enough to get him,' and Sarah cackled up a spit and with practised ease centered it into the glowing fire.

Roberto realised that the future of his son lay not in his mother's hands, but in those of his stoical grandmother. The child began to cry and Roberto jerked around at the strong, lusty sound of its voice. Betsy reached over and placed the baby to her full, blue veined breast. Suddenly he wanted to hold this child and he ached to kiss the back of Betsy's bending neck as she bowed over her cradling arm; but the rheumy eyes of the old woman were hard upon him. Sarah watched him steadily and as menacingly as an old lioness guarding a cub. Desperately he tried to sort out some order in his mind. Only this morning he had been planning a wonderful future for his and Maria's child but now in its place was an aching longing for this bastard son and the searing thought that he was unable to take him away from this hovel.

'Ma's not going back to sea again so between us we'll bring him up proper. Ma'll look after him when I'm down at the quayside.' Old Sarah, in her seal-skin coat, pipe in mouth, to be handling his baby son. He thought of the lovely little garments Maria was collecting, some of them especially prized because they had been made and sent by relatives in Italy. But he had to admit that this child was comfortably wrapped in a white woollen shawl, lying in its huge baby carriage.

'It's been a shock, Betsee, but I'm glad that you're all right. Give me time to think things over and maybe we can come to some arrangement.'

Betsy nodded her head over the suckling child but the old woman stood up tall and menacing. 'We've made our arrangements and there's no need for you to come back here again.'

Roberto accepted his dismissal and as he reached for the latch on the door, she said with a smear of a sardonic smile on her face, 'Well, isn't it time we had a man about the house?'

Clinging with hope to a last thread of involvement Roberto asked, 'Have you decided on his name?'

Before Betsy could reply there was a sharp rejoinder. 'No, but when we do he'll be christened in the Fishermen's Chapel.'

CHAPTER 46

Convinced that he held an ace in his hand, Reginald wasted no time in hastening downstairs to confront his father-in-law in the library. Determined on a showdown, with himself emerging as victor, he walked confidently in without knocking. With a malicious smile on his face he sat down opposite Sir Nathanial, laid back in his chair to examine insolently his shining shoes, and lit a cigarette. The older man's expression did not change but had Reginald observed closely he would have seen a slight contraction and a deepening of the seamed wrinkles on his face. He laid down his pen slowly and chin in hand looked coldly at Reginald. Subtlety was a word with which Reginald was familiar but something that he had never put into practice; for unable to bear the silence he blurted out, 'So Amelia wants to divorce me. Is she planning to marry that coal miner she's been spreading her legs for?'

The cold eyes became icy as Sir Nathanial slowly replied, 'Yes. My daughter intends to divorce and as to your question I must point out that her future plans will have nothing to do with you or anyone else.'

'Oh, but they have,' and Reginald, triumphant, leaned over the desk, 'I intend to take William away from her, for from what is now common knowledge she is not fit to be in charge of him. No court will award her the custody of the boy when the facts about her loose behaviour are brought into court.' With a 'how do you like that?' air, Reginald resumed his seat and faced Sir Nathanial. 'While that clever sod Tobias has been keeping tabs on me,' he mused, 'that randy bitch, my wife, and his sister has been in bed with a common pit man and dragging my son with her to their rendezvous.'

Confidently he waited in the long silence, leaning over to tap ash on to the tray on the desk. 'That's silenced the old bugger,' he thought, and wished he dared help himself to a congratulatory drink from the cabinet. Instead he coldly lit another cigarette – give the old sod time

162

to think it over and, as Reginald began to fidget impatiently, the elder man smiled thinly.

'Of course, today would be as good a time as any other. I'll ask Amelia to order William's clothes to be packed. You will also need to take Nanny with you to look after the child,' and he picked up his pen as a dismissive gesture. Reginald sat astounded. His precious ace had been trumped. He tried to control his raging anger as, throat tight, he said, 'You had better consult your daughter about that.'

'We have already discussed this possibility and we came to this decision.'

'You old sod – you are bluffing.'

Sir Nathanial winced but replied flatly, 'Try us.'

It was then that Reginald knew his hasty scheme had failed. They both knew he could not look after the child himself; had neither the money to pay the Nanny nor the desire to be encumbered with her or the boy. He realised he was homeless and would have to book into a hotel. He was desolate at the thought of leaving Drumrauch, for he loved the manor house and its lifestyle even if he hated the inmates. Always he had enjoyed giving the lodge keeper a gracious smile as the gates were opened for him. Even though he lodged at the back of the hall, life was very comfortable. He was still Mr Reginald to the staff, who looked after his every need. Having his meals sent up had been by his own choice, it was preferable to the stony contempt of the Dobson family. Now the feeling of desperation returned.

Without looking up Sir Nathanial spoke: 'My lawyers will be getting in touch with you. There will be a five thousand pound settlement assigned to you when the divorce goes through. He will explain the terms.'

So he was to be bought off – go quickly and give no trouble, he thought bitterly. Reginald was cornered and he knew it. As he wandered around the grounds of Drummauch Hall for the last time, the grounds where he had enjoyed playing the role of landed gentry, he was at last facing reality. He would have to move to a hotel, and grimly he decided he must hire a financial advisor. He had always hated having to think about money, happy only when it was in his pocket and making plans on how to spend it. He decided he would sell the hated Fanshaw Store, legendary in the town since his grandfather's day and now in a declining competition with the brash Co-operative Store,

163

luring away his customers with a dividend bonus. Yes, he decided he would sell because he had no intention of being tied to a drapery store. His grandfather's house, now willed to his mother, would fetch a good price. But while her mind was disordered, physically she was sound. She could last for years, especially the way she was tucking into Aunt Polly's excellent food. That was another problem. His aunt had extended Harriet's stay for another month but was adamant that that date was final. She was sick of Harriet's biting criticisms and mad outbursts. Her distressing habit of pleating the bottom of curtains, tablecloths and cushion covers, as well as her own clothes, unnerved Polly Platt. The long shadows from the tall trees in the park laced the green lawns when, finally, Reginald returned to his room to find his clothes piled high upon his stripped bed.

CHAPTER 47

Maisie's baby burped happily as her warring grandparents lined up at the font. Jamie and two of Maisie's friends were there as Godparents, proud but uneasy as the two grandfathers lanced each other with lowering looks. Olive had decided that she was only doing the neighbourly thing by attending, adding to herself that nobody could slight a child. She was annoyed that Roberto was late and when he finally arrived alone, tip-toeing up the aisle, she remembered that it was Marina's day off and Maria would be minding the shop. Agnes Cowen rustled her habit up and down the outer aisle, her eyes fixed on Father Antony while the grey mole moved places. She knew that the locum priest was just behind the reredos and she also knew that, after the Bishop's last visit, he had been sent to spy upon the man she loved like a son. Full of Irish charm he was, she thought sourly, but he was not a gentleman like Antony Howard. Deliberately she had housed the locum priest in a front bedroom, away from the sound of bottles clinking and sometimes shattering as they descended down the well.

The glowering interaction between the Marr and the O'Connor family was set aside, for there was now a united anxiety when Father Antony, looking white and ill, greeted them uncertainly. Shuffling uneasily, they glanced at each other, their family feud shelved at this bewildering situation. As the priest received the child into his arms he began to shake violently. The two older men, with raised eyebrows crossed glances, shocked by the mutual discovery. Suddenly the baby slipped from the Priest's arms and the little head banged against the rim of the font. Simultaneously a pair of hands plucked the screaming child from the water and with smiling, brogue-ridden sentences proceeded with the christening ceremony. Horrified glances were levelled at Father Antony, now still shaking and seated in a pew, his head bowed in his hands. Agnes Cowen rushed up and, whispering urgently, led him away.

'Well now, didn't we christen her properly?' the Priest said gaily, as though all that had happened had been a divine planning. He ushered them through the church door, kissing the baby, teasing the women by declaring he had never seen such a bonny mother and child, nor so handsome a grandmother.

'You'll not forget to wet the baby's head,' he chuckled genially as he slapped the men folk on the shoulder. No sooner had the christening party turned the corner than he rushed indoors to the telephone. Outside on the church steps, Danny turned to Albert O'Connor: 'Did you ever see the likes of that? He must have been on one hell of a bender to get into that state.'

Being men of experience they shook their heads disapprovingly. With a few hurried steps they caught up with the women, who were busy examining the newly christened Doreen Edith. Danny shrugged off their concern. 'Sure it's only a clout on the head – no harm done,' and as the little Doreen burped happily, she seemed to agree. Only an hour before Jonty had prophesied to Amelia that there would be skin and hair flying when the Marrs met the O'Connors at the christening. He was more than surprised to find the two parties amiably sharing beer between the men and port wine among the women folk. Having exhausted the surprising subject of the christening, their communal sharing of the amazing experience seemed to have dissipated their animosity. Edie politely removed an encrusted fly paper from the vicinity of Mrs O'Connor's hat, saying by way of explanation, 'It's the lads, they never shut the netty door.' The two older women were deeply engaged in matters maternal as Edie explained why nearly all her children had September birthdays. 'It's Danny, you know, he always gets a drop too much at Christmas time.' They gathered around the placid baby to remark upon the undeniable likeness to its grandmother Edie. If the O'Connors weren't too pleased at the monopoly of the Marr genes, they magnanimously put it aside to do justice to the beer and port wine. Slack Willie took a back seat, open mouthed, happily interpreting every compliment as a personal credit at producing such a beautiful child.

As Olive and Roberto followed the noisy comments of the party, she remarked tartly that the Marrs could not marry, bury or christen in their family without something out of the way happening. As Agnes Cowen had shepherded Father Antony down the aisle she had hissed,

'It's 'flu,' to Olive. Passing on this information to Roberto, Olive remarked that it was the strangest sort of 'flu that she had ever seen. Then she realised that Roberto had not spoken one word, not even about the bizarre happenings of the afternoon. She considered the coldness between them on their last meeting two days ago, when Betsy had let them down over the fish. He came in, she reflected, bouncing like a rubber ball because Maria was pregnant at last. 'I expect he's mad because I didn't do cartwheels over the news.' She was irritated because her curiosity about Betsy remained unsatisfied, for Jamie simply shook his head when she was forced to enquire. 'Any news of Betsy?' she asked Roberto, who, ignoring the question said, 'I'll go back with you to Inkerman Street and talk to you there.'

CHAPTER 48

Maria Delfino née Lobosco cradled her unborn child. For the first time since arriving in this cold country, she felt happy. Wistfully she wished she could have her baby back in her own country, where her many female relatives would share every stage of her pregnancy. Where the birth would be hailed with delight, where she would be showered with love and good wishes and encircled in the warmth of an extended family. The only concession on Roberto's part had been to agree to pay Zia's passage money to England to be with Maria at the birth. Reluctantly, he granted that she needed someone of the family to be with her during the labour. Zia was a widow, without ties and could extend her visit, here he grimaced, beyond her welcome. He remembered the conflict between Olive and Zia at the time of his wedding; at least with Zia in his own home he would be spared a repetition of that soured relationship.

Here Maria had tried to explain her homesick loneliness to Olive but she, awkward at dealing with emotion, had merely patted her on the shoulder, declaring that she would, 'Get over it and soon settle down.' Animatedly she pointed out how splendidly Roberto had absorbed the British way of life and how well he had done in business.

Nightly Maria prayed that Roberto would decide to return home. She knew that he was an astute business man and had made money. He seemed very clever at something he called stocks and shares. She sighed and thought how happy she would be with just a small shop or perhaps a café in Castiglione. His driving ambition frightened her for it was not what she wanted in a husband. Her family had impressed upon her that he was a good man and that she would learn to love him. Love – what was that? Surely it was something that would come with a growing family and perhaps this child would bind them more closely together. Roberto seemed often so cold and remote, insisting that she spoke in English and then correcting her when she did so.

Once her English speaking was good, then they would converse in Italian, he promised her. In the silence of the night she crooned silently to her unborn baby, 'I will tell you of springtime in the hills where you look down upon the glorious bay of Naples. I will tell you of beautiful churches, paintings and music. Not like this place where people live only for picture houses and the harsh music of brass bands.'

Zia wrote regularly and enthusiastically about a new political party headed by a saviour figure, Mussolino, a Rigorgimento who would make Italy a great power in the world. But Maria cared nothing for politics and longed only for *Bella Aprile* when her baby would be born, and counted the days until her aunt arrived. Although he lay silent, still she knew Roberto was awake and she puzzled over the change in him over the last few months. He had been like a happy school boy when her pregnancy had been confirmed. Immediately, he had rung up Luigi and ordered a special meal in the restaurant. The Taroni family had gathered round and toasted their good news and she had cried with happiness. Although every day he asked after her health, now he seemed once more remote and preoccupied. He had always been so careful with money, bordering on meanness, but suddenly he wanted to buy everything for the child. In spite of her protests he talked of buying a big house up in the square. It had previously belonged to the owner of that old-fashioned drapery store in the town and when he spoke of it there was a triumphant look in his eye. The news had dampened the elation over her pregnancy, for she had become accustomed to the living quarters behind the shop. Roberto had reproached her and declared that his children must have the best that money could buy. Maria sighed and eased a small pillow under her aching back; she worried in case the ship from Italy should be delayed.

Roberto also lay awake, conscious of Maria's efforts to find a comfortable resting place. He too hoped his passage money would not be wasted by the late arrival of Zia. Sleep evaded him as unhappy thoughts crowded in. He had a comfortable bank balance, was about to become a father, this time with a legitimate child and was yet desperately worried. He felt the change of attitude towards him by the local people; a wariness tinged with suspicion. He understood the general disapproval of his country's war tactics in Ethiopia. Last year, at the news of mustard gas being sprayed over the natives, a brick had

169

been thrown through his restaurant window. He had not escaped a taunting from Danny Marr, sitting knees hunched up to his neck. 'By, them brave Eytie lads are doing well against them fuzzy-wuzzies.' For the first time Roberto flinched as the biting sarcasm hurt. Luigi Taroni was anxious and talked of taking his family back to Taormina. Despite Luigi's splendid gastronomic reputation, business was falling rapidly and he was disconsolate as he eyed the empty tables in the restaurant and the full pans in his kitchen.

Roberto's thoughts turned to the fisherman's cottage and to Betsy's child, now eight months old. Sometimes the longing to see and hold the boy tore at his heart. Once he had seen him tied by a shawl to old Sarah's back, the dark head clearly visible while his small hands clutched at her keelman's hat. He smiled that Granny's big shiny baby carriage wasn't much use in the narrow streets with numerous steps. He bought a Brownie camera and gave it to Jamie to take photographs, and even now in his jacket pocket there was a snapshot of a strong, black-haired baby perched on a pile of lobster pots. He was aware that Jamie knew he was the father; the face and features made that self evident. On the quayside it was sometimes the theme of high-minded concern and low-minded gossip. But Jamie, as always, was close mouthed and answered only Roberto's direct questions. He saw the little one daily on the quayside and was secretly proud when Betsy asked him to be godfather.

'But you can't – you're a Catholic,' Roberto exclaimed.

'Down at the Fishermen's Mission nobody cares about that. There they have sailors of all colours, creeds and coming from all over the world. If they don't mind then I don't mind.'

With a lump in his throat Roberto asked, 'What is his name?'

'George.'

George, George Haddick. It should have been Giorgio Delfino.

CHAPTER 49

Not for the first time Reginald Fanshaw decided that the whole world was against him. His visit to the Fanshaw Emporium, still bearing the name of Amos Fanshaw in faded lettering, depressed him. Even he would sense the air of defeat in the half-empty shelves and the prevailing shabbiness of the interior. The ancient wooden balls carrying cash and change rolled less and less frequently. As a young girl his mother had sat in the place where now an ageing, tired-looking female sat comatose. In his mother's time the store had monopolised the clothing and hardware trade in the town. Fanshaw's goods were always understood to be high class, to equal the status, in their eyes, of some of its clients. Everything from a pin to a complete wedding outfit, the latter guaranteed London Fashion, could be viewed comfortably as pale, young assistants bowed and served the more valued customers. Now, all the assistants looked middle aged; the women with their crimped, tonged hair made even the one or two print-draped models look young.

'My God, it's like a museum in here,' thought Reginald. Scorning trade associations, as did his mother, he had never taken any interest in the store or bothered to enquire the reason for its failing profits. Looking around him with angry eyes, he was also aware of an underlying scared feeling. His family had let him down; his mother, who, after all, had some knowledge of the trade; his lecherous old grandfather had traded his grandson's birthright for a country lass and sired a son to be cuckoo in the family nest. He cursed and blamed everyone of them, especially his wife and her fancy man, that back street pitman for his present predicament. Heading his list of hates was Tobias, Sir Nathanial's son, who with his spying telescope had nudged down this avalanche of trouble. 'I'll have his back teeth,' he swore. They had all contributed to his downfall and even that bloody old Aunt Polly was threatening to put his mother and her clothes out on to the street. His mother – he ground his teeth with exasperation – what a burden she was.

At first he had been delighted to hear from the Estate Agent that there was now a firm offer for his mother's house. Even though the offer was less than he had expected, he was anxious for the sale and sure that he would soon be able to transfer the money from his mother's pocket to his own without much difficulty. The old woman, he thought bitterly, had put the blight on any better offers by her mad wanderings around the house and gardens. It was the bitter knowledge that the offer was from that Italian Delfino, that brought the bile into his throat. That affair in Italy had been nothing at all and yet it had come back to haunt him. But, like all his unpleasant thoughts, they were easily shrugged off and forgotten. Yet like an uneasy dream or troublesome memory something kept worrying him every time he thought of or met the dark-eyed foreigner. The girl he remembered but faintly, he had forgotten her name, if he ever knew it and even the place, although it was somewhere near Naples. Why did he always try to recall something that was so importantly worrying whenever Delfino's name came to mind? He hated passing the smart restaurant, although it was with some gratification that when he had arrived at the shop, he had noticed the half-empty restaurant next door.

Reginald turned all his anger and frustration on to Joshua Milburn. And he kept the manager standing in the small office that Joshua had snugly made his own over the years. Sharply, Reginald demanded an explanation for the downfall of what was once a thriving business. Joshua nursed a sly satisfaction. He remembered the curdled humiliation he had suffered years ago when he was young and vulnerable at the hands of this arrogant sod – the boss's son. In his short time at the Emporium, he had taken a delight in persecuting the young Joshua. Constantly he insulted him in front of the other staff as he genially offered his childish jibes for general approval. Now as he listened to Reginald's blustering anger Joshua felt only a sweet revenge. Over the years he had carefully but cleverly syphoned off and banked a modest fortune as cynically he watched the decline of the house of Fanshaw. From the early days he knew that this old-fashioned business could in no way compete with the new Co-operative Store. Ignoring Reginald's spitting anger, he pointed out, oh so sadly, how the Co-operative Store had taken away trade. Their policy of shares and dividends, and here he dipped his head confidentially, the political bias of the new store had taken away many customers. How he regretted that the late Mr Amos had not been able to take a more active part in the business during these latter years. Piously he regretted also that Miss Harriet Fanshaw had not been persuaded to advise staff. 'And you, you big snot,' he said silently to himself, 'couldn't give a toss about the shop as long as your mother put money in your pocket.'

'The oily bugger,' Reginald fumed. 'I'll make him smart.' 'Well, from today you and those ancient crones through there are out of a job. This shop is going onto the market. And where will a failure like you get a job?'

'Well now,' Joshua replied smoothly, 'I've no doubt I could be employed by the Co-operative Society.' He omitted to add that he had been hand in pocket with the Manager of the Co-operative Store for years. With that prospect and his carefully filched fortune he could afford his sly arrogance. 'It will be difficult to sell a failed business.'

'Even if that were a difficulty this land is useful for any sort of development.'

Joshua savoured with pleasure the next few words. 'The land, Mr Reginald, does not belong to you or your family. It is owned by your father-in-law, Sir Nathanial Dobson and until it is sold you will have to pay ground rent.'

'Just get out before I wring your bloody neck.'

'Certainly, Mr Reginald,' and Joshua smiled smugly as he closed the door. For God's sake, what other disaster could hit him, Reginald implored the heavens. 'That old bugger Dobson offered me five thousand pounds blood money to divorce his sodding daughter, while all the time my family has been paying him ground rent since God knows when.'

Reginald left the office and moved into the shop. He stood where his father Herbert, formerly Platt, had looked up at Harriet, the fair cashier sending wooden balls on their way and had fallen deeply in love.

'I see by the look on your faces that Mr Joshua Milburn has already imparted the good news,' he said sarcastically. 'You are all on a fortnight's notice,' and turning to Joshua he ordered, 'Get a closing down sale notice in every window.'

In a foul temper he returned to his Aunt Polly's house in Morden

Street and was very relieved to find her not at home. He looked at his mother without compassion. She, who had always been so fastidious, now looked as if she had dressed in the dark at a jumble sale. Always thin, she now looked gaunt as she sat pleating an old shawl hanging from one shoulder. He noticed with disgust her unlaced shoes were on the wrong feet; obviously that old cow Polly was neglecting her. 'Mother,' he said sharply and Harriet looked up startled, 'do you know who is going to buy Grandfather's house, that beautiful house in the square that you have always loved?' he taunted cruelly. 'That ice-cream merchant who used to live with your servant. You must remember those folks who lived in Inkerman Street.' He was surprised and annoyed that his stinging barb brought no response. Disgustedly he flung himself out of the house. His mother might have been deaf for all the notice she took and he swore as he walked passed the Delfino Restaurant to his waiting car.

But Harriet was not deaf and Reginald's every word had registered with a mind suddenly made crystal clear.

CHAPTER 50

Jonty and Amelia lay on the grass, talking quietly as young William slept near them. He looked over the hill top and down the valley. 'I wonder why the farm is called Bobbin Hill when it's so sheltered in the valley.'

'Probably because this is the hill and I love both the name and the farm,' Amelia said sleepy in the sunlight.

'Well, if you call a great kitchen with stone flags and an ancient kitchen range lovely, then it is.'

'Ah, I intend to have an Aga cooker in the scullery and keep the old range for an open fire.'

'Very romantic, have you thought what it's like in winter time out here?'

'I do know, I've ridden horseback over these moors every winter and loved every minute of it.'

'There're two hundred acres of arable land and twice that for sheep. Can you manage all that and a house as well?'

'I've already got promised help for the house. Remember the village is only one mile away and there're plenty of people there wanting work.'

'It's a bonny hard life you're taking on.'

'See these hands,' she said firmly and showed him a small shapely pair. 'They have been mucking out stables since I was old enough to hold a shovel.'

There was a long silence between them broken at last by Amelia saying tentatively, 'I'll need someone to help with the horses.'

Jonty took the long thin grass stem out of his mouth. 'I know just the man.' Amelia glanced up quickly. 'Harry Walters is looking for a job. He's expert with horses and worked with the big brewers' drays before he went down the Wilhelmina. Reckon he's had his fill of nursing half-blind pit ponies. He looks for the day when mechanisation will make ponies obsolete down there.'

There was a strained disappointment in Amelia's voice as she followed his line of thought. 'Wasn't he the man whose wife . . .'

Jonty interrupted, 'Yes, she waited long enough for a son that wasn't coming home, the son she lost her reason for. Well, death has joined them now and Harry's free. You have a nice room or two over the stable yard. Harry's a steady fellow – could be trusted with the crown jewels – only don't offer him smoked haddock for his tea.'

Amelia looked over to the dark smudge of the Cheviot Hills and wondered at the sudden change in her life. After seeing the sale notice in the local paper, she had ridden out to view Bobbin Hill and had instantly fallen in love with the place. This very morning she had answered, 'Yes,' to all William's happy questions as he raced around the house and outbuildings. 'May I have my own dog and will we keep sheep? Will we keep Patches and my pony Raffles in this stable?' The only 'No' had been when he asked uncertainly if Nanny would be coming. On the way to the farm she pointed out the village school that he would be soon attending. Her father had taken a more pragmatic view and examined carefully all the business details. He, like the rest of the family, was quite unmoved and took Amelia's decision to leave Drumrauch Hall as a matter of course. It was Sir Nathanial who, after examining the deeds of the farm, pointed out an amazing coincidence. Bobbin Hill, vacant since the last owner, a very old man and the last survivor of bachelor brothers, was William's great uncle. Bobbin Hill Farm was where his great-grandmother had met the pack man, Amos Fanshaw. Amelia was fascinated by the coincidence and became even more convinced that this was the right place to bring up her son.

Sir Nathanial instantly contacted his lawyers and was interested to find out that the old owner had died intestate. By a strange quirk of fate, the money Amelia had paid for the farm, plus the hoarded wealth of the dead brothers, would now go to their only blood relation, the farmer's niece, Harriet Fanshaw. Lying together on the hill top, Amelia told the amazing story to Jonty, adding that her father had angrily declared that the profligate Reginald would soon waste his mother's inheritance. But Amelia did not care, only glad to be free of him and that she, not his father Reginald, would take care of William's future. Since meeting Jonty she viewed her son through different eyes; she had become increasingly interested in William's development and anxious for his future welfare. Her great fear, that Reginald would carry out his threat, 'to drag her and Jonty through the law courts,' had largely disappeared. Whispers that Reginald was having an affair with her sister-in-law Celia, reached her ears and she wondered if her brother Tobias was aware of it. Looking at it through the mirrored debacle of her own marriage, she could in some way understand Celia becoming ensnared by Reginald. She knew well her cold, austere brother deeply immersed in his wholesale fish business. She recalled how Celia's life had been a boring round of shopping interspersed with golf; interested in nothing more than *haute couture*, with her reading matter confined to fashion magazines, Celia would fall easy prey to Reginald's charming banter. And wouldn't Reginald enjoy blacking the eye of a Dobson son!

Jonty picked up his jacket and laid it over the sleeping William, for there was now a cool wind blowing. As he watched the afternoon shadows laying longer figures over the valley he waited for Amelia to speak. Unsteadily she began, 'I can manage the house and the horses with a good man like Walters.'

'Harry,' he interrupted.

'Yes,' she conceded. 'Harry, but I can't farm two hundred acres as well.'

She waited but she knew he had no intention of helping her out. 'Jonty,' she pleaded, 'leave the colliery and farm my . . . the land.'

He laid back on the hill grass. He had known what was coming and had given it a lot of consideration. The land; to work the seed time and the harvest. It would be a dream come true. He had loved the planting and the crop gathering in his huge allotment. His prize vegetables were the talk and envy every year in the local shows and working his allotment had been a damned sight more pleasurable than working down the Wilhelmina. The pit had been only a means of earning a living. Walking home in the early dawns he would sit as black as the early risen crows alongside him on the fence; to listen to the Earth's awakening. Crossing the fields to work his night shift at the Colliery he watched the hedgerow creatures and the seasons' use of the land. All life and growing things intrigued Jonty; that was why, unlike the rest of his family he never visited Joe's grave. Death, he believed, was just a movement. He loved the woman and child beside him but he felt their hands were too full of gifts.

177

'Well now, Boss woman, are you offering me a job?'

'No, I'm asking you to be my partner,' and gazing over the grey purple hills she said quietly, 'Jonty, we could get married.'

Jonty rolled her over on to her back and looked steadily down into brown eyes. Gently he tapped her nose. 'Now then, pet, it will be when I do the asking.' He lifted the sleeping child. 'We'd better get going, it's a good walk to the station.'

CHAPTER 51

With the closing of the restaurant, Roberto was overwhelmed with sadness at the death of his dream. His ambition to have a string of restaurants throughout the North-East had seen only failure. Luigi had taken his family back home to Sicily, with the exception of his daughter Marina. Roberto had been called in to negotiate between the rebellious daughter and her parents. Marina was now engaged to a young man in the drawing office at Dobson Shipyard and refused steadfastly to leave him and Embleton. Despite her mother's tears and her father's anger, she pushed ahead with wedding plans and reluctantly, her parents attended the ceremony prior to a tearful leave-taking to Sicily. Aware of failing patronage to the restaurant and sensitive towards the growing hostility towards his country, Luigi Taroni and his family had finally departed. The ultimate decision had been made after the younger Taroni boys found themselves always targeted as the enemy in the school yard playground war games.

Roberto now wandered around the silent kitchen where Luigi had happily bounced from chopping board to stove. In the restaurant where Cecil/Cesare had practised his pseudo broken English to intrigued customers, there was a dreary emptiness. Olive had carefully folded all the table cloths and napkins and stacked them tidily in a cupboard. As usual she had given Roberto strong support over the trying business of closing down the restaurant. Everything looked very neat and very dead. As he locked the outer door he looked first at the 'Closing Down' notice in his restaurant window and then at the 'For Sale' in the windows of the Fanshaw Emporium. No one, he thought, could possibly have envisaged this strange turn of events. The downward slide in his fortunes and the unease he now felt in the community made him more distant than before. Although he had a neat fortune invested, the loss of the restaurant revenue grieved his careful soul. But the set-back to his ambitions troubled him more.

179

Since the day he had arrived in England he had worked to amass money, believing it to be the weapon to deal with his enemy. He now realized that that driving force had died sometime ago. Somewhere along the line he had grafted on to the culture of these people. The stinging urge of vendetta was out of place here; yet this would not be understood or forgiven in Castiglione.

Zia Lobosco was still in charge in Roberto's house, a year after their daughter, Lucia had been born. Every week she declared she would follow the example of the Taronis and leave for home, but was finally placated by a tearful Maria begging her to stay longer. Roberto could only watch as she depended more and more upon her aunt. The two chatted happily in Italian, marvelling every day at the beauty of the baby Lucia, totally engrossed in their mutual interest. Zia had visited Olive on one occasion since the wedding and had returned from Inkerman Street in a rage at being kept seated in the kitchen. She badly wanted to reappraise those sitting room treasures but Olive had ignored her thrusting gesticulations and the trying of the door handle. Frostily she told the uncomprehending Zia that it was not her day for the front room. Zia vented her anger and frustration by standing by each gate on her way down the street to give a caustic Italian commentary on the house, the occupants and the English in general. When Roberto was given a full account of her behaviour by the indignant residents, he pointed out the damage she was doing to his ice-cream parlour and ordered Zia to carry out her oft-repeated threat to return home. There had been a scene of hysterics and tears and Maria had flown at him, demanding that Zia, her only comfort in this benighted country, should stay. The nodding back-up by Zia of Maria's every sentence irritated Roberto beyond words, and, faced with their united lamentations and accusations, he fell silent. Maria, the formerly quiet, obedient wife, had, since the advent of Zia with her insidious pressures, given him an ultimatum – 'If Zia goes, I will go too and I will take the baby Lucia with me.'

That morning Roberto had received a telephone call from the Estate Agent requiring him to call at the office. Roberto anticipated that Reginald had agreed to the price for his grandfather's house in the square. He paused in front of the Georgian house which he had, in more settled days, planned to occupy and there to bring up his family. With the recent alteration in his business affairs he realised that this was not the time to buy property. He now felt uncertain about the future; such a feeling he had never known before. The militant mouthings of Mussolini and the growing union with Germany filled him with dread. He clashed with Zia constantly as she harped upon the great new regime, the Facisti, which was making Italy a great power in the world. Always Maria, urged by her aunt, put pressure upon him to follow Luigi's example and return to Italy.

Mr Winthrop, the estate agent, hugged his little secret. His ambiguous telephone call had been only a message asking Roberto to call. Reginald breezing in, had previously instructed him to tell Roberto that his offer was refused. He struck a patriotic pose as he arrogantly told Mr Winthrop that he was not selling his grandfather's home to a bloody Eytie. And Mr Winthrop gave his enthusiastic approval. In fact, Reginald would have enjoyed telling the Italian face to face but he had a pressing engagement with his brother-in-law's wife and Celia would not be kept waiting. Mr Winthrop's ire had been furthered by Roberto putting a closing down notice in the restaurant window instead of giving him the sale arrangements of the property. For Reginald, on the other hand, he had done very well. Although the Fanshaw shop premises had not been sold, he had negotiated a profitable lease of the premises to the Government as a storage depot. No doubt there was a sniffing of war in the air and it gave him strong satisfaction to deal his own patriotic blow at the Italian. Before Roberto got past a polite, 'Good morning,' Mr Winthrop announced coldly that Mr Reginald Fanshaw had withdrawn from the proposed contract. 'Is the house not for sale now?'

'Oh yes,' replied Mr Winthrop glibly, 'but not in the present situation,' while he longed to say, 'Not to you.' Roberto decided it would look like sour grapes if he said he had already decided to withdraw. He left the estate agent disappointedly guessing at the disinterested way he had taken the refusal. As Roberto departed Mr Winthrop remarked testily to his junior staff, 'It is not fitting that such a beautiful house in that respectable square should be lived in by a foreigner and an Italian at that.'

CHAPTER 52

Aunt Polly Platt tied on her apron before washing up the breakfast dishes. 'God,' she sighed, 'it has been a week and it's only Tuesday.' Her comfortable world had been overturned since she had been fool enough to allow her sister-in-law into her home. Reginald had since played a cat and mouse game with her, alternately pleading with her to look after his mother until he found a suitable house and since his improved finances, arrogantly stating that he would pay for her keep. So far, she reflected grimly, she had benefited by the magnificent sum of two pounds in hard cash and a volume of promises. Now he visited more often to direct Harriet's hand towards her cheque book. The wonderful windfall of his mother's inheritance from her uncle, resulting in the sale of Bobbin Hill Farm, brought him almost daily to the cottage in Morden Street. The cheek of him, thought Polly. He would arrive unannounced, open the front door and bound up the stairs to the back room where, nowadays, Harriet spent most of her time. He knows, she thought bitterly, that I cannot put her out on to the street, 'Not my dead brother's wife.' It had been a sad day when he married Harriet. Polly and her brother had shared a quiet, comfortable life together but Herbert had never known a day's peace since he left the cottage. Throughout the years of the marriage, Harriet and her son had ignored the existence of Polly Platt, but desperation on their part had brought the three of them together. It had been difficult to put up with Harriet's trying ways. Her cutting criticisms of the house, furnishings and housekeeping she had endured, not patiently but as an alternative to Harriet's tantrums. These were often followed by malevolent silences or muttered incomprehensible monologues. Harriet would sit pleating the tablecloth edges, giving sudden jerks making Polly leap up to rescue the trembling crockery. Thankfully Harriet was going through a quieter spell just now and spent much of her time in bed. Polly almost wished, like Reginald, that Harriet could be certified

182

and sent to an asylum but her doctor had bluntly told Reginald that sick people could not be put away for the family's convenience. He suggested that the alternative would be to place Harriet in a private clinic. He rather enjoyed watching the expression on Reginald's face as he read through the proffered leaflet and registered the cost of the service.

Quietly, Polly had carefully locked away knives and scissors, unnerved by the strange look that lately had come into Harriet's eyes. On Reginald's last visit, his aunt had pleaded with him to find someone else to care for his mother. Flinging two pounds upon the table he angrily reminded her that the very house she lived in had been bought and given to her by his father. Reginald, with easy access to his mother's money, had no intention of wasting it on her upkeep. He was now enjoying life, living in a good hotel and able to finance a bevy of toadies and hangers on; and Celia Dobson was his for the asking. Gratuitous sex with his sister-in-law was especially appealing compared to expensive evenings at Clarty Clara's. It would have taken only one other satisfaction to make his enjoyable life complete. He would have liked Tobias Dobson to be made aware of his cuckoldry, but Celia insisted upon clandestine meetings. He reflected with complacence on his improved financial situation. The huge, roomy Fanshaw Emporium was now leased to the Government for army storage purposes and this brought in a handsome, monthly cheque. His old fool of a mother was daft in the head and easily, as he guided her hand, signed for the repetitive fifty or hundred pound cheque. Sardonically he wondered just how long she would last and looked keenly for any sign of deterioration.

Reginald had been vastly surprised to learn that it was Amelia, his ex-wife, who wanted to buy the farm, Bobbin Hill; lately inherited by his mother. At first, he had been suspicious of her motives and then amused that she wanted to buy property formerly belonging to his ancestors. He was only lightly intrigued by the strangeness of events, but gratified that she had paid top price for the farm. To the family connection he was indifferent, regarding the property as an old, ramshackle farm house surrounded by bleak moorland, fit only for weathering scraggy sheep. A fitting hide-away for Amelia and her collier fancy man. Although granted reasonable access to his son, William, Reginald had made no effort to see the boy. He had no intention of encumbering his life with paternal responsibilities. Free from all ties except his exasperating old mother, he lived a carefree bachelor life, surrounded by sycophantic drinking companions. That old nuisance Nanny Benson had written to him, begging help to find employment; pleading that her life with her tetchy sister was unendurable. She plainly insinuated that some financial assistance would be welcome as remuneration for past services rendered. Damn it – past favours – she had only looked after his clothes and, after all, she had had a comfortable life at Drumrauch and comfort at the Hall, that was something for which he was well able to vouch.

Reginald gave a fleeting thought to his satisfying triumph over the Italian and wondered if he should share his feelings of exuberance with his mother. He decided it was a waste of time and effort talking to her, for the last time he had mentioned her father's house she hadn't heard a word he had said.

CHAPTER 53

Harriet certainly did hear Reginald's wounding words and the sudden clarity in her mind surprised her. For the past year her mind had worked in a clouded curtain of confusion, alternating with sharp bursts of anger as she railed against her present circumstances. Oblivious of her slatternly state, she threw out scornful remarks concerning the small cottage and its lack of facilities. Harriet refused to wash in the back kitchen and ordered Polly to carry hot water to her room. Each time Polly ignored her demands for room service she would clash the door and retreat to the window, murmuring threats as she spied down on Polly working in the kitchen. It had occupied her thoughts for many days, working out one revengeful scheme after the other. Making and rejecting plans became a jigsaw puzzle into which she was always trying to fit the pieces. She was determined to go to her father's house; it belonged to her now and she vowed no one else would live there. Reginald had told her that the Italian was going to buy it but she knew he was just a front for that woman in Inkerman Street. No, not a woman, Harriet shook her head, it was that girl – a girl in a shimmering green dress with a stolen crown upon her head. But just now she wanted to get back in her father's house. Harriet knew she must get in to protect it from the thief; she must guard it for Reginald. He would be so pleased with her efforts to defend it for him. It was naughty of him to have taken the keys from her; but then he wasn't aware of the secret. It had come back to her in an illuminating flash and that night she had danced around the bedroom euphoric with happiness. There was a secret place in the garden and Amos had once shown it to her, where he had buried a tobacco tin box, filled with oil and in it the keys to the back door. 'Remember,' he had stressed, 'where it is and if you ever forget your keys and it happens to be the housekeeper's day off – if one of us can't get in and, mind you, only in an emergency – you know where the spare keys lie. I want no windows or doors damaged by forced entry and only you and me will know what to do.'

He was clever, her Dad, but there was something he'd done wrong before he died – something about a will. Trying to remember, she sat with a worried frown and then she smiled, it didn't really matter. She would get those keys, but first she must get dressed to visit the big house.

Disregarding her soiled dress and worn slippers she looked carefully into the wardrobe mirror as she buttoned up a fine, light grey coat. She peered through the window at Polly washing dishes and silently stole down the stairs and out at the front door. At first she felt dizzy, for it was sometime since she had been outside the house and the traffic noise troubled her. But the urgency of her mission forced her to dash across the street, narrowly missing being run down by a van. Not one but several people stopped to stare at the outlandish figure pushing her way through the crowded street. Although it was raining, Harriet wore a fine straw hat pinned grotesquely above her untidy hair. Below her coat bare legs ended where her feet were covered in worn, red woollen slippers. Intent only on reaching the house in the square, Harriet ignored the stares and smiles of passers-by.

Outside the house she paused to get her breath. She was shaking as she sat down upon the low wall and tried to remember what she had come for. Ah! That was it – the keys. She walked around the side of the house, passed the kitchen door, and into the spacious lawn and garden. Harriet knew exactly where it was; there at the end of the terrace, under a white rounded stone. Over the years the stone had sunk into the ground and she looked around for a tool. Beside the summer house she found a broken slate and began frantically to scrape away turf, using her bare hands in her impatience to ease up the stone.

Although her hands were scratched and her nails torn and bleeding, she was impervious to pain. With super-human strength she heaved at the stone and shouted in triumph as it turned over, for there lay a rusted tobacco box. Brushing the soil off she could still trace the name – Bruno's Golden Cut Flake Tobacco. Using the slate point and her nails she strained at the lid which with surprising ease suddenly shot off and the dark, dank oil spilled down her grey coat. But that scarcely mattered to Harriet for there, still wrapped in oiled paper, lay the keys to the kitchen door. Triumphantly she rushed up to the door, where

186

the oiled key turned easily. As she passed through the rooms, panting with the exertion, she stripped off the dust covers from the furniture. Gloatingly, she fondled the fine brocade settee and chairs, leaving oily, dirty hand prints on all that she touched. Holding on to the carved stair hand rail she took a deep breath of satisfaction – she was home. For several minutes her harsh laugh echoed throughout the empty house.

There was only one more task; she must regain her crown. Harriet walked through to the kitchen and pulled open the kitchen drawers, scattering cutlery and utensils on to the floor. Finally, she chose a small, very sharp knife. Chuckling, she relocked the back door, placed the keys in the tobacco tin and rolled back the stone. Nobody, she told herself, would ever know her secret; only her father. She remembered that her father had impressed upon her that only the two of them must know.

CHAPTER 54

Olive looked out at the rain and decided that her time would be best spent on an afternoon's sewing. The house between the noon time fish frying and the evening time opening were very precious to her. Sometimes she wondered if, she was now worth the money Roberto paid her. For Jamie was so competent and they had lately employed Maud Thompson to help with the serving. Jamie was an excellent worker; keen and honest. Smiling slightly she had noticed how Maud raced to carry out Jamie's monosyllabic orders. Maud's adoration of the once written-off dummy gave Olive satisfaction; for she did not underrate her own role in the establishing of Jamie in Embleton society. Through the adjoining wall she could hear the 'Hey up,' of Danny Marr's loud voice as he tossed his adored granddaughter up in the air. 'It's a wonder that child has survived,' she thought, and gave a disappointed sniff, for hadn't Edie laughingly told her that Danny encouraged the toddler to sip froth off his beer. Imagine, she said sternly to herself, beer froth on top of boily, for bread soaked in warm sugared milk was the standard diet for a weaned child. The young Doreen thrived and confounded all her pessimistic predictions. Even Olive would hold the proffered hand of the angelic-looking, golden-haired, but usually grubby little one. Her thoughts strayed to Roberto's daughter; Lucia, her godchild. All too aware that Zia and Maria had not favoured her as godmother, she had been delighted that Roberto had insisted that she stood at the font for the baby Lucia. Zia had protested, listing a quayside length of Italian relatives who would, by proxy, be honoured to undertake the responsibility. For once the two women could not exert enough pressure to make Roberto change his mind.

Over the years Olive had hoarded her empty wooden cotton reels, deciding that one day she would find a use for them, even if only to fuel the fire. Now, painted in bright glowing colours, the cotton reels lay clustered on the table: two red, two yellow, two blue and two green. Patiently, Olive had given the wooden reels several coats of shining paint and now they were ready to assemble as a toy for the little Lucia. From the tidy contents of her work box she measured a length of elastic and threaded it through the coloured reels. Quietly satisfied she held up the circlet of colour, gently clicking the reels. The rain had stopped and the sun shining on the window picked out tiny coloured diamonds, enhanced by the glowing colours on to the wet panes. Olive took off the box top of her sewing machine and prepared to turn sides to middle, a sheet wearing thin in the centre.

Vinegar Lill bent her tall, thin body over the backyard gate to better view the startling sight of Harriet hurrying down the lane. *Haute couture* was rarely seen down Inkerman Street, but the sight of an oil-stained, head-dishevelled figure wearing old, red slippers was definitely unusual. Resting her bottle on top of the low wall, Lill was surprised to see the stranger pause and then push her way through the yard gate of Number Seven. Few visitors walked up Olive's clean backyard but this one was the most unusual of all.

Harriet put down the gate latch quietly, for she knew silence and caution were necessary to catch the thief. Through the back window she saw Olive seated at her sewing machine and on the table – there it was, her shining crown and immediately Olive's sober garments turned into a shimmering green gown. Quietly she lifted the latch on the back door and edged her way through to the kitchen. Intent on the rhythm of the treadle sewing machine, Olive did not hear or perceive the approaching figure drawing from inside her coat a sharp shining knife. When alerted to the danger it was already too late. With a savage cry, Harriet struck the knife deep into the jugular vein. She jabbed again and again as she remembered rending a white, silk dress, edged with guipure lace and scalloped at neck and hem with tiny rosebuds.

Coughing and gurgling blood, Olive tried to rise from her chair, only to fall, limbs twitching on to the floor, her head rolling against the shining fender.

Harriet, laughing gleefully, tossed her hat to one side and seizing the circlet of coloured reels, placed it on her head. Through the glass panes of the green wall cupboard, she saw herself crowned at last.

CHAPTER 55

When the weird figure re-appeared in the lane, Vinegar Lill backed away towards her back door, for the oil marks on Harriet's coat were now obliterated by blood stains. Clutching the ring of bobbins on her head, Harriet ran, singing gaily, down the back street. As fast as her weak legs would carry her, Lill ran into Edie's backyard. 'Next door,' she gasped, 'I think something terrible has happened there.' Edie dropped the pan she was holding and over the back lane she yelled, 'Danny, come here.'

'What the hell's up?' he called from the stable.

Edie had now reached the back gate. 'Hurry up,' she begged.

Danny slammed the stable door impatiently and began to walk down the garden path. At the sight of the worried look on the faces of the two women he began to run. 'It's not Jamie?' he mouthed. As he formed the words Edie shook her head and both women pointed to Olive's door. Lill halted at the gate as the Marr couple gingerly pushed at the half-open door. At the sight of the mutilated body lying across the mat, Edie fell to her knees, soundlessly covering her mouth with her apron. Horror stricken as she was, one strange thing registered in her mind; the sight of Danny crying, as he knelt by the body lifting an inert hand, he gently kissed it. He stood up and there was a ripping sound as he dragged the half-mended sheet from the sewing machine, breaking the needle. Lill, now a greenish tinge to her pale cheeks, was hovering at the back door. Danny called to her, 'Away and fetch the Pollis, this is a murder job.' Until the Police came Edie sat murmuring all the prayers she could remember, but Danny was strangely silent. Somehow the long afternoon was lived through. Edie sent for the handywoman, Bella Makepeace. Danny placed his arm around his wife's shoulder. 'Sure you and me are in need of a drop of whisky,' he said as they left the Police and Bella Makepeace in charge.

The driver of the Platt's heavy, dray cart surveyed his two horses with pride. Their well-brushed tails and manes were skilfully interwoven into ribboned plaits and their harnesses shone in the bright sunlight. He had worried about the early morning rain but now he sighed with pleasure, basking in the sunlight. Sitting high above the road, the supple leather reins in his hands, he looked contemptuously down at the crowds gathered by the roadside to watch his progress to Castletown Fair. He knew perfectly well that the horses were aware of their special day. When they tossed their proud heads there was a dancing light along the tinkling bells of the harness. He had served the brewery for many years and thought that it was good for the name of Platt to be displayed on the brightly painted side and tailboard of the dray. When Herbert Platt had died bankrupt and disgraced the new owners, knowing nothing of the region, had wisely decided to trade under the well-known name. They had invested in new machinery, copper vats and a smart advertising manager who, clever with captions, touched the hearts and memories of local people. One such, 'Platt's Perfect Pints', was posted on bill boards all around the region. Whole families gathered to admire the resplendent horses, the braver among them tossing time-honoured quips at the stony-faced, bowler-hatted driver.

At first, nobody noticed the hurried approach of a dishevelled woman with a ring of coloured cotton reels encircling her head and wearing a blood-stained coat. When they did, the crowd divided as she pushed her way forward. Harriet had with glee seen the approach of the dray with its splendidly bedecked horses. She knew immediately that it was meant for her; for her royal tour of the town. She had her crown and here was her magnificent equipage, just as it used to be on the days when she was crowned May Queen.

'Hey, Missus, watch where you are going and mind the bairns,' called a big hawser lad from the quayside, who looked on anxiously as Harriet shoved her way to the front. With a sudden movement she darted from the pavement and as the big shires passed, their hooves sparking lights on the grey stones, she leapt to reach the side of the dray. For a few seconds she hung there until her foot caught in the first yellow wheel, dragging her down under the second wheel.

Screeching and gesticulating, the onlookers' shouts pierced the haughty mien of the driver. With a frown he halted the horses. He had felt a small bump and as he descended he wondered why he had not seen an obstruction in the road. As he lowered himself down, still holding the reins, he noticed the surge backwards. Some of the people broke from the crowd to vomit on the grass. The body of Harriet Fanshaw lay on the road, while the bloodied brains were scattered like shining brambles among the coloured reels of the broken circlet.

CHAPTER 56

In the Coroner's Court, every female heart was full of compassion, with one exception, as they watched the handsome man struggling to contain his manly tears. Former unsavoury behaviour was forgotten in the wave of sympathy at the triple bludgeoning that fate had dealt Reginald Fanshaw. With the deaths of his grandfather, father and mother in so short a time, Reginald found himself an object of loving concern among the female population of the area. In the courtroom even the men turned to each other, shaking their heads in pity as Reginald confirmed that he had identified the body of his mother. Actually, he had given a sharp glance at the bandaged head and, with a quick affirmative, left the hospital. But for Aunt Polly there was only a grim cynicism as she watched Reginald sucking up every vestige of local sympathy. In addition to his bereavements, Reginald had spread the heartbreak of his wife's divorce; not forgetting to remind listeners of the type of man with whom she had decamped. Had Harriet lived, she would have been highly satisfied with the front page coverage by the newspapers heralding the triple tragedies. The further hints of a jinx on the Fanshaw family might not have been so welcome. Only Aunt Polly had not been deceived. Before his mother had even been buried Reginald had ransacked her room and, unable to find the key, had impatiently broken open a box kept locked in a drawer. To his delight he found all her jewellery and, what was more important, insurance policies that would bring him the handsome sum of ten thousand pounds. When Polly demanded that he pay for the months Harriet had stayed in her house, Reginald coldly replied that she could sell his mother's clothes and keep the money. Enraged, Polly tartly retorted that she would give the clothes to the Salvation Army, adding bitterly that if she never saw her nephew again, it would be too soon.

Wild with the dazzling prospect of wealth, Reginald decided to occupy his grandfather's fine house in the square. His new financial status and his prestigious home made him the object of much speculation. Mothers, daughters on their arms, would solicitously concern themselves about his welfare. Invitations flew, inviting him, respecting his state of mourning, to a quiet family tea or supper. Not only Reginald but the Police were baffled as to how his mother had entered the big house. There was no sign of entry, yet she had certainly been inside on the morning of the murder, and her subsequent death. Her finger prints were everywhere in the rooms as well as oil-stained hand prints on the expensive furniture. The knife that she had used to murder Olive Harman had been identified as taken from the kitchen drawer of the house. But nobody could offer a solution as to how she had entered and left a securely locked house.

With his ever increasing wealth came a dizzy feeling of power and Reginald determined to wreak vengeance on the Dobson family. And first on the list was his ex-wife, Amelia. It appeared, he thought sneeringly that she had had a rush of maternal feeling since she had shacked up with her pitman. At Drumrauch Hall she had seemed more interested in her damned horses than in paying attention to the youngster. Well, he decided, that ignorant coal miner was not going to usurp his rights as a father. He would, through the courts, take the child away from them; he could always send William away to a boarding school. He had approached that old crab of a lawyer of Pickering, Pickering & Shepherd, to be informed that he had accepted five thousand pounds as a divorce settlement. 'Moreover,' said the senior Pickering, 'you have not, over the years, visited nor sought access to the child.'

'Keep your damned advice.' Reginald threw out as he stormed through the door, but the older man had already turned his attention to other papers. Reginald, determined not to be beaten, had found in Castletown just the man he deemed to be a smart lawyer. It was through him that he had engaged a private detective to docket the details of Amelia's private life. His new lawyer pointed out that Amelia was living with a lover – a telling point with any Judge. Together they would dwell on this point as a reason for the change of custody, pressing home the immoral life style of the boy's mother. And this was just the beginning, he told himself. Next on the list was that sod Tobias Dobson. It was his prying and sneaking to his old man that had set in motion the whole disastrous chain of events.

194

But that was all over now and they would all be made to pay, for Reginald knew that at last he was in command.

CHAPTER 57

It looks like rain, Amelia thought, and that would bring the men in earlier from the hay making. There was always so much work to do at Bobbin Hill Farm and Jonty would normally work alongside the two village men until five o'clock. She stood back, floury from her baking and checked the Aga stove. Jonty, she knew, would break to bring William from the village school and she smiled as she thought of the strong bond between Jonty and her son. For William, proud in his new hob-nailed boots, followed Jonty everywhere. The farm was prospering for they worked all hours in the land. On autumnal moonlit nights she would see the headlights of the newly bought tractor as Jonty, unwilling to waste an hour, used the light of the moon to plough out. Occasionally she had pulled on a coat and found the tractor, still warm in the yard while Jonty slept soundly in the hay alongside the quiet cows. There were still blue coal scars, as deep as a tattoo, showing through his tanned skin, but regular work in the open air had made him as hard as a walnut shell. Even in the wettest weather he was out working; a corn sack turned in on itself, was-cowl shaped over his head and his protection from the weather. They still planned to run a stud farm and already there were two mares and a handsome stallion, called Nimrod, in the stables. Harry Walters, comfortably established in his own quarters over the stables, was as content as any human being could hope to be. The stallion, the mares, Patches and William's pony encompassed his world. His meagre weekly shopping list, augmented by the farmhouse kitchen, was taken care of and the eager young William would carry extra food to him for the joy of sharing Harry's work and expertise.

Amelia leaned against the kitchen table and decided Jonty would have to be told as soon as he came in. 'Oh God,' she thought, teeth clenched, 'it's the oldest trick in the world.' She looked out of the window at the beautifully tended garden. The profusion of flowers was owed to the devoted diligence of her mother. Lady Dobson would turn up in her worn garden clothes and wellingtons for a good day's gardening, accompanied as ever by Jasper, her faithful Jack Russell Terrier. The little dog shared her life and her bed and walked always just two steps behind her.

Despite the intimate sharing of their lives, Amelia had always the uneasy feeling that she lived in a tenuous situation. Since Jonty had turned down her open invitation to marriage, Amelia had been careful to avoid the subject. And now she was two months pregnant and would have to broach the subject. It would seem she was using their unborn child as a weapon; it might threaten the happiness she had known since living with Jonty. As the tender thoughts of her happiness glowed within her a voice brought her back suddenly to reality.

'My, my, aren't we the little country housewife.' Amelia spun round to see her ex-husband leaning against the door post.

Reginald's lawyer had warned him not to approach Amelia only to let the law deal with his appeal. But he could hardly wait to confront her and on this windy morning with rain in the air he drove up the Tyne Valley to find Bobbin Hill Farm. 'Good God,' he thought as he scoured the country lanes, 'this must be the road to nowhere. Imagine anybody choosing to live in such a God-forsaken hole.' That his ancestors had lived for centuries in this remote farm, tilling the soil and tending their sheep, interested him not at all. The sign 'Bobbin Hill Farm' creaked on the post as he turned down the lane. He smiled delightedly as two middle-aged women jumped into the hedgerow as he sped up the lane, but were too late to escape the muddy swirl of water thrown up from the rutted track.

He entered the farmhouse, quietly edging his way up the cool passage towards the kitchen. At first glance he could scarcely believe that this was the pampered daughter, lately of Drumrauch Hall. Amelia, warm and flushed from the baking, stood in front of a table covered with pies and cakes.

'What are you doing here?' she gasped.

Reginald lowered himself into the rocking chair beside the stove and began to rock himself to and fro. 'Surely I've a right to visit my son?'

'Why? You've never shown interest in him before.'

'Neither, I recollect my dear, did you when he was born.'

'You can't see him, he's at school.'

'Along with the village ruffians, no doubt. You see, I know all about your life and that collier fellow you live with. I've been having you watched for months.'

Reginald stared intently as her flushed face registered his remarks. 'I have applied to the courts for custody of William. I can offer them proof that you are unfit to look after him.'

Amelia held on to the table edge, white knuckled as fear raced through her body. 'You will never succeed, for William has a good life here.'

'Perhaps with you, but there are many people who can testify to the disgraceful reputation of Jonathan Marr.'

A voice interjected. 'Somebody talking about me?'

Both heads turned to see Jonty blocking the light from the kitchen door. Reginald jumped from the chair, causing it to rock violently back and forward.

'My business has nothing to do with you, even if you do share her bed; or is it a haystack?' he said derisively.

Jonty walked into the kitchen until the two men were face to face. 'It has everything to do with me, for this woman is shortly to become my wife.'

Intent on their eye-to-eye combat, neither heard Amelia's sharp intake of breath.

'You may legalize it now,' Reginald sneered, 'but it will not alter the fact that I intend to have the legal custody of William.'

'I'll float you down the Tyne before I'll let that happen.'

Reginald was not deceived by the quiet tone in his voice. He circled around towards the kitchen door. 'That threat will be noted when I take you into court.'

As the sound of his hurried steps receded down the passage Amelia turned in fury on to Jonty.

'You might have asked me first.'

'Asked what?'

'That we are getting married.'

'Oh! That,' he said carelessly as he poked the stove. 'I think we'll have a day out in Castletown.'

'Is that all I mean to you – a day out in town?'

Jonty laughed and pulled her on to his knee. 'Well, there's a registry office there, isn't there?'

'Jonty, there's something I must tell you – I'm expecting a child.'

For a few seconds Jonty surveyed the ceiling and then, smiling wickedly he said, 'Now surely it's we are expecting, isn't it? And it is about time too, for what is a farm without stock, love?' As he pulled off her apron he added mischievously, 'Surely it's usual for a lass in your condition to have a quickie wedding.'

'Oh, Jonty!' she laughed and as they lay together on the mat in front of the fire Jonty with a wry face murmured, 'You'll be let down, bonny lass, there'll be nobody there with a shot gun.'

Even as they kissed passionately there was still between them the unspoken terror of losing William; an unspoken blight on their happiness.

CHAPTER 58

There was a mean gleam in Reginald's eye as he relished the effects of yesterday's visit to Bobbin Hill Farm. He was delightedly aware that the cool facade of Amelia had been punctured by his threat to seek the custody of William. If he succeeded, only vague ideas flitted through his mind of what to do with the boy; probably boarding school would be the best solution. It would be a damned sight better than the peasant life he was leading in the wilds of Northumberland. But uppermost in his mind was the urge to wound his ex-wife for the ignominy he had suffered of being discarded for a pitman; he savoured the image of the fear he had provoked in Amelia's eyes.

Reginald was now where his mother had always planned he should be; living in style in his grandfather's beautiful Georgian house in the prestigious Embleton Square. If his neighbours worried about the numerous noisy parties lasting into the early hours, they were inclined to be indulgent to one who had suffered so much. For now, they speculated, he had emerged as a rich and eligible partner for one of the many unmarried daughters in the square. The tragic murder of Olive Harman and the bizarre subsequent death of his mother had bathed him in a mystical aura which fascinated the easily impressed young women. They entreated their parents to include the name of Reginald Fanshaw on their list of dinner invitations. And Reginald could turn on his easy charm to the clucking matrons who now, so frequently, invited him into their homes. Reginald had already decided to remarry but only with the most advantageous match in the area. After his marriage to Amelia and the life style of Drumrauch Hall, he had acquired a taste for aristocratic comfort and ease.

There was the Fenton family, with a bunch of lumpy daughters; they were top of the list, for the family owned two of the largest collieries and their black wealth extended in seams for miles under the North Sea. The second choice went to the Hardwicks, whose family owned huge engineering works sprawled, caterpillar like, alongside the river side. Rich with the pickings from wars around the globe, often supplying both sides, the Hardwicks employed the largest labour force in the north of England.

With these enticing prospects Reginald could afford to be a matrimonial dilettante. But nothing deflected him from pursuing a revengeful attack upon his Aunt Polly Platt. With the aid and encouragement of his suave new lawyer, he was determined to evict her from the little house in Morden Street. Although she held the deeds of the house, they were still in his father's name and there was no written evidence that they belonged to Polly Platt. Her resistance to his spurious charm and her disdain at the way he had treated his mother rankled deep with the nephew. The house itself meant nothing to him and if his Aunt had begged to be left in peace he might have considered dropping the case against her; but Polly Platt was incapable of hiding her dislike and distrust. With petty spite he determined, as he so vindictively put it, 'To see her out on the street.'

In spite of his many social commitments, Reginald was still deeply involved with his sister-in-law, Celia Fanshaw, although access and familiarity were beginning to bore him. His conquest had been too easy, he thought, for almost anyone with a modicum of charm could have gained Celia's affections. With such a husband as Tobias, as cold as the fish he sold, Celia had obviously been available to any smooth talker. It was the satisfaction of knowing that Tobias was aware of his cuckolding that eluded Reginald. Badly he wanted to taunt him as he had taunted Amelia and to face him with proof of his wife's infidelity. But Celia was cautious; she knew that one day their affair would end and that sooner or later Reginald would tire of their relationship. She was also aware that she had no wish to throw away her rich and comfortable life style. With Tobias spending long hours at his wholesale fish business and involved in a sharing partnership with his brother and father in ship building, he spent little time at home.

The tide would be running high in an hour's time and Reginald guessed that Tobias would be in his office watchtower, waiting to check on his incoming fishing boats. As he drove Celia down the dark road leading to the fish quay, she stirred uneasily in the car. They had dined well at an out-of-town restaurant and now, sleepily, she had thought that they were heading back to Reginald's house.

'Where are we going? I didn't want to come down here.'

'Come on, Celia, have a little romance in your life. There's nobody on the quayside until the boats are due in. Don't you like the riverside at night?'

Celia looked around the dark angles of the buildings and shivered. It was completely deserted and, apart from one bright security lamp shining near the edge of the water, gloomy with night shadows.

Reginald opened the car door. 'Let's have a breath of fresh air, Celia.'

Reluctantly she eased herself out of the car, and Reginald, arm encircling her waist, stationed her directly under the lamp. He turned her so that the light shone directly on to her face. 'You slimey sod,' he thought, 'once you watched me and told tales to your old man Dobson; now watch this!'

He made sure they were both directly in line of vision of Tobias' office window and easily began to slide up Celia's skirt. Worriedly she cried out, 'Not here, Reginald,' and struggled free.

'Oh! All right,' he said, holding up his hands. 'Let's have a cigarette.' He lit two cigarettes and, holding them aloft in his right hand as a gesture of defiance, kissed Celia long and passionately. With his arm still around Celia's shoulder he enjoyed a final stare at the office window.

Celia gave a sigh of relief as they settled down in the car seats. Laughing, Reginald said, 'Right, off we go.'

Forgetting his car engine was in forward gear, he pressed on the accelerator. The powerful car shot forward and nose dived into the inky black waters of the river Tyne.

It was seconds before Tobias saw the lights, still shining under water, dimmed into blackness.

CHAPTER 59

As he had done so lately, Roberto rose early, hoping to see Betsy and the boy opening up the filleting shed. Always, he hoped that each visit would appease the desperate longing in his heart, but it only left him empty of gratification. From the top of the quay stairs he would watch as a small figure darted in and out of the shed, tugging at fish boxes and climbing over lobster pots. The indistinct face of the child would appear from the warm bundle of his clothes as often he sat on the cracket outside the hut, drinking from a small mug. Today, to Roberto's surprise, there was an extra activity on the quayside. Divers surfaced to wave to a crane driver and Roberto watched as chains rattled downwards into the river. Taking the steps two at a time, he reached the quayside just as a car, gushing with water, was slowly winched upwards in a gentle, macabre swinging dance. He was waved back by the Police as the car was slowly lowered on to the quay. Roberto suddenly felt a gut gulp as he recognised the sodden body of Reginald Fanshaw being dragged from the driver's seat. From the other side he was surprised to see Tobias Dobson, waiting with a blanket that hurriedly he covered over the face and body of a woman.

Roberto's first reaction was one of frustration as he realised circumstances had outwitted his plans for revenge. At that time it was unclear in his mind whether this was accident or suicide, but in either case the end result relieved Roberto of a duty forged almost twenty years ago. Grimly he acknowledged the truth of the saying back home in Italy that, 'Time is a gentleman.' For days the local papers carried dramatic headlines, foraging among previous family deaths to come up with varying versions of 'The Curse Of The Fanshaws'. Even the powerful Dobson family could not gloss over the fact that Celia, 'the sister-in-law and well-known friend of Mr Reginald Fanshaw', was at midnight also a drowned victim. As neither Tobias nor any member of the Dobson family gave press interviews or any intimations to the

203

media, thwarted journalists made sure that daring hints appeared in local newspapers.

As the only close living relative of Reginald was his five-year-old son, it was left to Aunt Polly Platt formally to identify the body. She could feel no remorse as she nodded an affirmative over the still figure, the face so handsome even in death. She felt only relief that Reginald would no more threaten or vent his petty spike upon her and that now the ownership of her home was no longer in danger. Almost immediately she had received a letter of thanks from Amelia for her service of identification of the body. Aunt Polly realised that it was not only she who felt, with Reginald's death, the removal of a terrible anxiety. A few of Reginald's drinking friends attended the funeral service, which was as lacking in sincerity as the three previous Fanshaw interments. Already a juicy sex scandal involving the local Member of Parliament had deflected the local press from the life and times of Reginald Fanshaw. A few, a very few, remembered or commented upon the fact that there was still a scion of that ill-fated family living in the farmlands of Northumberland. It was only when the small figure appeared for the service in church, accompanied by his mother, that a hurried appendix was added to the obituary. Of the three who had known of the existence of Amos Fanshaw Junior, two were dead and the senior partner of the firm of Heslop, Heslop & Fairburn kept his saturnine thoughts to himself.

For Amelia and Jonty, absorbed in the work of the farm, there had been neither the time nor the inclination to leave Bobbin Hill Farm after their wedding. Sir Nathanial Dobson, arms resting on the flank of the stallion Nimrod, gave an amused glance at his new son-in-law. Used to subservient approaches, Jonty's cheerful indifference was refreshing. Watching his daughter, out in the stableyard, looking so well and happy, up to her ankles in what Jonty laughingly called 'plother', he was thankful. Thankful too, that Amelia was no longer living in terror that Reginald might obtain the custody of William. His ex son-in-law had, he decided, done them all a service when he plunged, with Celia, to his death in the waters of the Tyne. The embarrassment caused by the double death had become yesterday's concern. He watched Jonty, seated on the trailer, William beside him, drive out of the stableyard with a load of manure. It was, as Jonty called it, 'plugging muck' time – the season to return to the earth the goodness that crops had taken out of it. He felt a pang of pity for Tobias' children, who were not in such a happy situation. Strangely enough, neither they nor Tobias seemed overtly distressed at Celia's death. Their short holidays from boarding schools were spent on trips abroad with their cousins, Martin's children. All adolescent, their lives were filled with monetary demands to satisfy fleeting interests. The waters of the river had closed smoothly over the head of Celia Dobson.

Even his wife, mused Sir Nathanial, spent days at Bobbin Hill, delighting in bringing back order and beauty to the years of garden neglect. With Jasper, her beloved terrier, at her heels, the Lady Dobson, armed with bulbs and cuttings from the gardens of Drumrauch Hall, created loveliness from a wilderness. Plants chosen with care, to withstand the rigours of a moorland winter, thrived under the farmhouse windows.

CHAPTER 60

There was no outward hostility from the people he had known well and lived among for nearly twenty years, but there was an alteration – a diffidence in their attitude towards him. Roberto felt a cooling wind blowing in both his neighbours' attitudes and on his business affairs as European developments affected the local people. The unlikely alliance between Italy and Germany had caused some to looks askance at the foreigner in their midst. The loss of the restaurant had been a bitter blow to Roberto's plans and now he felt it was only the respect for Jamie that made the fish shop so popular. That, together with the high standards that Olive had incarcerated into Jamie, had made the shop such a profitable concern. The young Maud Thompson proved to be an eager learner, anxious to prove indispensable to the handsome Jamie. When contemporaries, assuring her of their anxiety for her welfare, pointed out his early years of silence and his strange alliance with his dead brother, her retorts were as crisp as the batter covering the fish. Roberto had longed to expand the fish business to Castletown and even over the river to the south side of the Tyne, but he knew the tide of goodwill was now against him.

The bank manager, Mr Callum Ogilvie, regarded Roberto's bank statements with a jaundiced eye. For sometime Roberto had been transferring his comfortable wealth to an Italian bank; something that Mr Ogilvie already considered as an act of war. Roberto might be a British citizen, but to the bank manager he was now the enemy; and he guessed quite rightly that Mr Roberto Delfino was preparing to return to his native country. And there was the strange matter of the weekly allotment to Betsy Haddick at Neuk End. With his ear to the ground, Mr Ogilvie knew just why. What did surprise him was that Roberto had made such an elaborate system to continue paying instead of just skipping out of the country.

What Mr Ogilvie did not know were the pressures under which

Roberto lived at home. The daily united chorus put up by Zia and Maria, together with business problems, had forced the issue. The continued threats by Zia to return home had coalesced into reality. She was not a British citizen and already preparations for her departure were underway. Maria in tearful desperation begged Roberto to wind up his affairs so that they could accompany Zia home before it was too late. In spite of political protestations there was an undercurrent of fear that war was imminent. Zia's dominance over his wife was paramount and Roberto knew that Maria was capable, even determined, to take the child, Lucia, and leave with her aunt. She complained that she was receiving derogatory remarks from customers in the ice-cream parlour. Since Marina had left, Maria was called upon to spend more time serving behind the counter. Marina's departure was looked upon as desertion. As soon as she had married her drawing office sweetheart, she discarded all association with the Delfinos and even with her family, now far away in Taormina. When Roberto was absent, Zia would draw up a chair alongside Maria to keep her company. While they chattered non-stop in Italian, Zia would scowl at the customers, coldly staring at them with her shoe-button eyes. Maria had long since given up the effort to learn English and Roberto had ceased to encourage or demand that she should. The language struggle had ended when Roberto realised that the word barrier precluded his womenfolk from the gossip of his quayside assocation. Now, even his child's first words were in Italian. Had Zia managed her heavybody on to the quayside, words would not have been needed if she had encountered a small dark lad already handling a flenching knife. Apart from church attendance and visiting Castletown by car, the two women rarely left the house. Zia disapproved of Roberto's integration into local life and blamed it, not unreasonably, on the determined teaching of his landlady, Olive Harman.

Roberto could find no consolation either at home or in church. A further bitter blow had been the removal of Father Antony Howard into a rehabilitation Catholic home. Just where it was no one seemed to know, although rumour had it that the disappearing Agnes Cowen had been granted permission to work in the same home. Roberto missed the Priest, for a mutually respectful friendship had developed between them over the years. It was not until the very end, at the extraordinary christening of the Marr baby, that he had realised that

Father Antony's gaunt appearance and frequent bouts of illness were due to alcohol. Roberto still diligently performed his religious duties but he could not relate to the gregarious charm of the new Priest. To most members of the church he was a great success; the veritable life and soul of the Catholic Men's Club and new hats flourished like summer flowers in the congregation.

CHAPTER 61

Roberto felt little joy at the thought of returning to his native land. The passing years had altered the impressionable seventeen-year-old foreigner. In that harsh environment he had carved out a prosperous living and to him the little town of Embleton was synonymous with success and held him with a strange affection. Perhaps, he wondered, life would have been easier if he had married a local girl, instead of reverting to the custom of his homeland. His life was full of 'if onlys'. Now, everything was stacked against him and with resignation he realised that the struggle of the past few months was over. There were still a few things to clear up. Jamie had requested a private meeting and this, he knew, was to be something more than just to say 'goodbye'.

Jamie Marr looked up as Roberto entered the fish shop and the smile, as always, was in his eyes. He nodded his head towards the back shop and Roberto, after greeting Maud, followed through. The old dog, Tyke, gave a token growl as it raised up stiffly on arthritic legs. Jamie gave a gentle rub onto the shaggy head and the dog subsided on to his bed with a little groan. The comfortable bed was made up against the wall immediately behind the warmth of the fish fryer. Roberto made an opening comment, 'He's lasted longer than his pal, Pilot.' Jamie nodded and pulled the woollen blanket up over the dog's hindquarters. The animal gazed at his master with an adoring look through eyes dimmed with the pain and discomfort of old age. He would end his days in a quiet peacefulness, dreaming his dreams of the days when he raced alongside the twins, always outrun by the now dead Pilot.

Jamie took off his white apron, as if what he had to say deserved a more suitable apparel.

'You know that Olive, Mrs Harman, left me fifty pounds in her will?'

Roberto smiled his approval. The news of the gift had been only mildly surprising for everyone was aware of Olive's growing appreciation of Jamie's worth. From the first day that he had trundled the fish barrow down on to the quayside, a gawky lad whose knee-length stockings never stayed at knee length, to his competent handling of both fish and customers; under the watchful eye of Olive Harman, he had become highly regarded. Roberto believed that Jamie had been badly affected by Olive's murder, but even he could not imagine the deep pain, bringing an arousal of the horror of his twin Joe's death. For several days after Olive's death he refused to speak and Edie watched her son anxiously. In the shop Maud carried on as if nothing had happened, discussing everyday happenings and business problems in a matter-of-fact voice as they carried out their daily routine. That night they had served the last customer and drawn the ashes from the cooling fryer. Jamie went through to the back shop. And it was there that Maud found him with tears welling down his face. Putting her arms around him she drew him down on to a pile of empty fish boxes. Without a word she dried his tears with the folds of her pinafore. Gradually their familiar footing was resumed and his mother thanked God for the sensible lass he had taken up with.

As if the two were not connected, Jamie said, 'Is it next week you're leaving?'

Roberto took some time looking out of the window before he answered, 'Next Wednesday morning.'

Jamie cleared his throat. 'Will you sell me the shop? I've another ten pounds saved and I'll lay down the sixty pounds. I can pay off the difference by instalments, although I'm not sure how to get it to you.'

In the silence that followed Jamie shifted uneasily in his seat, worried that Roberto already had other plans for the fish shop.

'I'm thinking of getting married next year,' he blurted out and then pointed to the front shop. 'She's a good lass.'

As if so many words had cost him much effort, he got up and refilled the dog's bowl at the sink. Although tears pricked his eyes Roberto was smiling gently. For what he was about to do was against all his business expertise and acumen.

'Jamie, the shop is yours. Look upon it as a wedding present from Olive and me. She would be happy about that.'

There was no effusion of thanks from Jamie as the two shook hands;

only the yellow triangle gleamed as Jamie took deep breaths. Suddenly he delved into the pocket of his coat, hanging behind the door, and handed Roberto a packet of snapshots. Roberto looked down into the laughing face of Betsy standing at the door of her hut, Betsy with the young George; the boy alongside the fishermen, and one of the lad seated upon an upturned boat.

'Is there any message for Betsy?'

Roberto mouthed a silent 'No.'

Jamie asked quietly, 'What time do you leave?'

Now in control of his voice, Roberto replied, 'On the morning tide – six o'clock.' He put the snapshots in his pocket and left the shop. Maud closed the door behind him.

CHAPTER 62

Roberto walked slowly down Inkerman Street. He passed Betty Mayhew, who had recently given birth to yet another child with a peach blossom skin. They must have a houseful by now, he thought, as he courteously called the time of day to the half face visible from a sideways shawl. As he entered Number eight he called the customary superfluous greeting, 'I see you're in, Edie.'

Edie laid the metal scoop with its wooden handle on top of the copper, where she had been busily scooping out broth from the set pot into a pan. 'Eeh, you're a sight for sore eyes, Robbie,' she exclaimed delightedly. 'Come in, lad, I was wondering when you would call. You've just missed our Maisie, she's out with the bairn.'

'Is Danny about?'

'No, it's Monday.'

Roberto remembered that Monday was lamp oil day and Danny would be walking the outlying areas with Old Boney, trading his paraffin oil and risqué chat to the housewives as he dodged their washing lines.

'Our Danny,' said Edie indulgently, 'he lights a lamp to troubles. Mind you, he's not so young as he was, neither is Old Boney, but you'd never notice it once the cart is laden and they are both on their way.'

'Nor when he's tippling his ale,' thought Roberto. Little had changed in the Marr kitchen. Where once the two dogs had sprawled over the mat in front of the fire, two marmalade-coloured cats sat leisurely washing their faces, ecstatically enjoying the generous heat. Roberto looked up at the empty space on top of the cupboard, where now only a moth-eaten fox fur tail wafted gently in the breeze from the back door. The spitting, anti-social cat was long gone. Edie filled the tea pot from the black kettle on the hob, using a folded terry towelling napkin as a pad, hastily pulled from the sagging clothes line stretching the length of the fireplace. 'Our Jamie says you're away on the Wednesday tide,' she said as she thoughtfully stirred the tea leaves in the tea pot. 'You'll be dropping me a line now and then, I hope. I'd be vexed if I don't get the scribe of a pen sometimes.'

Roberto paused in the act of lighting a cigarette. 'It might be difficult, Edie, but I'll try.'

Edie poured out the tea and Roberto saw the tears in her eyes as she sighed. 'It's dowly with the house empty next door – since Olive's gone. Her and me were never close you know – but she was always there. She was a good neighbour. Kept herself to herself mind, you could set the clock by her comings in and goings out to the fish shop.'

Roberto nodded; it was easier to let Edie talk on than to deflect her flow of conversation.

'I canna understand why that mad Fanshaw woman murdered Olive. Mind you, she said that there had to be three deaths in the street.' Swiftly she followed Roberto's puzzled look with an explanation. 'Three deaths, remember. There was our Joe, God rest his soul, then that Hilda Mason; she was three months gone, you know, when she laid her head on the railway line. It's hard on a woman, you know. A man can always put his hat on and walk away but a woman pays the price.'

There was a silence as Edie ruminated on the injustices of society. Roberto's thoughts ran in another channel. He was deflected from Edie's superstitious logic by the thought that, while Hilda Mason had ended her misery, Alan James would endure to the end of his days the spiteful retribution of his grinding wife. Edie broke into his thoughts with, 'Olive had to be the third. I blame myself, though. If I hadda went out a bit earlier I might have stopped that Fanshaw woman getting at Olive.'

'Nobody was to blame, Edie. There was something between those two that went deep into the past.'

There seemed to be nothing more to be said, so Edie changed course, anxious to acquaint Roberto with the updated family events. 'Things have changed around here; our Jonty's married – fancy, to that Lady Dobson. We've been up to Bobbin Hill Farm, our Maisie and me with the bairn, and nobody could have had a warmer welcome. Jonty and Amelia,' Edie hesitated as she tongued the name of her daughter-in-law, as if she were taking a liberty, 'met us at the station. Her bairn follows Jonty around like his shadow.' Edie eased her bust over the table to say confidentially, 'Mind, young William has come into fair-sized money since his father was found drowned in his car at the bottom of the Tyne. That lad will be well-to-do, you know. He'll need it, poor bairn, for he has been born with trouble on his back. Them Fanshaws are cursed. First his father drowned and his grandmother a murderess. My heart aches for him. But I'm glad our Jonty's married, though,' and here her voice dropped again. 'They were living on tally, you know. Our Michael says he'll never speak to Jonty again.'

'Why? I wouldn't have thought the two of them living together would have bothered Michael's conscience.'

'No, no, it's not like that and I'll tell you for why. It's the fact that he's married into the Dobson family. Michael says he's a traitor to his class. But he can say what he likes about the Dobsons, I'll never forget how it was her Da that brought our Joe's body home. In his own car and wrapped up in his overcoat.'

Edie lifted the tea pot lid by its top, the upper half of a china shepherdess, and refilled their mugs.

'Michael has his own house now. There's only Danny and me, Maisie and the baby and Slack Willie. He's taken over Jonty's allotment but he canna grow potstuff like our Jonty. Jamie's still here. It was grand of you to let him have the fish shop. He's planning an extension in the yard for when he gets married. You've met Maud, she's a nice lass.'

Suddenly Edie began to cry. 'I'll miss you, Robbie, you were always a grand lad,' she said as she dried away tears with her apron. 'They say that your country and ours are at variance, but it will never make any difference in this house. Remember how you used to sneak in here to have a fag . . . as if Olive didn't know?'

Roberto touched the plump hand encircling the mug of tea. 'I remember, Edie, and I'll often think of you . . . We've been through a terrible time. I've never felt such a loss in my life as I did on the day Olive died. She was a wonderful woman. She was strong and she shaped my life. I'll never forget her or cease to be grateful for the care she took of me over the years.'

With an unnatural restraint Edie resisted the temptation to ask about the other women in his life. As she wiped her eyes Roberto asked, 'Is there anything you'd like from the house as a keepsake?'

Edie knew very well what she would like, something that she had coveted every Christmas as she sat sharing the obligatory piece of cake and port wine with Olive. 'Do you think she would mind if I asked for the electroplated fire irons and fender?'

'Olive would be pleased for you to have them, Edie. Come across the yard and I'll pass them over the wall.'

CHAPTER 63

In the kitchen, denuded by the fire irons and the blood-flooded mat so thoughtfully disposed of by the handy woman, Bella Makepeace, Roberto felt the cold chill of the empty house. By placing his hand on the dividing wall he could just feel a hint of warmth from the Marr's generous fire back. He had tried to pay Bella Makepeace for the terrible task that she had undertaken in preparing Olive's body for burial. He knew that this was the woman who had helped to bring his son into the world and who had since, decently covered the horrible wounds of the woman he had cared for more than any other woman in the world with the exception of his long dead mother. When he had approached her, Bella told him in flat, clipped tones, 'You owe me nowt, lad. She left two pound notes wrapped in the finest linen I've ever seen, and with a note of thanks written in her own hand.' And Bella, as befitted her reputation, had left the house neat and tidy. Olive would have approved.

Roberto took the key out of the drawer in the green kitchen cupboard and went into the front room. The beauty of the treasures therein, and the care that Olive had expended upon them, caught at his heart. He sat down on the glowing red silk velvet seat of one of the gilded chairs. Maria had sat there resplendent in her white velvet gown on their wedding day, the other chair instantly appropriated by Zia. Olive had, in her will, left the house and its contents to him. She could never have imagined the dilemma in which she had placed him. How could she have known of the circumstances that would force him to return to Italy? But what could he do with the property, and her treasures that had stayed the same as Olive grew older? Beautiful things, carefully transported from across the world by two long dead seamen – the father and the husband of a now dead daughter and wife. The gas light popped uncertainly, as if little use had given a deflective flow through the pipes. Roberto covered the glowing chairs and sofa with bedspreads from upstairs. The plum-coloured velvet curtains were, as Olive had always kept them, serving the dual purpose of thwarting the prying eyes of Inkerman Street neighbours and the infrequent strong rays of the sun.

In spite of the cold, Roberto lingered in a house flooded with memories and reluctant to return home to the excited chatter of his family. All their luggage was already down at the quayside warehouse, but despite the inconvenience of the few shared chairs and cups, the two women were deliriously happy. They could not wait to set foot on the ship, for were they not going home! Zia had seen to it that everything packageable had been boxed or crated. Although she could not wait to shake off the dust of Embleton, she was equally determined that nothing should be left behind. Roberto turned out the gas light; the aged mantle burned off in a crimson glow and a last despairing 'pop'. He gave, with an aching heart, a final glance around the room. The room that had been the pride of Olive's life was now shrouded in shadows. He locked the door and with a sad smile upturned the small mat that Olive had insisted kept the dust blowing in through the gap at the bottom of the door.

In the back kitchen he took from his bag a tin box filled with olive oil. He placed the parlour door key in the box, stepped out and locked the back door and dropped the key beside the other. He slipped it into a pocket of oilskin, remembering the wise old shipyard men's advice on how to preserve metal. He groped down his bag for the remaining object and reaching out a small trowel put it in his pocket. Finally he hung the empty bag behind the coal house door and closed the gate of Number seven for the last time. Edie, still tearful, watching from her window, waved the napkin in goodbye. As he responded with a smile Roberto wondered if she would, as Olive so religiously did, cover up the fire irons from Monday 'til Friday. In the deserted churchyard Roberto stood, pansy plants in hand, as he looked down on Olive's grave. The gravestone he had had erected was a plain rectangle of grey granite bearing only her name, age and the simple message 'Rest In Peace'. At the top, near the headstone, he dug down and placed the box of keys, covering it with a layer of soil. Then he planted the pansies on the top. Olive had always admired pansies for they bloomed in winter when other plants had died. And they belonged to Olive, for weren't they also known as 'heart's ease'?

Speckled with the early morning mist, the two women walked ahead clutching their bundles of last minute necessities. Even Zia accelerated her usual elephantine tread to keep up with the eager steps of Maria. Roberto walked slowly behind carrying his small daughter. At the wooden dolly he stopped, remembering the wind-tossed figure of the woman who had given him shelter on that fearful stormy night when he had arrived in Embleton. He put down the child, who immediately became engrossed in a heap of broken brightly coloured pots left from a children's game. Her interest was deflected as, with wondering eyes, she saw her father cut a fine sliver of wood from the statue. To the uncomprehending child he said, 'It's supposed to bring you back safely to Embleton – but not for me, I'm afraid.' Opening his coat he took out a bundle of photographs and placed the wood sliver inside. Lucia, the child, had waited patiently but now raised her arms to be carried towards the ship, its lights hazed by the early morning mist. At the top of the gangway he handed the child over to her mother, who immediately went below to escape the clammy cold air.

As the ship smoothed out the waters of the Tyne, Roberto, still on deck, persuaded himself that it was Jamie looking out through the mist, from the top of the steps. But there was no light from the filleting shed. In spite of the quayside fervent belief in the efficacy of the wooden dolly sliver, Roberto knew he would never return. His country would be dragged into war as inexorably as the turning wheels of a tumbril.

CHAPTER 64

I n the warmth of an early July night it was still light enough to see
the beauty of the Bay of Naples. From the corner of the piazza
Roberto gazed down through the purple shadows on the hillside to
where the fading sun had left a golden goodnight upon the waters. But
the beauty of the night was lost on him for in his mind's eye he saw
only the grey glint of the Tyne waters. He had moved away as far as he
could across the square from the excited chatter of the two groups of
people; the men in one corner and the women in another. That young
fool, Mario Fettucci, was dominating the conversation as he shook the
cockscomb of feathers in his uniform hat. Roberto had noticed one or
two of the young girls making edging movements into the circle of
young males admiring Mario and his military accoutrement. The girls
had been sharply ordered back by the watchful eyes of the fathers and
the garment-plucking mothers. This was not the time for *passeggiata*.
High above the clamour of noisy voices he could hear Mario, sure in
his military ascendancy and informing all with certainty that Britain
was finished. That island would shortly be invaded and crushed by
the Germans and for Italy there would be the spoils of Southern
France. '*La Franchese*,' he shouted while making an elbow-high derisory
gesture, 'were finished.' Older men shifted uneasily but even as they
did so they could not escape the excitement of the day.

As usual Zia was expounding upon her days in North-Eastern
England. She described the cold days; how January was a wickedly
bitter month, when the wind came freezing off the North Sea and
funnelled up the mouth of the Tyne. Women, even on that warm night
drew their shawls more tightly around their shoulders. 'Surely, it is
not always so cold?' one more spirited young matron asked. Although
annoyed at having her first-hand experience questioned, reluctantly
Zia had to concede that some days were bearable.

'Look,' she ordered, pointing to Maria, 'she was never well when

219

she lived there and as for the people . . .' here only her upraised hands could adequately express her dislike of the English. On the quiet, to a few intimate members of the family, she expressed her belief that Maria's inability to conceive again was due to her exposure to that harsh climate.

How was it, Roberto asked himself, that a man could return to his native land and yet feel so unbearably unhappy? Maria and Zia had been reabsorbed into village life as if they had never left it. Strangely, the child, Lucia, had not settled down so easily. She would stand aside as the village children played their games, as if, like her father, she too felt herself an alien. Beached on the bay below were the family fishing boats. Roberto knew he could not join his brothers and cousins in fishing as a livelihood. Yet there must have been a seafaring strain in his blood that created the bond he had had with Betsy, her mother and the fisherfolk of Embleton. He sighed; the die had been cast and now he must forget Betsy and his son living in that other country, in that other life.

It had all been to avenge the seduction of his sister, and now he was burdened with the knowledge that the River Tyne had solved his problem. During the years in Embleton he had prevaricated, using time as a waiting game. Wait until he was established in the community; wait until he had made money to use as a weapon, and then the river had closed over his enemy, leaving him with a burden of guilt. When male family relatives questioned him, he would only reply, 'The man is dead.'

On a quiet spring morning he had walked up to the Convent and received permission to see his sister. In the cool reception room he thought that the old woman entering would be followed by his sister. With pain he realised that he was remembering a laughing beautiful young girl who, twenty-five years ago, had been seduced by the dead Reginald Fanshaw. The dull eyes looked out at him from a parchment-coloured skull. The hands resting on the polished table were as twisted and gnarled as those of a ninety-year-old crone. In a wave of pity he realised that they had both been caught in a web of village prejudice and revenge. But at least he had led a full life while the innocent instigator had been condemned to a lifetime of washing stone floors and latrine cleaning. Roberto, the tears streaming down his cheeks, said, 'Come back to the village and live in my house. I have money to make life comfortable for you.' For several determined seconds his sister shook her head slowly and, rising stiffly, she walked away and the doors closed silently behind her. It had all been ineffectual – a useless gesture, for he knew that the village women, like Zia, would never accept her into their society, shot through as it was with rigid condemnation and as virulent today as it had been in his youth.

Lucia tugged at her father's sleeve, demanding to be taken for a walk. Together they strolled through the lemon trees into the coolness of the church. The last of the sun's rays illuminated a patch of mosaic on the wall. Lucia began to trace the pattern with one small finger. Suddenly, she turned to her father with a puzzled frown as if trying to remember something – something almost forgotten. Pointing to the coloured stones in the wall, 'Boodies,' she said, and together they began to laugh at a shared remembrance. Roberto was delighted that she had carried this childhood image from her birthplace. As they left the church he decided, 'I won't let her forget. I'll teach her English,' as he had been taught by that stern teacher now lying in Embleton churchyard.

The voices on the piazza were still shrill with excitement, for on this day, the tenth of July, 1940, Italy had declared war on Great Britain.